Proteus

Simon Hawkins

ZSAZSEVA PUBLICATIONS
hello@zsazseva.com

First published in Great Britain
In 2014 by Zsazseva Limited
© Simon Hawkins 2012

ISBN: 978-0-956577122

Simon Hawkins has asserted his right under the
Copyright, Designs and Patents Act 1988 to be identified
as the writer of this work.

To Penny, the love of my life.

Acknowledgements

I have many people to thank for helping me write and finish this book.

Most important of these is my wonderful wife and best friend Penny who has supported this madcap idea of mine throughout and ensured it reached this conclusion. As Penny's an established cookery book author, she also lovingly edited and re-edited this book at least five times if not more (so all spelling and grammatical mistakes are hers not mine) and of course kept me well fed throughout.

Other people to thank are Barbara Thomson who read the book and gave me much encouragement and Pat Edwards for being a great neighbour, reader and maker of the perfect gin and tonic. Simon Firullo for his help with the cover. John Makin for giving it a final professional polish. Then there is the lovely Sam at Jellyfish without whom this book would not be sitting in front of you now.

Above all though I must thank Tom Cecil and Ben Cresswell, my extraordinary surgeons, and their team in Basingstoke. Without their bravery and incredible skills I would not have been alive to finish the book. Additionally two very special friends Mark Pollock and Ben Delamare who also have to bear the brunt of the blame for my continuing to live and breathe!

There are so many more, such as lifelong friend Stephen Cook and all those who visited and indeed looked after me whilst I was in residence on Ward C2.

Finally, I would like to thank some special friends whom until recently I had never met but had spent so much time chatting with online; Si and co at *The Liverpool Room*. These idiots kept me amused and positive when I was bedbound and everyone thought I was 'dying'. Their constant cheerfulness, and belief that No.19 was just around the corner, kept me going and looking forward. Thanks guys! YNWA

The contents of this book have come purely from my own imagination and its shortcomings and inaccuracies are purely my responsibility and can be put down to a combination of age, heavy medication and artistic licence.

I am no Charles Dickens, I just want people to have a little bit of fun and relaxation. So settle back and enjoy.

I would love to hear from you. If you'd like to get in touch email me at simon@simonjhawkins.co.uk or check me out on the various social media networks.

Proteus (noun)

. . . a minor sea god who had the power of prophecy but would assume different shapes to avoid answering questions . . .

Oxford Dictionary

The Prologue

Friday 18th/Saturday 19th September 2009

Elland Road is hardly the most romantic of places. Situated in a drab and depressing part of Leeds, the area is dominated by the famous football club Leeds United and its notorious and occasionally violent followers.

Shirley Swift, a local resident, lived barely a stone's throw away in one of the many dreary terraced houses opposite the football ground. She had done everything she could to make her two up, two down as comfortable and accommodating as possible.

Well, internally, anyway.

The outside of the property showed serious signs of neglect, particularly the garden, which hadn't seen a spade or fork in years. Weeds ran amok and curled themselves around and between such extravagant items as a decrepit supermarket trolley and the rusty remains of at least two old bikes.

Inside was very different, for Shirley had made a real effort and it looked like a catalogue for one of those online shopping channels, a testament to the credit card debt that had driven her to the edge of bankruptcy.

There were floral decorations everywhere, knick-knacks on all the tables, sideboards and even the window-ledges. She liked to think it was designer living but in truth it was twee and tasteless.

A former council worker, Shirley had been unemployed for the past four years. She liked to blame Margaret Thatcher and the poll tax for her predicament but in reality Shirley was fat and lazy.

Since her divorce ten years earlier, Shirley's weight had ballooned to over two hundred and sixty pounds, a remarkable nineteen stone. She now spent her life indoors eating and surfing the net. The innovation of internet shopping and home delivery by the supermarket chains meant that Shirley hadn't actually left the house for nearly a month. Her son, Tommy, had given up on her and called her a fat, lazy cow.

Shirley had always enjoyed a voracious sexual appetite although sadly her current obesity precluded the real thing. Not to be deprived, Shirley now used the very latest technology to find other ways to satisfy her carnal energy and imagination. Cyber sex wasn't like the real thing but it was better than nothing.

It was Friday afternoon and as was usual for this time of day, Shirley sat naked on her extra-comfort chair (bought online) seeking a frustrated male happy to watch a large woman pleasure herself in front of a webcam.

Her bedroom was a temple to cyber sex. It was dominated by a large table on which, in addition to a large PC screen, were three webcams (just in case two failed), and a plethora of sexual toys.

She had been surfing the net, unsuccessfully, for some time when

PING

An instant message from someone.

HUSKY23: *Hello Needaman.*

Needaman was Shirley's screen-name. It was self-explanatory and had proved extremely popular in her daily quest for cyber satisfaction.

Shirley perked up. She had met Husky23 nearly four months earlier and they had got on very well. So well in fact that Husky23 had suggested a business arrangement.

Husky23 had explained that he was a producer of porn films and was seeking to recruit male extras for his latest film. He suggested that in return for a weekly retainer, Shirley might be interested in surfing the net on his behalf to find suitable and willing participants.

All Shirley needed to do was be herself, attract men to her online and vet them. Husky23 had not really laid down any firm criteria for the search, merely saying that he was looking for well-endowed men who were desperate for sex, tall and dark haired. Oh and preferably Eastern European as they were cheaper.

When Shirley found someone she thought might be suitable she would ask for a photo of their face and their body, preferably naked, and a brief description of themselves. She would then email the information to Husky23.

Husky23 and Shirley would meet online every Friday afternoon to discuss the previous week's prospects and Husky23 would then give Shirley instructions for the week ahead. It was a simple enough arrangement.

Shirley couldn't really believe her luck. She had landed her dream job. She was now being paid £200 a day to do the thing she loved doing best. Her weekly money arrived tax-free every Friday straight into her bank account from some island in the Caribbean.

She had of course been sad to dump some of her regulars as she had grown very attached to them, but she needed the money and it was also a bit of a relief to start being selective.

She had little new to report to Husky23 so their online chat had been brief. She stayed online a bit longer but it was very quiet and she was just starting to think about signing off and having supper when

PING

LONELY ROMAN: *Hi Shirley, how are you today? It is very cold here and I long to be in the UK with you.*

NEEDAMAN: *Oh Tomas I have wonderful news for you. I have just spoken to my boss and he has selected you to come over to the UK for an audition.*

LONELY ROMAN: *That is wonderful news.*

At that very moment Tomas was sitting in a cold, lonely and smelly flat in Prague enjoying his one pleasure of the day, surfing the net on his rickety and ancient PC. He had joined the internet in the hope of finding an English woman. Shape or size was irrelevant.

Now it seemed that his dreams were about to come true.

Adam Batstone was sitting in his one bedroom, city centre flat in a mixed state of excitement and dread. Tomorrow was a massive day for him: he had an interview with the investment bank, Proteus, in Mayfair.

Adam was 38, short, slightly over-weight, ginger-haired, with freckles. He was a plain man with plain looks whose main interests in life were plane spotting and statistics. He had long since realised that he was not at all attractive to the females of the species and now followed his asexual role in life with a begrudging acceptance.

Adam had worked as an accountant for the Royal Bank of Scotland since leaving school at 16. The bank had always been very good to him, including supporting his studies whilst qualifying, but he had always been fascinated by the world of high finance. The allure of London and the celebrity status of Proteus were irresistible. He kept having to pinch himself that he was actually in with a chance of working there.

The people at Proteus had informed him that they were expanding and had a number of positions available, at least two of which, they believed, would suit him perfectly. They seemed very keen indeed to employ Adam and had even insisted he take a full medical in advance of his interview.

The medical had taken nearly all day at a nearby private hospital and included blood and urine tests and a full dental check including x-rays. He had to hand it to Proteus: they were certainly thorough.

In his striped M&S pyjamas and ready for bed, he returned to his wardrobe for a tenth time to check his suit and that it wasn't creased. He wanted to look his best when he met Proteus co-founder and investment director, Stewart McMillan, tomorrow.

He also felt inside his jacket pocket for a tenth time to check that the two forms of ID Proteus were requesting were there. They had been quite specific. Because of the nature of his work and their regulation by the Financial Services Authority, they needed him to prove his identity with his birth certificate and his passport.

He had already googled McMillan and knew a lot about him. He had read how he had started Proteus with his friend and fellow Oxford student Michael Defreitas whilst they were still undergraduates. In those days they were investing their fellow students' loans and grants. Now Proteus was the hot fund for attracting the rich and famous.

He shined his shoes for a second time. All that was left to decide was which tie to wear. Red or blue? He decided red – more powerful – but suspected he would change his mind again in the morning.

Tomorrow was Saturday, an unusual day for an interview but then Proteus was no ordinary business.

It was going to be a very special day for Adam.

Mayfair, London, at roughly the same time that evening

Oliver Price, senior partner of the auditors Gerrard, Ashurst and Price, sat in his large wood panelled office. He was in the ubiquitous chalk-striped, flamboyantly lined City suit with striped shirt and a slightly garish silk tie and enamel cuff links.

He had been staring at the same page of the report in front of him for ages when he was shaken from his reverie by his mobile phone going off. The screen told him it was *Home Calling*, yet again. He let it go to voicemail.

Oliver was in his early sixties and he and his much younger wife, Felicity, had rather different views of their marriage. In fact they hadn't really got on for years.

Oliver had married late in life to the surprise of many who thought he was either gay or disinterested. The difference in age, over twenty years, had been easily overcome to start with by the arrival of three sons in quick succession. *Triplets the hard way!* His friends used to laugh. When the boys went to boarding school, it had become obvious that he and Felicity had little else in common.

He knew Felicity missed the children and she took her empty nest despair out on him. He had tried to talk to her about their problems on a number of occasions but she had turned to Chardonnay for comfort. In return he chose to spend more time at the office, a tendency that enraged Felicity even more, especially once the level of the wine had reached below the label on the bottle.

He reached for his phone and checked his voicemail. No message. God that was so irritating! One of the many things that annoyed him about Felicity was that she rang him at least five times a day but never left a bloody message.

Oliver was about to ring her back when he heard a noise from the office outside. One of the annoyances of working late was being disrupted by the cleaners. He went back to the problems in his life. There were two really, a grumpy, possessive and totally unreasonable wife and the report in front of him outlining a very difficult ethical problem with his best client, an investment fund.

Who should he ring first? His wife, or the client? Either call would be very difficult especially on a Friday evening when he should be at home embracing the first of many single malts.

Delaying, he decided to get himself a coffee from the machine in the hall. It was a decision that solved his dilemma. When he pressed the button for a double espresso the machine exploded, plastering Oliver's body parts all over the corridor of his posh Mayfair offices.

––––––––––

It was 4am and Pete the Plumber sighed.

An habitual criminal for most of his life, Pete had shared a cell with a plumber from Ruislip during his last stretch inside. This had inspired him to 'learn' the plumbing trade and he had promised his wife and family that he was going straight. He had tried so hard to keep his promise but the money on offer for this job was just too tempting and it was just such an easy job. He took a deep breath and decided to go straight tomorrow.

Pete's other concern was that he liked working alone and tonight he wasn't alone.

Normally Pete wouldn't be nervous about being caught on the job but the stranger worried him. He seemed professional enough but Pete couldn't escape a feeling of uneasiness about him.

In his late fifties, Pete wasn't the most athletic of men although he could certainly handle himself in a fight. He was finding breaking and entering increasingly demanding physically as his waistband thickened and his health deteriorated.

Despite these physical challenges, the two men had successfully broken into the doctor's surgery in East Street and now it was the dentist's in the High Street. Gerrards Cross, GX, as it was known by its residents, was very quiet at that time of night and rarely patrolled by the police. Pete still felt exposed.

His job was easy; he merely had to break into the two properties, disarm the alarms and then find and rob the drugs cupboard. He would then wait outside for the smartly suited stranger who had gone in with a briefcase.

He asked no questions whatsoever although he did wonder why his final task at each job was to smash a window, making his perfect break-in look very amateurish indeed.

Still he cheered up slightly when, with the jobs complete, the stranger handed him £1,000 in cash and disappeared into the night. Not a bad night for Pete, cash and a few prescription drugs. It had been too easy, should he be worried? He pushed the thought away.

Wednesday evening, 14th October 2009

Marylebone Station, London

Marylebone Station was starting to calm down after the usual rush hour pandemonium. There were still some be-suited commuters rushing red-cheeked for their trains clutching the *Evening Standard*, their numbers now dwindling, becoming increasingly interspersed with sight-seers and socialisers.

Most of the travellers were wrapped up in their own little worlds but still couldn't fail to notice a large lady in an equally large and bright pink coat standing beneath the main station clock.

The large pink lady was Shirley. She was very pleased with herself. She had actually arrived early for her meeting with Tomas. This made a nice change from her terrible habit of being late for everything.

I'll meet you under the main station clock at 8pm, in a pink coat.

That's the promise Shirley had made Tomas and she now stood waiting apprehensively.

She had reason to be apprehensive. She had never met anyone via the internet before and she hadn't actually told Tomas that she was nineteen stone. It was a *large* and deliberate oversight she was now regretting.

She had hinted to Tomas on a couple of occasions that she was a 'big barrelled lass' but according to her doctor she was obese. He was right, she was. She had convinced herself that her size wouldn't matter. Tomas had always been so nice and, besides, they were soul mates.

Of course it will matter, she now thought. No man had given her a second glance in years, in fact no man had fancied her since her weight had ballooned after her son Tommy was born. Why on earth had she thought this man would be any different? Because he was foreign and desperate?

Shirley looked around the station and just saw the faces of strangers staring and her doubts grew. *What on earth was she doing here and why did she decide to wear this bloody stupid coat?*

Because she was being paid to meet this man and her employer had been so impressed with her for finding the perfect candidate. That's why I am here.

There was even talk of a bonus if things worked out well. But surely there was more to life than money especially if it meant standing here in a garish pink coat being stared at by strangers whilst waiting for a man she had never met.

Just as she was managing to talk herself out of the whole thing, a man approached her nervously. He was tall and wore a hat. He was one of the most handsome men she had ever seen.

'Good evening my English beauty, are you waiting for someone?' He drawled in a deep foreign accent. She felt like a film star from a 50s black and white romance.

'Yes dear sir, I am an English rose waiting to be plucked and appreciated.' She said, using the pre-agreed code.

'Oh you are appreciated my darling Shirley.'

'Oh Tomas it really is you,' she said as she threw herself into his arms.

———

Gerrards Cross, Buckinghamshire

Later that night

It was just after 2am and Gerrards Cross had settled down for the night to its twinkling lights and warm afterglow. There was no sign of traffic and all the late night dog walkers and pub revellers had found their way safely home, hours ago.

West Common is situated close to the town and consists of a mixture of grass areas, overgrown bushes, the occasional tree and a criss-cross network of pathways and tracks. It is sandwiched between the outskirts of the residential area and the A40. Inevitably, the common is very popular with walkers, their dogs and the occasional horse rider but deserted and a bit spooky at this time of night.

The black Hummer had turned off its headlights as it quietly edged its way down the wide pathway that dissected the common. Making full use of the bush cover, the large vehicle made its way invisibly into the nether regions of the overgrown expanse, before coming to a gentle halt.

The nearby houses showed no noticeable sign of life save for the occasional outside light that sparkled out over the frosty October night.

Two men, dressed in black from their balaclavas to their shoes, climbed out of the Hummer and opened the rear hatch. Laid out in the back was the third occupant, a man dressed immaculately in a dark Savile Row suit, crisp white shirt, silk tie and handmade leather brogues. In fact the only thing missing from the image of this very smart City gent was his head.

Moving swiftly, the two men lifted the body carefully out of the Hummer and carried it into the bushes where it was laid down gently, almost reverentially. One of the men pulled a wallet from his back pocket and placed it in the inside jacket pocket of the dead man.

'Goodbye Michael,' he whispered quietly.

Under the balaclava, the man smiled and gestured to his colleague for him to return to the vehicle.

Wednesday 14th/Thursday 15th October 2009

Detective Chief Inspector (DCI) Thomas Sparks, known affectionately by his friends and associates as Sparkie, when they were being polite, sat in a traffic jam drumming his fingers on the steering wheel. The police radio crackled and popped with static.

Tom was an old-fashioned policeman who was lucky to be based in such a virtually crime-free area.

Gerrards Cross is basically a gynaecocracy, run by women who can only be described as Stepfordesque. They are typically blonde and skinny and spend their time flitting between the gym, the favoured hairdresser of the moment and the latest trendy wine bar where they spend a bitchy hour or two pushing fat-free food around a plate, drinking coffee and sometimes a small glass of Pinot Grigio. All this flitting about is of course done in huge 4 x 4s – the GX tractors, over which they have little control. Their driving deficiencies are allied to a total disrespect for all other motorists and pedestrians. This makes Gerrards Cross one of the most dangerous places on earth at 8.20am each weekday morning during the school term.

Tom was in his early forties and not your typical policeman. He was tall, slim and good-looking, his classical looks, a cross between Ralph Fiennes and Hugh Grant. What also made him very different was that he had been to 'school'. Like many of his fellow Old Etonians he, and his mother, lived in a large house on a private estate in Gerrards Cross, in his case the Woodhill Estate.

His background was really far more appropriate to a politician, diplomat or banker than a policeman but Tom had always been fascinated by crime and mysteries stemming back to when he was a boy. He had loved the Famous Five and other mystery books of Enid Blyton.

He liked to think of his family as having old money but it had been dwindling fast since his father, a merchant banker, had died ten years ago. Tom realised that soon he was going to have to talk to his seventy-eight year old mother about money and the inevitable sale of the family home. He knew it would break her heart so he kept putting it off.

Tom was single, well divorced, and his lack of success with the opposite sex was spectacular. He had two ex-wives and a string of failed relationships behind him and had moved back with his mother nearly a year ago when it became clear that the house was becoming too much for her. Not that he was much of a handy man but his job always gave him an excuse to avoid doing things around the house.

Tom's problem wasn't attracting women, his problem was keeping them. Either he didn't understand them or he was attracted to the wrong ones. Probably both.

Despite Tom's appalling track record on the romantic front, his looks and apparent wealth made him attractive to the opposite sex and he was frequently invited to local parties as the spare man. At first the invitations were exciting and eagerly accepted but he now found the whole scene shallow and unattractive.

He was sick of trying to make conversation with middle-aged blonde divorcees with chips on their shoulders about the fact that their husbands had left them for a younger model. As a result he was no longer an A-lister on the dinner party circuit and spent most nights watching TV or having a pint at his local pub, The Apple Tree.

He looked at his watch again. It was now 7.56pm. Damn, damn, damn. The bloody M40 was closed again and the normally quiet A40 was jammed up.

Nothing else for it, he sighed to himself, as he reached into the passenger well and grabbed the blue light, placing it on the roof with one swift, well-practised movement.

The immediate blue flashing beam and the whoop whoop of the siren worked like magic, clearing a gap down the middle of the A40 through which he sent his car hurtling towards GX. He took a swift left turn at the traffic lights, followed by a right and then another left into a quiet suburban road. One final right turn brought him to the white, gated entrance of the Woodhill Estate.

Through the gates, he slowed to the private speed limit of 15mph. The last thing he needed was for one of the neighbourhood watch do-gooders to report him for speeding. Finally he turned into the double driveway of a large Georgian house. He skidded to a halt on the gravel and rushed through the already open front door.

'One day you are going to be too late!' The tired, frail female voice shouted from the lounge. Mother and Tom usually watched *Midsummer Murders* together. She insisted it was essential research for his job. He didn't have the heart to tell her he had never investigated a single murder in GX. There simply hadn't been any under his watch.

He threw himself into a worn leather armchair and let out a deep sigh as the programme started. He kept promising himself Sky+ but never seemed to find the time to sort it out. He'd get round to it next week. It seemed like it was always next week.

Whilst force-feeding his boredom-numbed brain on ITV escapism, Tom's mind started to wander.

How had such a promising life become so dreary? he asked himself as DCI Barnaby unmiraculously solved his next murder and predictably Tom had got it wrong; the murderer had been the long lost brother, not the mysterious stranger next door. He sighed and thanked his lucky stars that GX was a murder-free zone.

He must have nodded off as some time later he woke to find himself watching some awful bingo-style quiz programme with a cheesy host who was encouraging people without a life to ring in and spend a fortune per minute in the scant hope of winning thousands of pounds.

Tom for a brief moment was tempted to go back to sleep but eventually rose from his chair, sighed heavily and switched the

TV off. He had always wondered who watched such crap and now realised it was people like him. He poured himself a glass of water and shuffled off to bed.

————

Gerrards Cross, early next morning

Dawn had finally made an appearance over Gerrards Cross and was mistily starting to cast its light over the slumbering town. The early commuters were making their sleepy way towards the first trains of the day, to their destinies in the City and an early coronary.

Vicky Steadman – she had been christened Victoria but everyone called her Vicky much to her parents' chagrin – loved this time of year. In mid-autumn the air was crisp and the light was liquid. When the weather was good she would often get up early and, with the dogs, go down to the stables to see her horse Penelope.

It was 6.45am and after some skilful planning, she had managed to engineer enough time to take Penelope and the dogs for a quick hack on West Common.

Elsa and Henry, her Bernese mountain dogs were, as usual, steaming ahead looking for interesting smells and hopefully the odd rabbit while she guided Penelope along the narrow track across the common. She cherished the tranquillity and solitude of her early morning rides.

As she and Penelope trotted on, Vicky noticed something had caught the dog's interest. They were pawing at what looked like a bundle of clothes on the edge of a large bush. She steered Penelope over to where the dogs were getting themselves into a bit of a frenzy.

As she peered through the early morning mist, she realised it was more than just a bundle of clothes. She made her way even closer to where the dogs were frantically barking and pawing and the horror of what they had found became apparent.

Vicky screamed.

She pulled Penelope back, took some deep breaths and tried to calm down. She called Elsa and Henry to heel and amazingly they obeyed.

It was only then that she felt composed enough to pull out her mobile and dial 999.

Tom had not had the best of nights.

Mother's usual unpalatable dinner had come back to haunt him repeatedly during the night. He couldn't help thinking that it was no wonder his father had died at an early age. Tom immediately felt guilty about being so flippant about his father's early death. He had loved his father and missed him very much. He thought about him every day.

The combination of mother's cooking and Tom's general ill humour had conspired to make sleep slow in coming. He was however well and truly in the land of nod and having the most bizarre dream about being a contestant on *Who Wants to be a Millionaire?* but the host wasn't Chris Tarrant it was his boss, Deputy Chief Commissioner Jane Protheroe. He had got to £500,000 and was just one question away from the million and he had taken the option to phone a friend. But the friend wouldn't answer and the phone just kept ringing. It must of rung at least ten times before he recovered his consciousness sufficiently to realise it was his own phone ringing. It took him a moment to shake off the sleep, work out his whereabouts and find the phone. He fumbled it to his ear and mumbled sleepily.

'Sparks.'

'Oh hi sir,' a female voice crackled. It belonged to his Detective Sergeant, Jane Newsum.

'Sorry to disturb you so early sir.'

31

'What is it Newsum?'

'We have a dead body on the common sir.'

'We have a what where?'

'A dead body on the common sir, a man, we are pretty sure he has been murdered.'

Tom paused. A murder in Gerrards Cross?

'I'll be there in one minute.'

Ignoring his full bladder, Tom threw his clothes on and rushed out of the house. He got halfway to the car and paused. He shot back into the house and the cloakroom before again rushing to the car and speeding off.

Tom had no difficulty finding the crime scene as the normally quiet woodland of the common was a mass of activity and lights, most of which were blue and flashing. The road had been sealed at both ends by the Crime Scene Investigation team and there were four police cars and an ambulance crowding around a single point.

In addition there were three more unmarked cars, one of which Tom recognised to be the silver Audi sports car of the local pathologist, Doctor Helen James. Rather surprisingly, there was also a horse, a woman in riding gear, and two very large dogs.

A smartly dressed short, slim, ginger-haired woman in her mid-twenties was strutting around and was obviously keenly awaiting his arrival as she shot over to his car the moment he pulled up. His right hand woman, Newsum.

'Okay Newsum what have we got so far?'

'Dead white man, tallish but impossible to determine his actual height, medium build, expensively dressed. Possibly a commuter?'

'Why the height problem?'

'Oh forgot to mention, his head is missing.'

'Easy thing to overlook.' Tom answered with a bemused expression. He liked Newsum.

'CSI guys are now photographing and beginning their routine search.'

Tom kept moving towards the cordoned off area where a number of people in white suits – The Crime Scene Investigation team - were bustling about erecting a tent. What was almost comical was that they seemed to be trying to erect the tent around and over a tall figure dressed from head to toe in white.

'What's that bloody woman doing here?' Tom said pointing at the tall white tent pole of a woman.

'We don't get many murders sir and Helen is the local pathologist. I think the attraction was too great, can't harm can it sir?'

'I suppose not.' Tom sighed.

The tall white figure in question was Helen James. An attractive blonde, she was not only a fine pathologist but also Tom's most recent ex.

He sidled up to her.

'Hello Helen, nothing better to do at this hour of the morning? Who is making your early morning tea these days?'

Tom thought her normally beautiful face looked like a slapped arse; just one look could kill with a single glance. Tom stifled a giggle, deciding perhaps now was not the time for flippancy.

'Cause of death?' He said, plucking his best policeman's tone.

'Difficult to tell really, but my best bet at the moment is that it had something to do with the fact that his head has been chopped off.'

'Chopped off? As in, with an axe?' Tom was stunned. 'Unbelievable, beheaded? Here on the common? In GX?'

'Actually it looks more like it has been sawn off although I am not an expert on the subject. This has been stage-managed. The body was moved here in its decapitated state very recently.'

'How can you be so sure?'

Helen gave him a withering look of sheer disgust and spat out, 'Do you want it alphabetically or numerically? Lack of blood at the scene is a bit of a give-away. In fact there is a total lack of any evidence that such a savage murder took place here. Any other stupid questions?'

'A-a-anything else of interest?' Tom stuttered hoping to quickly change the subject.

'Yes, although there are no formal forms of identification, there was a wallet in the dead man's jacket pocket which appears to belong to a Mr Michael Defreitas'

Tom paused for a few moments. The name was familiar to him but he couldn't think why.

He played for time racking his brain for a meaningful question.

'Which pocket?' was the best he could offer.

'Inside left, but I really don't see what difference it makes which pocket it was in,' said an increasingly aggravated Helen.

'The devil is in the detail my dear, the devil is in the detail.' Tom smirked, much to her annoyance.

Helen, he knew, prided herself on her attention to detail. Tom was delighted that he had clearly managed to wind her up whilst being condescending at the same time.

Then it clicked.

'Michael Defreitas eh? I think I met him a couple of years ago at one of those infernal social things I used to attend. Wealthy banker and very handsome, definitely your type Helen.' He winked and she scowled.

There was an uneasy silence, which Tom broke.

'Any sign of the head?'

'No.'

'This has professional hit written all over it. Formal identification could take some time unless we get lucky with the fingerprints. The wallet might speed things up. Can you please get it over to us the moment forensic have finished with it?'

'Especially as it was in the left inside pocket.' Helen sneered.

Tom turned to DS Newsum who was standing behind him.

'Who found the body, Newsum?'

'A horse rider called Victoria Steadman.' She said looking in the direction of the pretty girl and her horse.

Tom took in the sight of the immaculately dressed rider and decided to investigate further.

'Victoria Steadman?'

'Yes.' She answered frostily.

'Detective Chief Inspector Sparks, Uxbridge Criminal Investigation Department more widely known as the CID. Based here in GX. I hear you found the body.'

'It was my dogs actually, Henry and Elsa.' She said pointing at the two slobbering dogs at the feet of the horse.

'I know that you have given a brief statement to DS Newsum but do you mind if I ask you a few more questions?'

'Officer, I only wish I had time but I must get to work. Really, this is just too much!'

'Please call me DCI Sparks,' Tom responded somewhat tetchily. 'Are you refusing to answer my questions?'

'I have to get Penelope home and get to work.'

'Penelope?'

'My horse, I am due at work at nine and I have to get her back and settled before I go home and get ready. I have an important day ahead.'

Tom sighed and found himself gazing in admiration at this splendid albeit irritatingly feisty woman. She was clearly blonde although this was partly disguised by the black riding hat and hair net she was wearing. He found his gaze repeatedly returning to her thighs. *Shame they are being wasted on Penelope*, he thought.

He sighed again and tried to clear his mind of everything except the job in hand.

'Mrs Steadman, I really must insist that you stay and answer my questions.'

'Sergeant, I will do no such thing!'

'I can insist, you know. In fact I can even arrest you and take you down the station!' Tom half-shouted and half-stuttered.

Tom heard a snigger from behind him and realised they had an audience. Newsum and Helen were being thoroughly entertained by the exchange of words.

'Mrs Steadman, I am actually a Detective Chief Inspector not a Sergeant!' He felt his voice getting louder and its tone much sharper.

'And I am a Miss not a Mrs!'

'Sir can I help at all?' Newsum interceded deciding to finally put her boss out of his misery.

'Ah Newsum, yes can you please obtain the number of Penelope's work, ring them and tell them that she will be late as she's helping the police with their enquiries.'

'You make it sound like I am a criminal!' Miss Steadman shrieked. 'You really are a contemptible little man DCI Sparks! I am off, and for your report, it is my horse that is Penelope, I am Miss Steadman, Miss Victoria Steadman!'

At that she bounced onto her horse, called her dogs and rode off into the morning mist. DS Newsum turned to her boss and smiled, saying. 'Don't worry sir, she's probably suffering from shock, after all it isn't every day you come across a headless body. I have all her contact details, I'll contact her later and get a full statement from her.'

'Thank you Newsum.'

Tom stormed off and decided to inspect the crime scene again. *Bloody women.* He muttered to himself.

Wembley

Peter Robinson was an overweight man who had managed to squeeze himself into one of his rarely worn suits and was now sitting ruddy-faced and sweaty on the 8.38am from Beaconsfield to Marylebone. He was due to arrive at 9.15 barely leaving him enough time to get to his appointment. He had meant to catch the earlier train but an emergency at work delayed him and he was cutting it fine, very fine indeed.

Peter was nervous; he had a very important meeting with his new bank manager.

Peter's company manufactured specialist car parts and was struggling. The business relied on the good relationship he enjoyed with his previous bank manager who had just retired. He was anxious to be on time and kept glancing at his watch.

The train had just left Wembley station when it ground to yet another halt. Peter stared out the window trying to stay calm.

His gaze fell on something large and pink on the embankment.

When he realised what it was he sub-consciously reached up and pulled the communication cord.

Bugger, now he would never make his meeting on time.

———

Gerrards Cross

It was 9.45am by the time Tom entered Gerrards Cross Police Station. There was much to do; he had to set up an incident room and get his team of detectives to work. There really was nothing like a murder to get the old adrenalin pumping. Not that he had ever investigated a murder before.

He had just walked through the front door when he heard:

'Morning Tom, hear you've got yourself a murder.' In normal circumstances he supposed that the rich female voice would be considered sexy but not in this instance as it came from a very statuesque uniformed and incongruously high-heeled lady, Deputy Chief Constable Jane Protheroe, the star of his unfinished dream.

'Morning ma'am, you're well informed.'

'I try to be, what do we have so far?'

'Well we're waiting for more information from the Crime Investigation Team and the pathologist' he hesitated, then continued, 'but it looks like a male, white, well dressed, oh and headless.'

He hesitated again to let the information filter through.

'Murder took place about three days ago. Apparently the body was then moved to West Common where it was discovered early this morning. A woman out with her horse and dogs.' *And great thighs,* he added silently.

'Any ID?'

'Not as such although there was a wallet on the body which seems to have belonged to a Michael Defreitas who, if he is the Michael Defreitas I have met, is a very wealthy banker.'

'Yes, I have met him a couple of times, bit of a smoothie. First impressions?'

'Well it has all come as a bit of a shock really but it has professional hit written all over it. Possibly organised crime.'

'Last thing we need, organised crime moving into GX. Be careful on this one.'

There was a pause as his boss cleared her throat almost apprehensively. 'Now, about Helen, are you two going to be able to deal with each other in a professional manner?'

'Of course.'

Tom blushed; the DCC and Helen were friends.

'We need a quick result Tom, I've already had Harry on the phone.'

Damn, Tom hadn't been thinking about the implications of Harry Smith, the Chief Constable, living in Gerrards Cross. That was all he needed.

'Tom, Harry doesn't want his wife worrying about the effect that a protracted murder investigation might have on house prices.'

'Don't worry Ma'am I'm on the case.'

'Good man, now off you trot and keep me informed.' She said with a giggle. Tom flinched at the horsey reference and wondered who had told her about his less than persuasive interchange with Victoria Steadman. Then she was gone, disappearing down the corridor to the loud click clacking of high heels on the tiled floor.

Tom sighed and shuffled slowly down the corridor to his very untidy office and grimaced at the pile of paperwork he had ignored over the past few weeks that was now dominating his desk.

Newsum arrived with life restoring coffee and pain au chocolat.

'Sir, thought you might need these.' Newsum knew that he lived with his mother and that she was not a cook by any means. Bless her. He devoured the hot chocolaty bread as Newsum informed him that they had been summoned to the Pathology lab.

They arrived as Helen James, dressed in all green, now, was carving her way down the chest of the murder victim with a saw. He sensed Newsum pull away and look out the window. Her first murder too.

'Must say green suits you Helen, matches your eyes.'

'Ah, Sparks,' she said coldly.

'So, what have you got for me?'

'I'm just getting started but I can tell you that he is white, probably European, height is difficult to be 100 per cent sure of, but likely to be about six foot. He was fit, probably about twelve stone. Any other information is severely restricted by the lack of a head. He was however wearing a very expensive Savile Row suit and leather brogues the soles of which are stamped *custom made by Robinson's Shoemakers*.'

'When did he die?' He said with a patronising smile. *Everything else you have told me is a bit bleeding obvious*, he thought.

'I estimate the time of death to be Monday afternoon between 3pm and 6pm. We've run blood tests and fingerprints which sadly revealed nothing of use. There are however signs of a recent manicure as the nails are immaculate, although the cuticles aren't quite as good as I would've expected.'

'Meaning?'

'Sometimes even a well-buffed and manicured set of fingernails can give us clues.'

'And in this case?'

'A poor upbringing.'

'Well see what else you can find out please.' Helen continued. 'At least we have a wallet which hopefully belonged to the victim. There was no jewellery.'

'Thanks. Have forensic finished with the wallet?'

'No.'

'Can you hurry them up?'

'Of course.'

Tom sensed he had out-stayed his welcome but, determined to wring what he could out of his far from helpful ex, he continued.

'Any other evidence found on the body?'

'No'

'Anything else cropped up?'

'No.'

'Pity, well thanks for that. Fancy a drink later?'

'I don't think that's a good idea do you DCI Sparks?'

Tom sighed a good-bye and left.

———

Wembley

Detective Inspector Brian Tooley sat in a standard issue blue Vauxhall Vectra watching his overweight CID colleague DS Wayne Porter buy bacon rolls and coffees from their favourite roadside cafe. Well, to be precise, it was actually his cholesterol junkie colleague's favourite cafe.

Tooley was a veteran of nearly 25 years, 20 of which had been spent in CID during which time he had solved numerous murders and other serious crimes. He had however failed to solve a couple of big cases recently. Rumour had it he'd lost his touch.

He had joined the police force from school and all he had ever wanted to do was catch criminals. He hated admin and the system, he was an instinctive cop, a dying breed in the new paperwork heavy, politically correct police force.

A promising footballer in his teens, Brian was now 43 and starting to show signs of middle age. His trousers had waistbands that seemed to shrink every year and his haircuts took less and less time. He had read somewhere that after 40 your waist grew by an inch each year. Surely that couldn't be true, could it?

The police radio blared out and he took the call. He jumped into the driver's seat and yelled for his colleague to get a move on. Porter moved surprisingly nimbly for his size, despite being laden with bacon rolls and coffee, and soon they were racing towards Wembley rail station with their blue lights flashing.

As they screeched to a halt outside the station, Tooley was relieved to see that uniform were already policing the location. Constable Ian Fisher was standing at the entrance making sure that no one could pass. He acknowledged Tooley and Porter and directed them towards a stationary train some two hundred yards down the line from the station. There was already a crowd of rubberneckers starting to gather on the embankment opposite.

Tooley mused about what type of person enjoyed looking at crime scenes and how they got to hear of them so quickly. *The power of the Blackberry* he decided. The crowd was being marshalled by Fisher's colleague, Constable Bob (Robert) Jones, with great difficulty when they arrived and looked most relieved to see the non-uniform reinforcements.

Jones introduced the two CID men to Peter Robinson a red-faced man who seemed quite agitated and who had apparently raised the alarm. Aware of the potential problems that would be caused by holding up the train any further, Tooley took his details and said he would contact him if he wanted further information. A relieved Peter returned to the train which finally continued its journey to Marylebone.

Tooley turned and went to see what all the fuss was about. He quickly took in the sight of a large lady in a bright pink coat who had clearly been dead for some hours. Bent over her in a white mask and uniform was a tall thin man in his 50s, Roger Townsend, the pathologist. Just Tooley's luck; they had crossed swords before.

'So they sent *you* did they?'

'Nice to see you too Townsend, what've you got for me?'

'Haven't been here long myself but we have a dead, obese middle-aged woman, blonde from a bottle, awful dress sense and by the way, it is *Doctor* Townsend'

'Time of death?'

'Sometime yesterday evening, probably 9pm onwards.'

'Cause of death?'

'Strangulation.'

'Any clues as to who she is?'

'Oh yes she's Shirley Swift, ironic name for a woman her size. Lived in Elland Road, Leeds. We found her handbag next to the body. Had her picture on her driving licence.'

Tooley shuddered at the mention of Elland Road. He regained his composure quickly.

'Is her purse still in the handbag?'

'Yes, fair bit of cash in it, couple of hundred pounds at least. So we can certainly rule out robbery, unsurprisingly no sign of sexual assault either.'

———

At that very moment, a Lear Jet was climbing overhead having just taken off from Northolt airbase. The only passenger on board unfastened his seat belt, poured himself a hefty scotch and sank into one of the plush leather seats.

The forecast was good. He would be in Malaga in one and a half hours.

He absent-mindedly touched his cheek with his right hand. It was still sore from where that fat bitch had scratched him.

He thought of where he was going and smiled to himself. He started to relax and let his mind wander back to when he was living in Czechoslovakia and how things had changed so much for him.

Gerrards Cross Police Station

It was 12.30pm and Tom was addressing a hastily called meeting of the Uxbridge police and CID. The room was buzzing with everyone talking at once about murder and headless bodies. There was clearly a great sense of excitement.

'Okay everyone, settle down. We have a dead white male, probably European, just under six foot tall and apparently fit. Identification is going to take longer as the head had been removed although we did find a wallet on the body belonging to a Michael Defreitas. We've made some initial calls to verify the whereabouts of Mr Defreitas but as yet we have no formal form of ID and we're currently trying to trace the him through his medical records and fingerprints.'

'The body was found on West Common in some bushes having been moved there some time after the murder. Time of murder is not precise but is likely to be sometime on Monday afternoon but we think the body was only moved to West Common last night.'

'Any questions so far?'

'Yes guv, think it was a professional hit?' Came a voice from the group in front of him.

'The fact that the head was removed would indicate so.'

'Surely sir, West Common is a pretty public place to dump a body?'

'Good point, this adds further weight to the theory that it was a professional hit and they wanted the body found quickly.'

'Any other questions?' Silence.

'Okay we need to question the residents of the common to see whether anyone saw or heard anything suspicious over the last couple of nights. Check and see who walks their dog regularly there. Someone must have seen something.'

'What about the woman who found the body, sir?'

'Victoria Steadman's statement is taken care of.'

Although she remained silent, Tom could see DS Newsum raise her left eyebrow in puzzlement.

Tom quickly continued. 'It may be a red herring but let's find out all we can about Michael Defreitas just in case even if just to eliminate him from our enquiries. On a slightly different subject, any progress been made on the break-ins at the two surgeries last month?'

'Fraid not sir, very amateurish, looks like druggies desperate for a fix.' Came a voice from the back.

'Well keep your eyes and ears open on that one, but it looks like a non-runner unless we get lucky.'

'Okay everyone, let's get cracking, we really need an early result on this. Oh and one last thing, find me that missing head!'

––––––

William Thornton was a worried man.

He had tried to speak to Michael Defreitas on Monday just before lunchtime but Michael fobbed him off saying he was late for a meeting and would see him the following morning.

That had been three days ago and Michael seemed to have vanished into thin air. No one knew where he was and he needed to speak to him urgently.

William had been the finance director of Proteus, the investment bank, for the past five years. It had been a period during which he had been forced to show great patience with Michael for his unorthodox methods and many times had even had to lie or turn a blind eye to things. But their annual audit was due shortly and William could foresee problems. The figures just didn't balance.

He had tried speaking to Stewart McMillan about Michael but had come up against a brick wall. Stewart was a geek, a financial genius but a geek all the same. All Stewart worried about was the market and what the market was doing.

Stewart had listened patiently to William and then assured him that Michael would turn up in the office on Monday morning sporting a smug grin and a huge hangover.

William had known Michael since they were at Oxford together in the late eighties. They had lost touch until bumping into each other again at a Bank of England do when out of the blue Michael had offered William the job of finance director. The fact that they were so close was actually a problem for William because of the way that Michael conducted his business.

He worried that Michael was declaring bonuses that were too high and that the fund's performance was being exaggerated as a result.

Proteus was of course *the* fund for the great, good and trendy. Anyone who was anybody wanted a piece of the action. Michael was a showman and made his investors feel so lucky and privileged to be able to share his expertise. William however did have reservations about dealing with quite so many professional footballers and their wives.

William's greatest concern however was not the WAGs, it was the amount of business they did with Tony Marciano and his group of companies. Whilst he realised that Tony had been Michael's first really wealthy client, he still worried about where the money came from. The regulators were so hot on money laundering these days.

It also hadn't escaped William that recently Michael had changed. He'd started being very secretive, spending more and more time with Julian Travers, the new IT manager. William suspected they were up to something, possibly something fraudulent.

The fund was under-performing due to the credit crunch but then all funds were. Michael, however, had insisted on declaring record-breaking dividends that William knew were untrue and which the fund could not afford.

The high dividends had attracted an influx of new investments, but William couldn't see how they would make the books balance for the audit. To make matters worse the regulators were due in next month for a compliance visit.

William needed answers from Michael now.

William was furious with himself for allowing Michael to compromise him like this. He was party to a massive fraud and he could go to prison!

He rang Michael's mobile again and got his voicemail again.

Where the hell was he?

————

Gerrards Cross

It was now late in the afternoon and Tom was staring at his desk. Well, to be accurate the paper that was completely covering his desk. In fact he couldn't even remember what his desk looked like beneath the months of paperwork that had built up since his promotion last year. It was the lot of the modern policeman to be better at form filling than detection. Sadly his talents started and ended with detection.

He thought about Helen, the beautiful Helen. He just couldn't work out where it had all gone wrong. It had been a whirlwind romance that started when they were introduced to each other at a charity function. They had previously met professionally on a number of occasions but had never really spoken at any great length until then.

They hit it off immediately; she had a wonderful sense of humour and seemed to genuinely like him. There was clearly a chemistry between them that seemed to grow and grow as they got to know one another. They became lovers and Tom knew he was in love, truly and deeply. Then suddenly one day Helen just announced that things weren't working and she was ending it.

'Sir!'

Tom returned to the present abruptly to find Newsum standing in front of him waving a piece of paper.

'You okay sir? You seemed a bit out of it.'

'Yes I am fine, what is it Newsum?'

'The wallet has finally arrived from forensic and I've been running a check on its contents and in particular Michael Defreitas. I Googled him. He's an investment banker in the City. Co-founder and 50 per cent shareholder of Proteus Investment Group. They're running a more detailed check on him as we speak.'

'Excellent, any news on the fingerprints?'

'We haven't found a match for the fingerprints, but that isn't really a surprise. People like that rarely have their fingerprints on record. I have sent them to all the usual agencies including Interpol but it will take time, as usual.'

'Well done, anything else?'

'I rang Proteus and spoke to the finance director, a Mr William Thornton, who wasn't very unhelpful. Stated that Mr Defreitas was out of the country on business and he'd get him to call on his return. He was very keen to know the reasons for my call but I thought it best to say very little until Defreitas has been formally identified.'

'Good thinking Newsum.'

'Just one other thing sir. There was a very interesting business card in the wallet. It was for a florist in Clerkenwell called Tony Marciano.'

Tom snapped to attention.

'Big Tony? Interesting. He's a well-known fixer for organised crime and is especially well known for his money laundering activities. The Met have been trying to nail him for years. He's listed as a person of considerable interest. Wonder what he was up to with Defreitas?'

'Do you want me to follow up on the Marciano connection sir?'

The potential involvement of a well-known mob financial man was worrying. Tom remembered the warning from the DCC and decided to err on the side of caution.

'I will need some time to think about that one Newsum – Tony Marciano is a dangerous man with very good connections. We will need to tread carefully. In the meantime continue digging and finding out all you can about Michael Defreitas.'

'Yes sir.'

Mayfair

William Thornton may have been worried before but now he was in a blind panic. He had just come off the phone from Detective Sergeant Jane Newsum of Uxbridge CID. She had asked to speak to Michael. William blurted out the first thing that came into his head about Michael being abroad on business. The policewoman had thanked him and asked to leave a message for Michael to call when he returned. He tried to find out why she wanted to speak to Michael but she wouldn't tell him.

William sat at his desk for a long time just staring out at the Mayfair street scene. He didn't know what to do.

At that moment his mobile phone bleeped, a text message. His heart raced as he read it.

Tonight?

His concerns were briefly forgotten as a tingle of excitement shot through to the tops of his thighs. William was gay but was very careful to keep his sex life private. He didn't want an actual homosexual relationship – he just needed sex with a man about once a week. He particularly enjoyed one-off sexual encounters with complete strangers. He had recently joined an internet site that specialised in bringing together men with similar desires.

He sent a text back

Age, description and photo?

Within a minute the information arrived via his phone. The man was 21, 6ft 3, slim, and his photo showed him to be blonde and handsome in a rugged way. Perfect in fact!

He thought for a brief second and then replied,

Hampstead Heath at 9pm by the HOLLOW OAK TREE. I will be wearing a black hat and coat.

The response was immediate.

Okay, see you then

William felt a tingle of anticipation as he looked forward to tonight. With all the problems with Michael a good seeing to would do him the world of good.

Friday 16th October 2009

Canary Wharf

Detective Inspector Jeremy Ward of the City squad was in bed with the wife of his best friend when his mobile rang.

Reluctantly, he grabbed the phone and barked into it. It was the desk sergeant from the station. They had a dead body in Mayfair. He even more reluctantly kissed his gorgeous blonde bed mate on the cheek and begrudgingly started dressing.

Mayfair

The Mayfair offices of Proteus International were situated in a Grade II listed Georgian townhouse in Mayfair. It was one of many in a narrow road that had been cordoned off by two uniformed constables who waved Ward through when he arrived.

His partner and best friend Mick, officially DS Michael Brunton, was already there, looking agitated.

'Where the bloody hell have you been?'

'DS Brunton, is that any way to speak to a senior officer?' He winked at Brunton with a grin. 'I told you I was having a breakfast meeting with my old boss. What's the problem?'

'Financial director, William Thornton was found dead in his office this morning by his secretary.'

'Suicide?'

'Well in a way yes, although the coroner will probably announce it as death by misadventure. He was naked and had suffocated in the plastic bag he had tied over his head. He was sucking an orange.'

'Ah, masturbation gone wrong. What a wanker.'

'His secretary is here if you want to talk to her. She is very upset.'

They left the office and left the Crime Scene Investigation Unit to do their stuff.

In a much smaller office next door, sat a pretty, petite blonde girl in her twenties. She looked up at them and Mick introduced his friend and colleague.

'Melanie, this is my boss Detective Inspector Jeremy Ward. Jeremy, Melanie here is Mr Thornton's PA, has been for the past five years.'

'Hi, Melanie, I realise this is probably not the best time but can I ask you a few questions? I will keep them as brief as possible.'

'Of course,' she sobbed. 'William, I mean Mr Thornton, was such a nice man. I can't believe that he would do this. It is such a shock.'

'Melanie, what time did you find William?'

'I came in at 8am as usual and was surprised that his office light wasn't on. I assumed that he had gone to a meeting because he was always in at the crack of dawn. He was such a happy man, he loved his work and he was so kind to us all. I can't believe what he has done, it is such a shock.'

'What was William's role at Proteus?'

'He was the finance director, he joined the business the same week as me five years ago. He was an old friend of Michael's.'

'Who is Michael?'

'Oh sorry, Michael Defreitas is the managing director.'

'Is Michael here at the moment?'

'No he isn't, I don't know where he is. In fact, Mr Thornton has been trying to get hold of him for a couple of days and was starting to get very worried.'

'Thank you Melanie, I suggest you go home and leave us to continue with our investigations. Who is in charge in the absence of Michael?'

'Well normally it is Stewart McMillan, the fund's co-founder, but he is away today so it would be the office manager Mr Davis.'

'Please tell Mr Davis that we would like to see him and will be with him shortly.'

Malaga

William Dean arrived by taxi at the austere white building in the hills some 50 miles outside Malaga. His mobile went as he stepped from the car.

He could see the taxi-driver listening to his rapid Czech dialogue and looking totally bemused.

That will teach you to eavesdrop, thought William.

The news on the phone was good. Things at home were on schedule and going to plan. The clinic was expecting him and they were ready. He couldn't wait for a nice rest. He would need it. It had been a long week.

Gerrards Cross

Tom had seen more of Helen in the past 24 hours than in their last month as a couple. It was weird. He wasn't sure how he felt about her but found himself looking forward to his visits to her lab.

He was currently sitting in her office sipping a mug of piping hot tea that she had kindly, if coolly, offered.

It had always been Tom who had made the tea, every morning religiously, two mugs by her side of the bed when she woke up.

He snapped back to the present; he really had to stop this daydreaming about her. Helen was in mid-flow.

'. . . so that is what we know so far.'

Tom, realising he had missed everything she had said had no choice. He clutched his tea and feebly responded.

'I am sorry Helen can you run that past me again?'

'Oh for God's sake, Tom!'

The room had turned to ice and all Tom could do was stare into his mug.

'Oh very well then, the body is believed to be that of Michael Defreitas an investment banker and GX resident. We have just received confirmation that the blood type of the body matches that on the medical records of Mr Defreitas. Interestingly, the man's blood group is AB negative which is a very rare blood group. Less than one per cent of the population, surely it is too much of a coincidence?'

Tom shuddered at the use of the word coincidence and wondered whether Helen was getting her own back for the 'devil is in the detail' jibe from the previous day. Tom's suspicion of coincidences was legendary in the Uxbridge force.

'Not totally conclusive Helen, but good enough for me to continue my investigation of Defreitas. I have my team currently investigating his private life, business life and background. Do you have anything more for me?'

Helen turned to him and smiled weakly.

'As per my original opinion I can confirm that the man died on Monday afternoon and was likely to have been strangled although the exact cause of death will not be established until the head turns up. There is bruising around the wrists and ankles which would indicate that he had been bound before death.'

'Is there any way of knowing how long the man was tied up?'

'Sorry, it is not an exact science.'

They finished their tea in virtual silence. Tom, feeling uncomfortable, rushed it, scalded his mouth and beat a hasty retreat.

Newsum was waiting by the car. 'Any more information Sir?'

Tom grunted, 'not much, really seems to be pretty much as per Helen's initial assessment. How are we getting on with the background checks on Defreitas?'

Newsum pulled out her notebook and started to recite.

'He is 43 years old, educated at Jesus College, Oxford, which is where he met Stewart McMillan. He and McMillan set up Proteus, a very successful investment fund whilst still at Oxford.

Defreitas is very high profile and a bit of a celeb. He has attracted a lot of celeb money especially from footballers.'

'Are his parents still alive?'

'I found no records of any next of kin, nor in fact, any records before his days at Oxford.'

'Keep digging, we need to have the full picture.'

'The Proteus office is in Mayfair and I rang again and this time was put through to John Davis the office manager who was in a right old state. I asked whether Mr Defreitas was back from abroad and he said that he had not seen him since he went to lunch with a client on Monday and that this morning the finance director had been found dead in his office.'

Tom shot forward in his seat. 'That makes two directors now dead! Wonder whether it was suicide? Interesting. This might be a very, very short murder enquiry.'

'Or a long complicated one sir!'

Tom ignored the pessimism. 'Who is dealing with the death of the finance director?'

'DS Brunton of Mayfair, don't you know him?'

'Yeah he's a good mate, we trained at Hendon together. Haven't spoken to him for a while, last time it seemed he was having wife trouble – in fact we both were.'

He grabbed his phone and scrolled through his address book until he found the number he wanted. The mobile was answered gruffly on the third ring.

'Brunton.'

'How is the soft life?'

'Who is that?'

'It's me, Tom Sparks, Can't believe you have forgotten me already!"

'Oh, hi mate not the best time to call. Got a dead one here and the wife is up to her old tricks.'

'Suicide?'

'Not my style, I think that's the cowards way out. I am going to tough it out and confront her. Start again if I have to.'

'No, no, not you, the body!'

'Well sort of, some masturbation technique that went wrong. Ended up suffocating himself whilst his head was in a plastic bag and he was sucking on an orange. No doubt the coroner will declare it as death by misadventure. Why the interest?'

'Well we are investigating the murder of a banker in GX and Jane, my DS, discovered that his finance director died in Mayfair earlier today, just putting two and two together. Better come down and check it out, is that okay with you?'

'Course, we're at the office now. See you soon.'

Tom turned back to Newsum.

'What have we got so far on Proteus?'

'Clean although something slightly unusual did turn up. The name Proteus cropped up in a missing person's report about three weeks ago. Man called Adam Batstone was due there for an interview and never turned up. Hasn't been seen since, his family is very concerned.'

'Maybe nothing, but you know me, I don't believe in coincidences, better check it out.'

Tom sensed that something was up with Newsum. 'Something troubling you Newsum?'

'Not at all sir.'

'Mmmm. That's not what your face is telling me.'

'Well sir, it is about Victoria Steadman.'

Tom sighed. He had hoped that subject had been forgotten but had as usual under-estimated Newsum's curiosity. Time to prevaricate.

'Oh that bloody woman. I was hoping I'd heard the last of her.'

'But sir she found the body.'

'I know, I know. I am being a coward that's all. Truth is she scares me to death. No offence but it really needs to be me who takes her statement and I'm just not ready to do battle with her again so soon.'

Tom could see Newsum unsuccessfully suppressing a smirk.

Leeds

Tooley let Porter drive for most of the journey to Leeds. It should have only taken three hours but Porter stopped twice, once for a bacon sandwich, the second time for a scotch egg. *God the man was a human dustbin and a dead cert for a coronary* Tooley thought as he watched Porter polishing off the scotch egg.

Tooley spent most of the journey on the phone organising his team. He had ordered door-to-door enquiries of all the houses in the Wembley station neighbourhood and for incident boards to be put up at both Marylebone and Wembley stations.

Finally they arrived in Leeds and made their way to 16A, Elland Road. Tooley took a moment to stare at the Leeds United Football Ground. He felt an involuntary shudder as he recalled the night when a reckless tackle ended his dream of being the best footballer in the world. Porter belching brought him back to reality.

Despite their stops to stoke the Porter fire, their early start had enabled them to arrive by mid-morning. They had arranged in advance for a search warrant and were meeting the local CID at the house.

The Leeds CID man was a typically dour Northerner who introduced himself as Detective Constable Jack Smith. He handed them the warrant and departed with not so much as a by your leave.

The house was situated in a cul-de-sac adjoining Elland Road and was a narrow terraced house similar to those often found near football grounds. The terrace had been built in the 30s and was in need of some TLC, especially a lick of paint.

They strolled up the garden path, if it could be called that, and knocked on the door and waited. They were just about to give up when a spotty youth appeared at the door. He had lank, greasy hair and was clearly half stoned.

'Morning lad, we are from the police, is your mum in?'

'Nah my mum's in London gone to meet some bloke.'

'Can we come in?'

'If you must.'

As he let them in Tooley asked, 'What's your name son?'

'T-t-t-ommy Swift,' he stuttered.

He looked scared, he was probably sitting on a hoard of drugs or pot.

They followed him in and sat him down and gave him the bad news. He took it quite well but then he was half stoned.

'Do you have a photo of your mum?'

'Somewhere, I'll try and find it,' he went to rise from his seat.

'Not yet, do you mind if we ask you a few questions?'

'Sure.'

'You said your mum had gone to London to meet some bloke.'

'Any idea who?'

'Yeah some foreigner called Tomas, came from Russia or somewhere.'

'Where was she going to meet him?'

'Dunno, London I think, they met in a chatroom on the internet."

'Were you and your mum close?'

'Not really, we hardly saw one another, she used to spend all her time in her room on the internet. Chatting to people and eating.'

'How long was your mum going to be in London for?'

'Dunno, she just gave me a wad of notes and said she'd see me soon.'

'Anything else at all?'

'Well she seemed to have a lot more money recently, she'd bought herself a load of new clothes.'

'Such as a bright pink coat?'

'Yeah, awful thing, how did she die?'

'She was strangled and I'm afraid we are going to have to take you back with us to identify her body. Mind if we look around?'

'No, feel free.'

The house was clearly suffering from being left in the care of a half stoned teenager. They ducked into the kitchen and quickly ducked out again. There were pots and pans and uneaten meals dotted all over the place. They went upstairs to the bedrooms, Tommy's was a typical teenager's room but the real eye-opener was Shirley's which was clearly something else entirely. The room was dominated by a large desk on which sat a large flat screen monitor. It was flanked with three digital cameras and sex toys of various shapes and sizes – a veritable temple to sex.

Tooley made a mental note to invest in some Ann Summers shares.

They returned downstairs and told Tommy they would have to take Shirley's PC with them along with the cameras and her personal papers.

Tommy shrugged and went into his bedroom to collect his things. Tooley found his indifference to his mother's death disconcerting, but knew that everyone dealt with grief differently.

An hour later they had what they needed all bagged up and ready to go along with a rather unhappy Tommy.

Drugs, what a bloody waste of time and money thought Tooley.

Malaga

William Dean came to and could feel the Spanish sun beating down on him through the grill on the window.

He looked around. The sparsely furnished room was brilliant white with a vase full of flowers on a table in one corner. A wall-mounted TV was gibbering away in Spanish in the other.

He was hot and thirsty. There was a button by his bed and he pressed it. Nothing happened. He pressed it again, still nothing. He would just have to wait. He took in his own circumstances especially the fact that his head was almost totally wrapped in bandages and his leg was strapped up and hurting severely.

His self-assessment was finally interrupted by a nurse ambling in to the room.

'Good afternoon Meester Dean welcome back, I will go tell the doctor you are awake,' disappearing again before he could tell her he was dying for a pee.

He waited another 15 very uncomfortable minutes until the nurse returned with a man in a white coat, William presumed he was the doctor.

The man smiled at William and said, 'The operations went well and we hope to be able to let you see our handiwork tomorrow. In the meantime your amputation was a complete success. Just one word of warning. It is not unusual for you to continue to feel the bottom part of your leg even though it is no longer there.'

William grimaced at the realization that he had sacrificed the bottom part of his leg to complete his plan. It had seemed such a good idea at the time.

Finally the nurse arrived with the very necessary bottle and he relieved himself.

The whole thing was turning into a nightmare. Lying in a very uncomfortable Spanish hospital bed in massive pain had not really featured that strongly in William's plans. How the bloody hell was he going to last in here for another four weeks whilst he healed? This was not the long awaited rest he had longed for.

Four weeks he decided was also too long for other reasons and he started planning his next move.

———

Tom and Newsum found the offices of Proteus easily but parking was another matter altogether. In the end they decided to throw themselves on the mercy of the local constabulary and parked on the double yellow lines in the cordoned off street leaving a note on the dashboard.

The offices of Proteus were picture perfect English Heritage set on four floors. The front of the house was a mixture of cream render and black woodwork and said one word to Tom. Expensive.

He strolled inside the building with Newsum and slapped the back of the dark haired man in the check sports jacket waiting in reception. God Terry never changed, not even the fashion of his clothes.

Terry turned and gave Tom a big bear hug.

'Good to see you mate, this is my DI and partner Jeremy Ward.' Pointing to the man he had been talking to before Tom's arrival.

'Hi Jeremy, I'm Tom Sparks and this is my DS, Jane Newsum.' He gestured at the now blushing and suddenly coy DS who had gone all girlie. Looking back at Jeremy he could see why. He had the dark, brooding looks that have a devastating effect on women and clearly Newsum was no exception.

'So what have we got?'

'William Thornton, the finance director was found dead this morning by his secretary. Apparently she came in at her usual time of 8.00am and went in to tidy his office and there he was. Lying on the floor, naked, plastic bag over his head an orange jammed in his mouth.'

Tom interrupted.

'I don't know about you boys but this is a new one to me although I do seem to recall a couple of high profile deaths, especially that Conservative MP.'

The two Londoners shrugged indifferently, which said it all really and made Tom realise what a sheltered career he had in GX. Jeremy interrupted Tom's interruption.

'I understand from Mick that you are investigating the possible murder of Michael Defreitas, the co-founder and managing director of Proteus.'

'Yes, we are still waiting for a positive ID but we are 90 per cent sure our body is that of Defreitas. Have you questioned the staff?'

'Obviously your news has changed things, Tom. What looked like a straightforward non-suspicious death is now starting to look a bit more sinister. We have so far only spoken to Thornton's secretary who is in a right state. We had a quick chat with her and sent her home – she knows very little about the business side of things. The other director, Stewart McMillan, is unavailable today but the office manager John Davis is here and we are about to interview him, want to sit in?'

'Sounds good, Newsum can you do a little bit of sniffing around?'

They entered a plush oak-panelled office and a small wiry man stood up from behind his desk. He had the look of a civil servant about him. Plain grey flannel suit, white shirt, blue tie and shiny black lace-up shoes. The only real concession to modern day living was a pair of frameless glasses perched on the bridge of his nose.

'Mr Davis? Mr John Davis?'

'Yes officers.'

'I am Detective Inspector Jeremy Ward from City CID and this is my colleague Detective Sergeant Terry Brunton. The third officer is Detective Chief Inspector Tom Sparks from Uxbridge CID.'

Davis seemed bewildered.

'Why such interest in this death? It is pretty clear what happened. Poor William, how humiliating.'

'Well I don't suppose he is feeling particularly humiliated now sir.' Jeremy quipped.

Tom interjected.

'Mr Davis, we have considerable joint interest in your firm since not only has Mr Thornton died but we are investigating the possibility that Michael Defreitas has been murdered. We believe that we may have found his body yesterday morning in Gerrards Cross.'

Davis sat down with a thump and went as white as a sheet.

'What? Both dead?'

'Yes – strange coincidence, isn't it? Tell me how did Mr Thornton get on with Mr Defreitas?'

'You don't think – surely you don't think that William killed Michael?'

'I'm not thinking anything at this stage but you must admit that it's strange that your managing director gets murdered and the next day one of his co-directors dies in bizarre circumstances.'

'But William was such a nice, gentle man. I don't believe it.'

'How is the business doing at the moment Mr Davis, having any problems?'

'I have little to do with the financial side of things my role is operational office manager with responsibility for the staff and general admin. The Board deals with all financial matters. I do know however that we had a lot of new funds come in recently and Michael was very excited for the future.'

'Okay. I expect this has all been a bit of a shock to you, we're going to be here for some time. Feel free to go home if you wish but please make sure that you leave your contact details with one of the officers.'

Tom continued.

'Mr Davis, we're going to have to search all the offices and investigate the accounts thoroughly and this could take a number of days, I hope we can rely on your full co-operation.'

'Of course officer, of course.'

As they got up to leave, Tom turned and said.

'Oh by the way Mr Davis, were you due to interview Adam Batstone here three weeks ago?'

Davis flinched.

'Adam Batstone?'

'Yes he was due to have an interview here and never turned up, hasn't been seen since.'

'Oh I did hear about that, no, he was due to be interviewed by Stewart McMillan, the co-founder.'

'Is Mr McMillan available?'

'I'm sorry officer he's away on business and won't be returning today.'

'Do you know where he is?'

'No, although his secretary would probably know but she is on holiday, she is getting married tomorrow.'

'We'll need to speak to Mr McMillan. Can you please give us his contact details?'

John Davis opened a desk drawer and rummaged around for a moment and then handed Tom a card.

'That's Stewart's business card which has all his contact details.'

'Thanks Mr Davis, that will be all although just a word of advice. Be careful, Proteus seems a very dangerous place to work at the moment.'

Tom felt he had achieved as much as he was likely to at the office, especially in the absence of Stewart McMillan and, finding Newsum, announced he was returning to GX. He turned to the two City detectives shaking each firmly by the hand.

'Great to see you again Terry, shame about the circumstances. Good to finally meet you too Jeremy.'

'Give me a call when you're in London next Tom maybe you can give me some marriage guidance?' Terry replied.

'With my track record Terry?' Tom grimaced, 'it would be good to catch up though, I'll give you a call. Come on Newsum, back to civilisation and sanity.'

Tom turned to go and then stopped.

'Oh just one last thing, either of you ever heard of Tony Marciano?'

Jeremy's head jerked towards Tom. It was an involuntary movement that Tom noticed with interest although Jeremy quickly recovered his composure and calmly replied.

'Tony Marciano? Now that name does ring a bell, not one of ours but I think the Met have had him on their radar for years. Why do you ask?'

'It's probably nothing, his name cropped up earlier today, we're checking if there's a connection to our murder.'

Wembley

After a long journey back from Leeds, again punctuated by Porter's dietary needs, this time a fry-up at motorway services in Nottingham, they took a now tearful Tommy to the mortuary to identify his mum. Tommy had come down and sobered up completely and Tooley realised that he was a nice lad and felt desperately sorry for him.

So, Tooley reflected during the journey, they had a woman from out of area meeting an unknown man she met on the internet. Hardly a rare occurrence in these days of cyber romance but it was really very rare for any harm to result. He needed to know what secrets were stored inside Shirley's PC and quickly.

He picked up his mobile and dialled a number. The response was fast, barely two rings, the voice young, cheerful and very female.

'Hello, big boy.'

Tooley felt himself blushing.

'Oh hi Mog.'

'Got something for me?'

The blush deepened. *Too right I have* he thought and then tried to concentrate on the reason for the call.

'Yes as a matter of fact, you busy today?'

'A bit but I always have time for you, where and when do you want me?'

If only, Tooley squirmed in his seat.

'On my way back from Leeds should be at the station in about an hour, shall we say two hours from now unless I ring?'

'Sure Tooley, see you then.'

Mog was his secret weapon. Mog was short for Margaret and she was a little stunner, black haired with lovely green eyes. Shame she was half his age.

Two hours later, she swept into his office wearing a floral gypsy wrap around skirt with a slit at the front that tantalised but didn't reveal.

Mog was a computer genius. He had met her when he busted a computer scam based in the Tottenham Court Road four years earlier. Taking a liking to her and spotting her obvious potential, he had made a deal with her. She came clean, got a suspended, sentence and worked for him on demand.

He pointed to Shirley's PC tower and screen saying, 'There you go, somewhere on there is the greatest unrequited love story since Romeo and Juliet. How long do you need?'

'Give me an hour and a half.'

Just over 90 minutes later, Mog returned.

'Steamy or what!' Mog said, round eyed. 'Tooley, I'm not sure a married guy your age can cope with the details, this woman was hot, hot, hot, with a capital H. She had over 100 online lovers!'

'I think I can take it, I know what she looked like.' He grunted, 'so tell me more, did she have any special boyfriends?'

'Well there is one guy Tomas who lived in the Czech Republic who she'd got very fond of over the past few weeks. In fact, they were due to meet at Marylebone Station on Wednesday night, under the clock.'

'How can you find all this out in 90 minutes?'

'I am a computer genius and a speed reader,' she said through a cheeky grin. 'Why are you so interested in Shirley?'

'Because she was murdered two nights ago by a person or, more likely, persons unknown.'

'Tomas?'

'Well he seems a good bet. Can you print off all the communications between them?'

'Sure but I will warn you there are a lot of them and they are very near the knuckle some of them.'

'Anything else of interest on there?'

'Well she had over £15k in the bank.'

'How do you know that?'

'I went into her online bank account. She was being paid £1,000 a week. Transferred into her account every Friday without fail. Bank in the Cayman Islands.'

'So our Shirley was more than just an online lover then? Tell you what, print off all her emails and cyber chats dating back to four weeks before the payments started.'

'But Tooley there are thousands of them.'

'Well the sooner you start the sooner you will be finished.'

Three hours later they had hundreds of emails and cyber conversations sitting in front of them along with a copy of Shirley's last six months bank statements.

'Porter!'

Porter appeared, munching on a Mars Bar.

'Porter, got a little job for you, start reading all these emails for anything suspicious.

Gerrards Cross

Newsum drove them back through the heavy Friday evening rush-hour traffic giving Tom time to reflect and plan. It was well known that the first 48 hours of every case were crucial and Tom was pleased with his progress but also aware that this threatened to be a very complicated case.

Growing up, Tom had taken little interest in the financial world despite living in an area of affluence and coming from a fairly wealthy family. He had always ducked economics classes. In fact he had ducked as many classes as possible. He had hated Eton with a passion.

He needed specialist assistance, so Tom phoned DCC Protheroe and asked for a member of the fraud squad to meet him at Proteus the following morning to check out their computers and books. He also phoned in to order his team to wait for him so they could have a close of play meeting to update the case.

The journey seemed interminable and he ran out of people to ring. *How on earth do people do this everyday?* He asked himself as they finally arrived back in GX. It was now 6pm which only left him an hour with his team as the DCC had asked him to be present at a press conference at 7pm.

He now stood in the incident room and gazed over his motley crew of detectives who clearly were anxious to start their weekend. They were fidgeting and checking their watches as he checked the notes he had hastily made on the journey back.

Apart from Newsum he had four other detectives in his team, all constables.

Julia Andrews was the youngest and also the keenest and smartest. She was, however, well aware of her abilities, very ambitious and had a tendency to be a bit of a loose cannon. Julia was a pretty brunette, small and athletic with a cheeky smile. Apart of course from Newsum, Andrews was Tom's favourite and everyone knew it.

Mel, or Melanie as her parents intended, Taylor was not as bright but was enthusiastic and a real steady Eddie. Every team needed one. She was particularly good at trawling through pages and pages of detail and doing the mundane jobs no one else wanted. She would sit there all day staring at her PC through the giant lenses of her horn-rimmed glasses, nibbling chocolate and drinking Diet Coke. Mel also looked the part, a bit lumpy and built for comfort not speed. Definitely not the best in a chase.

Jez Bryant was a young man in a hurry. He was in his mid-twenties and had joined the police from a local bank. His main interest was fraud and he longed to join the fraud squad. He would inevitably want to be involved with the investigation of Proteus and its finances.

Bill Thomas was the old pro of the team. He had been there, seen it and done it. In his late forties he was now in his twenty-eighth year on the force and still loved the job. He was an old-fashioned cop who was the one that kept the others in line and the first they went to if they had a problem. He was only three years from retirement to the cottage by the sea he had always wanted.

They might have been a motley crew but Tom trusted them and wouldn't swap any of them. They were a small tightly knit team and Tom liked it that way. He could never understand the need for some of the DCI's to surround themselves with huge teams.

'Okay team, how did we got on then?'

As usual, Bill was the spokesman.

'We've conducted house-to-house enquiries and no one heard anything unusual on the night the body was discovered. We do however have a report of a black Hummer being seen passing through West Common in the early hours. Local householder with a prostate problem got up for a constitutional and spotted it out of the window.'

'Okay let's check up on Hummers. I want to know everything about them, particularly if any have been reported stolen but let's also get a list of all black Hummers registered locally. Is that it?'

'I spoke to the neighbours of Mr Defreitas.' Mel piped up. 'He has owned his penthouse flat from new but it had been empty for two years until he moved in about three months ago. Kept himself to himself.'

'Strange he left it empty for so long, wonder why? See what else you can dig up Mel, speak to the local estate agents. I want to build up a complete picture of this man and what made him tick.'

Tom paused.

'Anything else of interest?'

'Yes we found Mr Defreitas's Aston Martin in the car park of GX rail station. Strange thing is that it is the car that was caught on the CCTV camera near one of last week's break-ins, the doctors surgery.'

'Mmmm probably a coincidence.' He turned to Newsum, 'any history of drug abuse on his records?'

'Well he does have a file. He was arrested as a student at Oxford. Some kind of anti-government protest.'

'Any fingerprints on file?'

'No sir, he was let off with a warning'

'One last thing, can someone please contact the Met and Serious Crimes and run a check on what we know about a man called Tony Marciano. Based in Clerkenwell. I want to know everything about him.'

Clerkenwell

Tony Marciano, Big Tony to his mates, sat back in the rear seat of his Roller and puffed on his Havana cigar, rolled on the thigh of a virgin no doubt. He had been told so many times to give up smoking but in his occupation so few people died of natural causes he couldn't see the point.

As befitting his nickname, Tony was huge, Italian and a genius at laundering money, this made him very valuable to a syndicate of families that ran organised crime in London.

Tony was officially a florist, although the only flowers he ever sent were to the funerals of people who had crossed him. Tony was Mob with a capital M.

Now in his fifties, Tony had inherited 'the business' from his father who had met an untimely end 20 years earlier. He had grown it into what it was today, fifty per cent legit, fifty per cent illegit. Tony liked to think that he mainly ran the legit side but the fact was he frequently had to cross the line to the very profitable dark side.

A key part of Tony's operation was Proteus and especially Michael Defreitas.

Tony had first heard about Michael Defreitas and Stewart McMillan in the late eighties when they won an investment competition organised by *The Sunday Times* whilst they were still at Oxford. Intrigued, he had sought them out and made them an offer they couldn't refuse.

Now it seemed that one of them had been murdered and Tony was a very worried man. Tony punched the keys on his phone and spoke briefly into it.

'It's Tony. What the bloody hell happened to Michael?'

He listened and then barked, 'I don't care, just find out! Bribe a policeman! I pay you to keep your finger on the pulse. If anything goes wrong I will blame you.'

He then listened for nearly a minute before shouting. 'What! You have got to be having a giraffe! Thornton dead too? This is a fucking disaster. Now get me that information and fast!'

He rang off without waiting for a reply. His cigar had lost its allure and he hurled it out of the window.

Mayfair

In Mayfair, John Davis, sat staring at the now dead mobile phone feeling queasy as he contemplated Big Tony's anger.

He just couldn't understand what had happened. Everything seemed to be fine until Monday. They had just attracted two new celebrities, Chelsea's newest overpaid foreign player and the latest one-minute wonder created by *Britain's Got Talent*.

But then it had all gone wrong, Michael had failed to come back from lunch with a client and then been found murdered in Gerrards Cross. Then William had been found dead in such bizarre circumstances. What on earth was happening?

John had been nervous of Tony Marciano from the start but had needed the money to pay off his gambling debts. The £1,000 a week in cash that Tony paid him enabled him to play roulette once a week and all he had to do in return was keep an eye on things at Proteus and keep Tony informed. In particular, he was to let him know if anything was happening that could raise any eyebrows.

John needed access to the computers but the police were everywhere, crawling all over the files and computers.

He knew something was badly wrong and needed to find out what and fast!

Wembley

It was also early evening when Tooley called his team together in the incident room. He waited patiently while they trooped in and settled themselves. Unlike Tom Sparks, he had a relatively large team that consisted of two detective sergeants and six detective constables.

Call it ego.

He recapped. 'So we have a dead woman who started an online affair with a Czech called Tomas. They arranged to meet at Marylebone Station, under the clock. He is obviously the prime suspect but why did he murder her?'

'Maybe he was upset when he discovered how fat she was?' Porter interrupted.

The rest of the team sniggered at the irony of Porter referring to someone as fat.

'Possible.'

'Maybe he was allergic to pink?' interjected one of the DC's to a chorus of giggles.

'Okay okay okay, let's just settle down shall we. Any luck with your door-to-door enquiries round Wembley?'

'A bit. A witness was walking his dog at just after 1am and he saw a black Hummer on the road by the station. We don't get many Hummers toodling about in the wee hours around here,' said Porter who had taken the role of reporting on behalf of the team.

'Number plate?'

'Sorry too dark. The Council now switch the lights off after the last train has gone through. Locals are up in arms.'

'Don't blame them, it isn't nice having a dead body turn up in your garden.'

'No, no, they aren't happy about the Council cutting off the lights at 1am!'

'So whoever dumped Shirley knew about the lights going off, could be local then. Do we know of anyone locally who owns a Hummer or any reports of one having been stolen?'

Silence.

'Okay can someone do a check on that and see if there was a Hummer parked outside Marylebone station at any time during the evening? Anything else of any interest?'

'Well I am not sure if it is relevant sir,' continued Porter, 'but I was checking the missing persons reports and a Harrow landlady has reported her lodger missing. He arrived from Eastern Europe two weeks ago and disappeared a few days later. His name is Tomas.'

'You wonder whether it is relevant?' An old saying occurred to Tooley. *You can be thought stupid or open your mouth and remove all doubt.* He returned to the present.

'Okay can someone go and see the landlady, no, on second thoughts Porter, you and I will go and talk to the landlady first thing in the morning. You lot get humming.'

A hummed chorus of *Always look on the bright side of life* reached his ears and he smiled and shouted. 'Bloody comedians! I meant go find that effing Hummer!'

Malaga

William Dean settled down for the night as best he could. He'd had all his hair removed by electrolysis earlier in the day and two days ago he had full facial plastic surgery and part of his left leg removed.

How settling could that be?

Gerrards Cross

Tom finally got home and tucked in to a take-away curry and a can of Stella. He usually preferred wine with his evening meal but the day had been long and he hadn't had time to stop in The Apple Tree for his usual Friday constitutional pint. So beer it was.

Finally, he thought *the weekend.*

Well not quite, there was the small matter of meeting the fraud squad in Mayfair. After that he had nothing to do except sit and veg in front of the telly or go down the pub and have a drink with the lads. It was at times like this that he missed Helen most; in fact he realised he always missed Helen the most.

Mother had disappeared for an early bath and then bed so Tom settled in front of the television. He channel-hopped and eventually selected an episode of *The Good Life*, a poor choice really in view of his inertia towards the badly needed garden activities.

He must have dozed off because he was woken by *You'll Never Walk Alone*, his mobile's ringtone. A present from some joker in the office at Christmas knowing he was a fanatical Liverpool supporter.

'Hello.' He answered sleepily.

'Tom its Helen, I just rang up to check how the investigation was going.'

His adrenalin rushed and his heart leapt. *Stay calm man and be professional*, he told himself.

'Thanks for the call, you still at work?'

'No, finally got away at seven and was just sitting having a glass of wine and was wondering how you were getting on – with the case, that is.' she hurriedly added.

'Well we've run checks on Defreitas. He seems to have disappeared, even more curious is the fact that one of his work colleagues also died last night.'

'You know me. I don't like coincidences. I have the fraud squad checking the Proteus books. We're also looking for a black Hummer that was seen near the common that evening.'

'I think you're right, it does seem too much of a coincidence for one of them to be murdered and then the other one dies in such bizarre circumstances. But then, Tom, things are never as they seem.'

'You usually have lots of theories of your own Helen. Any ideas?'

'Well seems like a professional hit to me and maybe the business card for that Italian may not be a coincidence. Well, thanks for the update, sleep well and have a good weekend.'

And then she was gone.

Tom climbed the stairs to the accompaniment of his mother's snoring that not only filled but shook the house, which was some achievement. It was a big house.

As he drifted off to sleep he kept replaying his conversation with Helen. Something wasn't right, but what was it?

———

In Wembley it was late and Tooley and Porter had just finished their beer. Tooley went home and Porter went to the chippie.

It had been a bloody long day especially for Tooley. Hopefully a long hot bath would wash away the memory of Elland Road. God he hated the place.

———

Chalfont St Peter

Pete was reflecting on what had been a brilliant week.

He still had most of the cash and drugs from the two jobs he did for the stranger and now this, he and the missus had won a fortnight's holiday for the whole family in a luxury villa in Marbella on the Costa Del Sol, wherever that was. Free travel, including a chauffeur-driven car to and from the airport, and even a grand's spending money.

The letter had arrived yesterday congratulating them on winning the competition they had entered at the shopping mall in Uxbridge. Inside were airline tickets in their names and a cheque payable to him for £1,000 from a Cayman Island bank account. Neither of them could remember entering any competition but it was probably the wife as she was always filling out surveys and forms and things whilst out shopping.

It was very short notice because the flights were the following Saturday but what the heck. The missus was so excited and had spent the day in Uxbridge buying suntan oil and a new bikini.

After so many years of strife and disappointments it seemed that their luck had changed.

Saturday 17th October 2009

Tom slept in for a change and woke to the smell of his mum's stew, or, more accurately, the odour of overcooked cabbage. He rolled out of bed musing that the only thing he had liked about School was being rescued from his mother's cooking. School food an improvement? Now that was saying something.

He looked out of the window and contemplated the garden that needed his undivided attention. Problem was he wasn't a gardener and his mum suffered from a sticky chair. They did have a gardener but he had been with them for over 40 years and was now in his 80s. He worked very slowly and his stoop meant he could not attend to anything over five foot in height which gave the garden a rather odd top-heavy look. Tom made a mental note to go into the garden tomorrow armed with a pair of secateurs and a stepladder.

Tearing his gaze from the garden, he looked skywards. It was one of those glorious British autumnal mornings when he wished he played golf. So, what should he do on this wonderful Saturday morning. Which pub would he honour with his presence?

He decided The Apple Tree was calling. He had to meet the fraud squad officer at Proteus at eleven and it was only half eight, he had time to kill.

Tom showered and dressed then walked into Gerrards Cross for a quick coffee. His route took him past West Common and he couldn't resist the temptation to step into the woodland and check out the crime scene again.

He was about 20 yards from the spot where the body was found when he realised that someone else had the same idea as him. She was tall, blonde and Helen. His immediate reaction was not to be seen so he dove behind the nearest bush before she spotted him.

Why was Helen here in the common? Her domain was in the lab. His curiosity was so peaked he didn't see the large

Doberman lumbering toward him, closely followed by its middle-aged, middle-class, rather prissy looking mistress.

It was too late to run, all he could do was posture himself for the inevitable tussle with fur and fangs and invent a quick excuse for being caught ogling an attractive woman from the bushes.

Then just as teeth were supposed to meet flesh, nothing happened.

He slowly opened his eyes and saw the Doberman and its owner staring at him. 'I say what on earth are you up to in there? You're not some kind of pervert are you? Sabre is trained to sniff out perverts.'

He glanced around and could see Helen heading their way. Only one thing for it, he thought as he flashed his warrant card and said loudly. 'Police officer searching for evidence.'

'Oh I am so sorry I didn't realise. Come on Sabre let's leave the man to it.'

By now Helen was a yard away and his cover was blown. No avoiding this one and her fangs looked even sharper.

'Are you stalking me, Detective Chief Inspector Sparks? If you are I'll have to call the police immediately.'

'I'm told the local CID are superb and thoroughly recommended.'

'Hummm, so what exactly are you doing here?'

'I was going to ask you the same thing.'

'Well, I . . .'she hesitated before continuing, 'I wanted to see the crime scene in the light.'

'You're taking a lot of interest in this case Helen, late night calls and off duty inspections.'

'Well it isn't everyday we have a headless man dumped on our doorstep and I want to make sure we don't miss anything.'

'Very commendable.' Tom said. *But hardly credible*, he thought. 'Fancy a coffee?' Helen had a strange look on her face and didn't reply; he knew from past experience not to dig too deep.

He took in the crime scene himself for the first time, in particular the mass of yellow tape with which uniform had re-decorated the area. Nothing sprung out at him.

'Find anything?'

'What?' Helen said with a jump as though she didn't realise that Tom was still there. 'Oh no, nothing at all. Seems we did a thorough job the other night, as always. Well I better be off now. See you soon Tom.'

'No coffee then,' Tom murmured to himself.

Tom stood still for many minutes trying to gather his thoughts in particular why Helen was acting so strangely. Again he thought back to the previous evening and tried to recall why their conversation then, and now, made him so uneasy.

In the end, he concluded that she was still struggling with the closeness they had shared and which she had shattered out of the blue.

Tom shrugged and headed off to the high street for his coffee. Latte always helped him think. His gut shouted *delusional*. He didn't believe in coincidences.

Harrow

Tooley loved the weekends when he wasn't working. It was a time he could spend shopping with his wife before, brownie points earned, disappearing down the pub to watch football and have a beer.

Today, sadly, was not one of those days. Tooley and Porter were in Harrow, the High Road to be precise. Porter wasn't eating for a change, although he did look a bit restless. Tooley had however already had to witness him consume a huge fry-up at the greasy spoon where they had met earlier that morning.

Maureen Jones lived in a former corner shop that she had converted into a boarding house. Wonder if she has planning for this? Tooley thought as he rang the front doorbell. *Land of Hope and Glory* chimed loudly to announce their presence and soon a very short skinny lady was at the door.

'Mrs Jones? Detective Inspector Tooley and Detective Sergeant Porter. We've come to investigate your missing person.'

'Oh how good of you, fancy a cup of tea?'

'Please, one with no sugar, one with four, both white'

'Chocolate biscuit?'

'No thanks we are both on diets.'

Porter frowned at his boss.

'Well take a seat while I put the kettle on and then we can have a nice chat.'

Porter and Tooley took their places on chairs at the scratched kitchen table and waited for Mrs Jones. The chairs had seen better days and the last thing they needed was to be filled by the like of DS Porter. His chair groaned and seemed about to collapse but finally settled into an uneasy truce with the large man.

Mrs Jones came back with tea in Wallace and Gromit mugs and said 'Four sugars for you Detective Sergeant Porter?'

'No ma'am that one is for the DI – I am watching my figure,' and winked at her.

'Have you been taking lodgers for long Mrs Jones?' Tooley asked.

'About ten years, since my dear old Reg went.'

'Oh I am sorry, may I ask how old was Reg when he died?'

'Oh he isn't dead, he just moved in with that scrubber down the road.'

Tooley quickly changed the subject.

'Do you take in many foreigners?'

'These days yes, it seems there are more of them than us at times. My friend Mavis blames it on the Common Market'

'Don't you mean the EU?'

'Probably, it is all a lot of nonsense if you ask me.'

'Where did Tomas come from?''

'Oh one of those eastern European places, Prague I think.' She paused, 'Yes it was Prague definitely.'

'When did he arrive?'

'He arrived on the Monday'

'Which Monday?'

'The one before last, would have been the 5th.' she said consulting the calendar on the wall that had clearly been a present from a local Chinese take away.

'Did he have a job?'

'Nothing definite, he was hoping to move up North with some lady he had met on the internet.'

'If she was up North any idea why he was down here?'

'Well apparently he knew someone in London who was going to help him out, find him a bit of work and things. In fact, he had been trying to get hold of them all that week and only managed to speak to them last Sunday. After the call he shot out the house and I haven't seen him since.'

'Any idea at all who this person was?'

'He never told me his name only his nickname which was something like Starsky, or Husky.'

'Did he tell you anything else about his friend in London?'

'No we didn't talk much. His English wasn't very good and what English he knew was disguised very well by his very strong accent. It made conversation very difficult. Although he could do a mean posh English impersonation which would have me in stitches. Apparently he used to watch a lot of old black and white romances.'

She paused, mainly Tooley suspected so her lungs could reload themselves with oxygen.

'Did he talk much about the lady up North?'

'Oh yes, he was always talking about her and their plans for the future.'

'He tell you her name?'

Oh yes he told me on his very first night that he had a gorgeous girlfriend who lived in Leeds and was called Shirley. He said he would be meeting her on Wednesday evening at Marylebone Station. He was so very excited.'

'I see.'

'Has something happened to Tomas? Is that why you are here?'

'We don't know for sure but we do know that his gorgeous girlfriend Shirley was murdered on Wednesday night. We don't know for certain whether Tomas did it but we would like to speak to him most urgently. Mind if we check his room?'

'Oh how awful, please, this way.'

'No fing way I would be a guest here.' Porter muttered breathlessly as they climbed the stairs following Mrs Jones.

Tomas had been given a room in the attic, it was just big enough to fit the smallest of beds, a chest of drawers and a wardrobe. The wardrobe could not be opened at the same time as the drawers.

There was a battered suitcase, some papers and a half empty water glass. A check of the chest of drawers yielded his passport, two very worn checked shirts, a pair of tatty jeans, some underwear and socks. The wardrobe held only a jacket.

Tomas had travelled light.

'Well he's still in the country sir.' ventured Porter as he checked the passport. 'Not a bad looking bloke really, wonder what he saw in fat Shirley.'

'Escape and freedom probably. Thank you Mrs Jones.' Tooley said as he started back down the stairs.

As they were leaving Tooley turned to Mrs Jones and gave her his card.

'We are going to keep his papers for now and would ask you to ring immediately if you hear from him or if you think of anything else that might be useful.'

Mrs Jones smiled pensively as she saw them to the door.

Back in the car, Tooley sought an update from Porter on the emails and cyber conversations Mog had printed off for them the previous day.

'Enjoy your evening's reading Porter?'

'Riveting sir. It really is amazing the lives that some people live. I showed some of the more fruity bits to the wife and she came over all romantic.'

'Lucky you,' Tooley said trying to blot out the image of Porter and his equally portly wife getting frisky. *Bumping uglies*, he thought cringingly.

'Maybe I should borrow them and let my wife read some of them. Anything revealing?'

'Well apart from carnally, very little although it did become clear what Shirley was up to and how she was earning the money from the Cayman Islands. There were a number of conversations with a guy who had the screen name Husky23. Seems she was employed by him to recruit men for porn movies.'

'Porn movies?'

'Yes she was required to find men of a certain look and height. Preferably East European.'

'I wonder why their looks and nationality were so important. I always thought that successful porn stars needed other far more upstanding attributes.' They both laughed.

'Yeah bit of a mystery all round really. Probably comes down to money, it usually does.'

'True, Eastern Europeans are definitely cheaper.'

'Would help if we could find Tomas. He can't have gone far without a job, money or passport. Get the picture on his passport blown up and circulated. Maybe we'll get lucky.'

Something clicked.

'Porter, did you say Husky23?'

'Yes, why'

'Sounds like if we find Husky23 we might solve this whole thing.'

'Of course – the friend who rang.'

Malaga

William Dean was still in considerable pain. The drugs were helping but wore off too quickly, leaving him to endure hours of agony between doses.

He lay there with his thoughts.

Thorpe Park

At that very moment Julian Travis was having fun. He and his wife, Louise, had taken the kids to Thorpe Park for the day. Kylie was fourteen and Wayne was eleven and they were now the size and age when they could enjoy all the rides and attractions.

Louise had just taken them on the rollercoaster and Julian was waiting for them to come back. He was so relieved to finally get a chance to relax after the past few months.

He loved his work and had thrown himself into his new job. The world of investment banking was new to him but he had taken to it like a duck to water. After all he was the IT whizz kid and IT was pretty much the same whichever industry you were in.

He was still a little stunned at how things had changed for him so dramatically, so quickly. One minute he was stuck in his humdrum job with Ranger Life Assurance the next he was in the exciting world of investment banking.

Strange really, Louise was always giving him stick for spending too much time in the bar of the Bull Hotel with Michael Defreitas yet she had soon changed her tune when Michael had offered him a job.

So, he was now happily working for Proteus and earning £200,000 a year, a salary that was twice the industry norm. Everyone at school always called him thick and picked on him. They wouldn't think he was thick now, would they?

Truth was, Julian *was* thick and that was the very reason Michael had chosen him and agreed to pay him such a princely sum. Michael knew Julian would do as he was told and wouldn't ask awkward questions. The perfect arrangement for both of them, a win-win.

Julian worked mainly from home and only went into the office on Tuesdays and Thursdays. He rarely bought a newspaper and as they had left very early that morning, Julian didn't realise that his dream job was about to become a nightmare.

Clerkenwell

Tony Marciano chewed on yet another Havana as he watched his horse triumph at Ascot. Good old Chalky!

Richard Chalky White trained Tony's horses and was the perfect trainer. Well, perfect for Tony, as he knew everything about fixing horse races. He had assured Tony that his five-year-old gelding, Fat Roller, would win and had duly done so at 25 to 1.

They had been holding the horse back for months, watching the betting odds rise with each failure until the time was right. Big Tony did the maths. He had won nearly £100,000. Chalky would get a nice bonus.

Tony's pleasure didn't last long. Proteus was like a storm cloud hanging over him. He had to find out what had happened. He had been laundering money through Michael since the beginning. Stewart was a genius and legalised all his ill-gotten gains without even realising it. Michael had a hold over Stewart who did whatever he asked. It was an elegant arrangement.

But all good things come to an end and it looked as though Proteus was dead and buried like Michael and William Thornton. Well, dead anyway. He made a note to send some flowers.

Time for damage limitation, Tony picked up the phone.

'Jeremy mate, how are you? About that favour you owe me . .'

Mayfair

Saturday had started as a lovely day for Jeremy. He had been out the night before to his favourite club and managed to pull. She was not the most attractive conquest, but boy was she grateful. The less attractive ones always were.

He had kicked her out after a hurried breakfast amid promises of a call later and then gone down to the Proteus offices to check on the progress of their enquiries. There he met DS David Browne from the fraud squad who had arrived before him and was already hard at it, systematically working his way through the Proteus files on one of the desktop computers.

After introductions, Jeremy quickly turned to business.

'Found anything interesting yet?'

'No, not yet. All pretty mundane stuff really. Share transactions, price movements, what you would expect. Proteus had a large amount of money under management and its portfolio was very widespread. There are however a number of locked files.'

'Can you open them?'

'Not me. I have asked the staff and apparently the files have been locked by Michael Defreitas and he is the only one who knows how to unlock them. I'm just a number cruncher, you need a hacker for that kind of work. I know someone if you want.'

'No don't worry, I have a guy.'

Jeremy left the office and was scrolling through his numbers when he received a call, *withheld number*. He knew immediately that he would regret answering but knew he had to.

'Jeremy mate, how are you? About that favour you owe me.'

'Oh err . . .' Jeremy hesitated before continuing with more confidence.

'Hi, how are you?'

'Not good to be honest Jeremy. I am hearing some very disturbing stories about Proteus. Are you investigating the deaths?'

'Well I am in charge of the investigation into the death of William Thornton but Defreitas was murdered out of area and technically out of my jurisdiction. I have however already had a meeting with the officer in charge up there and we will be working very closely on this.'

'Well that isn't perfect but it will have to do for now. It would really be much better for all concerned if you were to take sole charge.'

'I am working on it. In the meantime, I have a problem that you might be able to help me with. I am at the Proteus offices and I have a gentleman from the fraud office with me and he is having trouble accessing some of the office files. I don't suppose you know anyone who might be able to help us out?'

'I have just the man, he'll ring you in ten. You will ring me won't you Jeremy? Don't leave me hanging. I don't like to be left hanging.'

'As you say Tony.' Jeremy replied, secretly thinking something completely different which involved Big Tony and hanging.

Click.

Jeremy stared at the phone for a while and played the brief conversation back. Why was Tony Marciano so interested in Proteus and how was he supposed to sweep this elephant under the carpet?

His biggest concern was not his department; he knew how to deal with them. It was Tom Sparks. He seemed like an intelligent, good, honest copper. He would have to be on the ball at all times on this one.

Jeremy's thoughts were interrupted by the phone.

'Jeremy Ward.'

'Oh hi, I have been given your name and number by a mutual friend. He says you have some computer work for me.'

'Err? Oh yes, of course.'

'My name is Andy I live nearby. See you in five minutes.'

The phone went dead.

———

Gerrards Cross

Julian's relaxed mood had been ended by an item on the regional news that evening. He'd been pouring himself a decent claret to accompany his plate of rich and runny cheeses in anticipation of the late night film, when the TV blurted the word Proteus.

He dashed to the lounge in time to catch a photo of Michael on the screen. He found his Sky+ remote and rewound the footage to the start.

'Police have today confirmed that the headless body found in woodland on West Common in Gerrards Cross is believed to be that of investment banker Michael Defreitas. In a sad coincidence one of his business colleagues, William Thornton, was also found dead in his office on Friday morning. Police are refusing to comment further on the deaths at this time but would ask anyone who may have any information about either man to ring the number on the screen below.'

Julian was gobsmacked. He sat there staring at the TV thinking first about poor Michael. Headless?

He shivered.

What a dreadful way to die and so young too. He then thought of himself and his family. What would he do? Michael was the only reason he was at Proteus and so well paid. He knew that John Davis in particular did not approve of him and his overpaid position and would do anything to remove him.

Julian felt guilty thinking of himself at a time like this but couldn't help feeling a shiver of anxiety. In addition to his worries for his position there was another even more sinister reason for the sweat beading on Julian's brow.

Michael had been killed for a reason and he was sure that the reason had something to do with Julian. Julian knew that his overpaid work, if discovered, would lead to problems. Big problems.

But murder? Oh gawd.

Then of course there was William. Had he been murdered too? Julian continued to sit there in a daze as the awful thought struck him that maybe he was next.

He tried to ring John Davis but his phone was switched off. Julian put his phone down and re-ran the news report again. His claret and cheese sat next to him, untouched.

Monday 19th October 2009

Tom was in the office early. Big mistake.

DCC Protheroe was on the prowl and caught him as he came through the front door insisting on a complete update. He told her what he knew.

'So it is definitely Defreitas then?'

'As sure as we can be without the head.'

'I know his wife, Patsy. He's been a real bastard. Did the dirty on her with some blonde. How is it going with City CID? Bizarre about that other director Thornton isn't it? Hell of a coincidence, and you don't believe in coincidences do you Tom?'

She paused whilst he shook his head and then continued.

'Why on earth do people need to find such strange ways to have pleasure? What happened to good old fashioned sex?'

Tom wanted to say something but common sense got the better of him. Instead he remained very business-like.

'Well we're going back to London today to get an update. City CID are being helpful but are as much in the dark at this stage as we are. The business connection seems the best line of enquiry at the moment.'

'Well just get a result Tom. Any progress on the surgery burglaries?'

'Not really, probably local kids looking for a fix, although strangely, Defreitas's car was in the vicinity at the time of the burglaries.'

DCC Jane Protheroe frowned slightly when she considered this. Then turned to Tom.

'Small place, GX. Seem to be a lot of coincidences at the moment.'

Too many, thought Tom as the DCC continued.

'Well I hope your lack of faith in coincidences will serve us well, and quickly. Keep me posted.'

Tom's team dribbed and drabbed their way into the incident room.

'Right everyone. Where are we?' Newsum stood up.

'Michael Defreitas was separated from his wife, Patricia. She remained in the family home on Camp Road whilst he moved into a penthouse flat in the centre of town. There are rumours of a blonde girlfriend but no firm ID. Last seen leaving his office Monday lunchtime. His movements after that are unaccounted for.'

She continued.

'His body was moved after death and left on the common in what appears to be a deliberate attempt to have it found quickly. We've conducted a fingertip search of the common. Still no head I'm afraid.'

Newsum paused.

'Defreitas's car, an Aston Martin Vanquish was found at the rail station where he'd left it on Monday morning. This would indicate that Defreitas did not return to GX under his own steam. We have no suspect and no motive.'

Tom sighed, reminding himself yet again of the well-known fact that most murders are solved in the first 48 hours. They were now at hour 96 or thereabouts. They were getting nowhere fast. Newsum was right, no suspect, no motive.

'Okay guys we have to find ourselves a motive and a suspect and fast. I'm coming under a lot of pressure from above. I want to know everything there is about this man. Mel,' Mel jumped at the mention of her name, suddenly on full alert. 'Find out as much as possible about the mysterious blonde girlfriend. Talk to the other residents in the flats where he lived. Someone must have seen her.'

'Yes sir.'

'Newsum and I are going to conduct a search of the flat and then go back to his office in Mayfair. Bill, I want his bank statements checked. Julia, I want a copy of his medical and dental files. I want to know everything about this man. Have his car and flat been fingerprinted yet?'

'No sir.' Newsum replied sheepishly.

'Well tell them to hurry up!' Tom sighed and cursed himself for not being more on the ball.

'How about the Hummer?'

Silence.

'I want that bloody car found and fast!'

Tom thoughts turned to Tony Marciano. He was still undecided about the potential mob connection and how hard to push.

Last thing GX needed was a dead copper.

'How are we getting on with Tony Marciano?'

'We have put calls in to both the Met and the Serious Crimes division but apparently this guy is top of their wanted list and most of the information is classified.'

'Okay, thanks. Leave that one with me. Anyone got anything else of interest to report?'

Tom broke yet another silence.

'Come on Newsum we're going to check out his des res.'

The penthouse flat was typical of modern design and style. Open plan, with rooms at a minimum, it was massive with wonderful views. Tom looked out of the large windows that looked out over the Misbourne Valley and sighed. It really was another world. Still, money doesn't buy everything.

He and Newsum had systematically gone through the flat and were waiting now for the forensic team, specifically the finger-printers, to arrive.

They had found little of interest. Some bank statements and other personal paperwork. Disappointingly but unsurprisingly, no laptop nor desktop computer. No phone, either land or mobile.

Tom sat on the leather sofa staring out over the valley wondering where the man's laptop was. He wasn't so surprised about the lack of a phone as few people used landlines these days and he was most likely to have his mobile on him at the time of his disappearance but he had hoped the laptop would have turned up.

The finger printers arrived and found nothing. The flat had been wiped clean. That was weird. Suspiciously weird.

Wembley

Tooley's Monday wasn't going much better really.

He too had hosted an early morning briefing and listened to Porter's case update.

'Shirley Swift, a big lady from Leeds was strangled and dumped on the railway embankment near Wembley. She had been due to meet a Czech called Tomas at Marylebone on the evening of her death. Mrs Swift's son has identified her body.'

'We believe we have identified Tomas is Tomas Kopecky from Prague. Kopecky was reported missing by his landlady after he disappeared from his lodgings in Harrow a week ago and hasn't been seen since. Apparently he was off to meet a friend, nicknamed Husky or Starsky who had offered him some work. A full- scale search is out for him.' Porter passed around copies of Tomas Kopecky's passport photo.

'We are hoping that the Marylebone CCTV will confirm that Kopecky was the man who met Mrs Swift on Wednesday night.'

Tooley cleared his throat and took over.

'Porter and I went to Leeds and conducted a full investigation into Mrs Swift including a search of her home. She seems to have been a very curious lady that lived a surreal second life online.'

There was a comment and a giggle from one of his team that spread like a Mexican wave. Tooley let them have their thirty seconds of mirth before bringing the meeting back into a semblance of order.

'Okay, that's enough. There is little to follow-up on her except this Tomas and the mysterious payments she was getting weekly from the Cayman Islands. She seems to have been some form of male porn talent spotter for a man that we only know at this stage under his internet identity of Husky23. It doesn't take a rocket scientist to deduce that Tomas's friend's nickname was very similar and they are likely to be the same person. We are working on that as we speak.'

'How is our search going for the Hummer?'

'No Hummers reported stolen and we have a list of local owners to contact and question.'

'Good, Porter and I are now off to Marylebone. I want you all to report back to me by 5pm.'

Tooley drove and refused to stop en-route, ignoring the various sandwich and burger bars and the way Porter was wriggling in his seat like a drug addict desperate for a fix.

They arrived outside Marylebone and Porter shot out of the car, heading straight for the pasty stall.

Tooley went over to the Station Master's office and found it locked.

Bloody railways, he muttered to himself.

He joined Porter in the centre of the station and looked around until he could see the clock. He walked over to one of the guards.

'Detective Inspector Tooley, Wembley CID. Where is the security office?'

'Security office?'

'Okay where is the office which holds the CCTV tapes?'

'Oh you want the Station Master's office mate.'

'It's shut.'

'Yes mate, it's only open from noon until 3pm on a Monday. It's only 10.30'

Tooley sighed in frustration and led Porter back towards the car before having second thoughts and returning to the guard.

'Were you working on Thursday night by any chance?'

'I only do the early shift, 4am till 12.'

'How do I find out who was working that evening?'

'At the Station Master's office!' they all completed in unison including Porter and Tooley.

Enquiries at the ticket office, various shops and stalls at the station yielded nothing. Anyone who might have been working on Thursday night certainly wasn't working that morning.

Tooley decided he had no choice but to return later in the day between noon and 3pm.

So off they drove to Wembley rail station.

'Amazing stadium.' Tooley commented to Porter as they passed the new Wembley. 'Been to a game there yet?'

'Yeah FA Cup semi. Pompey last year. They have some great stalls there. Delicious pies.'

Tooley had forgotten that Porter was a south coast boy.

Their trip to Wembley station yielded no additional information. It merely confirmed that the station is unmanned from 10pm and the lights outside are switched off by a timing mechanism after the final train.

The uniforms were still conducting house-to-house enquiries but Tooley wasn't holding his breath. So far the only break had been the sighting of the black Hummer.

In the circumstances they decided to return to the station and re-examine the facts of the case so far. Tooley rang Mog and arranged to meet her at the station.

Mayfair

Jeremy Ward hadn't slept well. He was worried about Tony Marciano. God what a fool he'd been. He had always lived above his means. He especially loved fast women and fast cars or as his mates jibed, *fast cars and slow women!*

He had no trouble attracting the women, it was the cost of them that was the problem. The more up-market the bird, the higher the cost.

It had all started so harmlessly. In his early days as a motorcycle cop, Jeremy had caught a young man speeding in a Ferrari on the underpass by Green Park. He stopped him and realised he had been drinking. The kid was crapping himself begging Jeremy to ring his dad who was a solicitor.

Jeremy felt a bit sorry for the kid and rang the father who turned out to be Tony Marciano, who was in fact a florist, not a solicitor. At the time, Jeremy was in debt. Credit cards all up to their limit and in arrears with the mortgage on the flash flat in Canary Wharf he had bought at the peak of the market.

Tony Marciano had paid him to let the boy go and had been paying him ever since as insurance. Jeremy was now a DI in the City CID and a very useful source of information. Because of this, Jeremy knew that Big Tony would never release him.

At Tony's insistence, Jeremy had arranged for Andy, Tony's IT man, to inspect the Proteus computers on Saturday and introduced him to David Browne. David had done enough for the day and left shortly afterwards. Jeremy had decided not to be there whilst Andy did his stuff, so he left him to get on with things whilst he went for a long lunch.

On his return, he found Andy packed up and ready to go.

'Glad you are back plod, David has gone for the day and I didn't want to leave the place open. All the files are now open for David; I've done all I need to except for one thing. There seem to be some files missing. Any idea what they did with Michael's laptop?'

'Sorry no, is it important?'

'Could say that. The man will not be happy.'

It was the words *the man will not be happy,* that gave him a miserable weekend and ensured he got little sleep on Sunday night.

The inevitable call came in mid-morning on Monday.

'Jeremy we are in a fix.'

'How can I help Tony?'

'We need Michael's laptop and mobile phone.'

'We've looked everywhere, there's no sign.'

'Find them Jeremy.'

Click.

Jeremy called Tom at Gerrards Cross. He was out. *Bugger, bugger, bugger!*

Mick turned up looking like death. Jeremy felt a twinge of guilt, after all, he was the main cause of Mick's marital problems.

'Morning Jeremy.'

'Morning Mick.'

'Good weekend?'

'Yes, you?'

'Yes great, had another row with the missus. I am sure she is having an affair.' Jeremy ignored him.

'I was wondering, did the directors of Proteus have laptops?'

'We found one that belonged to William Thornton but Michael Defreitas's laptop is missing.'

'Mobile?' he asked hopefully.

'Ditto, have you tried DCI Sparks?'

'Good idea, I'll call him later. Anything of interest on Thornton's laptop?'

'No but his mobile is interesting. Very interesting.'

Geneva

No one knew Zolo's real name. In fact very few people knew he even existed. He lived in the shadows. Those that did know about him were the rich and powerful and even that was comparatively little except that he was expensive and offered guaranteed success.

For Zolo was the most dangerous man on earth, the most deadly assassin of them all.

He was shortish, and of very slight build. He had a nondescript face and was unmemorable, all virtues that contributed to his success. He was so unremarkable that he could enter and leave a busy room at will without ever being noticed, a great asset in his line of work.

Today he had just finished his daily 2-hour workout and checked his emails. There was a coded email from his agent Antonio. Antonio was the only one who really knew anything about Zolo and was trusted. He was after all, his brother.

Although from Algerian extraction, Zolo was a Swiss citizen and had always loved Lake Geneva. He had purchased the most beautiful chalet style house overlooking the lake. It was set up on high and offered incredible views and more importantly, great security. Its elevated position ensured that no one could approach within a half mile of the house without alerting him to their presence.

The house was accessed by a steep cobbled lane that he was now cycling down on his mountain bike to go to the local post office where he held a PO Box.

He had post.

He opened the box and removed the manila envelope inside and then cycled back to his mountainside chalet.

The manila envelope contained his next assignment. Gerrards Cross, England. He felt a tingle of excitement and went to pack. Shame he hadn't got this assignment earlier – he had only just returned from Hampstead Heath.

Tuesday 20th October 2009

Tooley gazed out over his motley crew of detectives and cleared his throat.

'Morning all, Porter, update please.'

Porter hauled himself to his feet and spoke, 'DI Tooley and I finally managed to arrive at Marylebone station at a time when the station office was open and were able to examine the CCTV tape. The tape clearly shows Shirley waiting under the clock and being met by a tall man in a black overcoat and hat. The hat obscured the face of the man and prevented us from obtaining a worthwhile image.'

'Yes, very clever if deliberate,' Tooley interjected.

Porter continued. 'The two spoke to each other briefly and embraced before leaving the station arm-in-arm.'

'Thank you Porter. So everyone, it looks like the evening started well for Tomas and Shirley. What we need to know is why and how did it all go wrong to such an extent that Shirley was murdered.' Tooley paused, then asked. 'Any luck with the Hummer?'

'We have narrowed it down to ten Hummers in the Wembley area and we are planning to interview the owners today. But we think it's unlikely that a murderer would use such a distinctive car unless it was stolen. However there are still no reports of one being stolen.'

Tooley brought the meeting to a close and left the station to grab himself a drinkable coffee and consider his next steps.

As he sipped his latte at the local Starbucks, he assessed what he knew so far. They had a dead woman from Leeds, a missing Czech who may or may not have killed her and the sighting of a conspicuous black Hummer near the murder scene.

He thought about the Czech connection and whether a trip to Prague would be useful. Undecided, he placed a call to his favourite pathologist. Roger Townsend answered in his usual gruff and unwelcome manner.

'Townsend.'

'DI Tooley here, just thought I would give you a quick call to find out if anything new has cropped up since we last spoke.'

'A little bit yes, Shirley was strangled and thrown on to the embankment. Time of death was about 1am. Forensic have come up with nothing on the body except some material that is likely to have come from a car mat.'

'Any idea what car?'

'Who do you think I am? Jeremy Clarkson?'

'Leave that with me. Anything else?'

'Shirley also had some particles of skin and blood under her fingernails. She must have struggled with her killer. I have sent it off for DNA analysis.'

'Okay thanks, when are you likely to receive the DNA results?'

'End of the week.'

'Thanks Townsend.' He said putting the phone down quickly to avoid the inevitable rebuke.

———

Gerrards Cross

It was after 10am when Tom and Newsum pulled into the driveway of a large detached house on the ultra posh Camp Road in Gerrards Cross.

'Christ sir, they have an in and out driveway and a roundabout! That's so cool!' 'Calm down Newsum.'

Was that a touch of a cynicism? Tom thought.

'We are here to see a recently widowed lady.'

'Sorry sir.' Newsum murmured as she dropped her chin in an attempt to hide a smirk.

The house was a rambling Charles Church Georgian-style property with two columns either side of solid oak double front doors. Alongside the doors was a large brass bell-pull that

Newsum insisted on giving a rigorous pull. A chime worthy of Big Ben sounded from inside the house and seemed to make the ground shake.

The door was opened by a Filipino lady, in a black and white maid's outfit.

'How I help you?' she asked in pidgin English.

'I am Detective Chief Inspector Sparks and this is my colleague Detective Sergeant Newsum. We would like to see Mrs Defreitas please.'

'I not know if possible, I go find out.'

'Thank you.'

To their surprise the maid then shut the door and left them standing on the doorstep for another couple of minutes before she returned.

'Mrs Defreitas say she see you, she down in minute,' she said as she led them into a very lounge area with enormous chandeliers, hanging down from a high ceiling, and a huge inglenook fireplace. The room was the size of a tennis court.

They perched on a large leather sofa and took in the sheer opulence of the room. There was a grand piano in one corner that had sheets of music spread across it.

'Ever tinkled the ivories Newsum?'

Newsum looked confused but before she could reply a glamorous woman breezed into the room.

'I am so sorry to keep you waiting, I was on the phone to the undertaker. There is so much to do, planning a funeral is like planning a wedding.'

Tom had risen from the sofa to greet the lady and was standing there speechless. He didn't really know what he had expected, probably a sad lady who was half-shrivelled in grief. Certainly not the awesome example of the female form in front of him who looked positively radiant and was totally intimidating.

She was typically blonde as was the GX norm and stunning. She was tall, slim with the most extraordinary blue eyes. She was the most beautiful woman Tom had ever seen.

Tom regained his composure to some extent and stuttered.

'Good morning Mrs Defreitas, thank you for seeing us at such short notice. I am Detective Chief Inspector Thomas Sparks of Uxbridge CID and this is my colleague Detective Sergeant Jane Newsum. May I first of all offer our sympathies following the death of your husband.'

'Oh don't look so worried Detective Chief Inspector, my husband was an absolute womanising bastard and was very well insured. To be honest I am bloody pleased to see the back of him. Saves a very expensive and messy divorce. Oh dear I am starting to sound like I have a motive. I hope you aren't going to arrest me Detective Chief Inspector?'

The final sentence was accompanied by a teasing smile.

'Oh I don't think you need to worry about that Mrs Defreitas, you're not on my list of suspects at the moment.'

'Oh that is a relief, may I ask who is?'

'I'm afraid I cannot divulge such information at this stage.'

'Of course, of course.' She mused 'Now how can I help you?'

'I really just wanted to ask you a few questions ma'am.'

'Ask away.' She said as she sat gently down on a leather chair that Tom estimated would have cost about three months of his salary.

'How long were you married to Michael?'

'Nineteen years. We first met at Oxford. I was studying classical music and he was studying women and economics, very much in that order. We met up again at an alumni get together about a year after leaving Oxford and the rest as they say is history.'

'What happened then?'

'Michael was then, and still is, a serial womaniser but he was so charming that I made the decision that I would prefer to live with his womanising than live without him.'

Patricia Defreitas paused.

'That was until this new woman arrived on the scene. She changed everything. He was head over heels in love with her. That was too much and so I kicked him out. Best thing I ever did to be honest.'

'I see, who is she?'

'That's the extraordinary thing Chief Inspector, I could never find out. I never met her and Michael would never admit to her existence but friends of mine had seen him with her in his car and things.'

'I am most keen to find this lady, can you think of anything else?'

'I know she is tall and blonde, but that's about it. One of my friends thought she was a doctor but was very vague about why.'

'Are you aware of anyone who might have wished your husband harm?'

'Oh there are plenty of husbands whose wives Michael screwed – the list is long but I would be surprised if any of them would resort to murdering him.'

'Well if you think of anything please let me know, here is my card.'

'Would you like me to identify the body?'

'No that won't be necessary I didn't want to distress you more than absolutely necessary so I have arranged for one of his co-directors to identify him.'

'Oh yes? Which one?'

'Stewart McMillan.'

'Oh that creep.'

'You don't get on with him then?'

'No, he is a complete nerd. I had to be nice to him at company functions and so forth and hated it. That's something else I won't miss!'

She stared out the window briefly before continuing, 'Any idea when I will be able to hold the funeral?'

'That is very much down to the Coroner.'

'Death certificate?'

For the insurance company no doubt, Tom thought with disgust.

'Again, the Coroner will be the one who will decide when to release the death certificate.'

At that she rose and showed them to the door. 'Well I mustn't take up any more of your valuable time Chief Inspector. You have a murderer to catch.'

'Thank you Mrs Defreitas. Just one last thing, do you know anyone who drives a black Hummer?'

'Please call me Patsy, and yes I do. Stewart McMillan.'

Mayfair

Tom was excited, was this the break they had been waiting for?

When they got into the car, he turned to Newsum and told her it was his turn to drive. As they tore down the A40 heading for the Proteus offices, he turned to Newsum.

'Tell the office to get everything they know on Stewart McMillan as quickly as they can.'

'Will do sir.' Newsum looked worried.

'What is it Newsum?'

'Well it is about the identification sir. I wasn't aware that you had arranged for Stewart McMillan to identify the body. I mean wouldn't Mrs Defreitas be a safer bet?'

'Mmm, bit of a spur of the moment thing, Newsum. The identification of a headless body is hardly an exact science and would not stand up in court without other unique identifying marks. Such as moles etc.' He realised that was one thing he hadn't asked Helen and made a mental note to do so. 'Besides the blood group makes the identification practically unnecessary.'

Tom paused.

'Of course my main reason is to see Stewart McMillan's reaction to the body.'

Ten minutes later they were sitting in a traffic jam in Acton when Newsum's phone rang. She frantically scribbled down a couple of pages of notes. Tom waited trying to hide his impatience while she finished her call.

'Well?'

'Well a lot of it we know already sir. Stewart McMillan is the other co-founder of Proteus and a director. In fact the sole surviving one. He met Defreitas at Oxford and they started a fund investing their fellow students' monies. You know the rest about Proteus so I won't bore you with it.'

'Is that it?'

'Oh no sir I was just getting to the personal stuff. He is single, lives in Gerrards Cross, in fact in the same block of flats as Defreitas. He owns one car, a 911.'

'No Hummer?'

'Fraid not sir, although the Hummer could be a company car?'

'Good point, remind me to ask when we get to Proteus.'

'Anything else? Does he have family? Where did he go to school?'

'Not really sir in fact the background on him before he went to Oxford is non-existent. Bit like Defreitas. Tom grimaced, another bloody coincidence. We do know however that he plays golf and is a member of the local club in Gerrards Cross.'

'Oh well that is all we need then, let's arrest the man!'

They finally arrived at the offices of Proteus. Stewart McMillan was at lunch but and due back within minutes.

Whilst they were waiting they had another look round and bumped into Detective Sergeant David Browne of the fraud squad. Browne looked less like a copper than anyone Tom could imagine. He was short, thin and basically could almost be described as wimpish. He was dressed in a city suit and looked more like an accountant.

'Afternoon David, another lovely day wading through reams of paperwork and computer charts?'

'Yes sir.'

'Found anything of interest?'

'No, all seems above board so far. DI Ward managed to find someone to open the locked files for me but they contained nothing new. It will all be in my report which will be with you by Friday'

'Okay, well you have my number if anything turns up in the meantime.'

'Yes sir.'

At that moment Stewart McMillan entered the room and was rather taken aback to find them waiting to interview him.

'Sorry to bother you Mr McMillan but I would like to ask you a few questions.' 'But I have spent all morning answering the questions of those two City detectives – what do you lot want now? I am a busy man you know.' He said indignantly.

'I can understand your frustration sir and please be assured I won't keep you any longer than absolutely necessary but I am sure you are as anxious to get to the truth as we are.'

'Indeed, so how can I help?'

'Firstly sir, how long have you lived in Gerrards Cross?'

'Oh about five years, I moved there from Fulham.'

'I understand that you own a flat in the same block as Michael?'

'Yes we bought them together as an investment just over two years ago. Michael bought his to rent out but I chose to live in mine.'

'Any idea why Michael's was empty for two years?'

'Well Michael found it rather useful have a little *pied-à-terre* so he always managed to find an excuse not to let it out. Besides he hardly needed the money.' He said smugly.

Tom had taken an instant dislike to Stewart MacMillan, but continued his questioning calmly.

'Are your flats near one another?'

'They are next door actually, the penthouses.'

'So you must have seen a lot of Michael since he separated?'

'No not really, we never mixed socially. I like to get home from work and read or watch television. Michael was a party animal and would be out until all hours.'

'Did he have a girlfriend?'

'He had many. That's why his wife kicked him out and not before time either.' 'Was there anyone special? We understand that he had a tall blonde girlfriend. Possibly a doctor?'

'They were all tall and blonde. That was Michael's type. I am neither aware of anyone special nor what they did for a living. Sorry I can't be of any more help on that one.'

Tom opened his notebook to play for time.

'What car do you drive?'

'I actually only drive quite rarely. I commute into work each day on the train and walk to the station. By the time I return at night I am usually too tired to want to go out again. At the weekends when the weather is good I like to drive my 911 convertible.'

'Do you own any other cars sir?'

'No but I do sometimes drive the company Hummer which we bought a couple of years ago but I haven't driven it for ages.'

'Where do you keep it?'

'Well it's kept in the company garage here. It is used mainly to pick up clients and as a fleet car for anyone who needs it.'

'Do you keep any records of who drives it and when?'

'That isn't really my domain, I leave things like that up to John Davis the office manager. You've met him I believe – may I suggest you have a word with him?'

Tom was torn, he felt that McMillan could be the key to the whole investigation and he wanted to know lots more about him and Proteus but he also wanted to investigate the Hummer. There were too many coincidences cropping up in this case and it was time to start eliminating some of them. He decided to put his other questions on hold and see John Davis.

'Yes thanks, I think that will be all for now but I'll be back to ask you more questions. I would also like to make arrangements with you to identify the body.'

'Yes of course but I thought that it was usually the next of kin?'

'Not in this case sir.'

Stewart Macmillan looked a bit surprised but then shrugged, 'No problem just let me know when and where'

Tom left Stewart McMillan's office and immediately sought out John Davis who was sitting in his office staring out of the window.

'Mr Davis, I understand that you look after the company Hummer, could I see it please?'

'Yes of course. It's in the garage about 400 yards away.'

'Okay, let's go.'

John Davis walked alongside Tom.

'Do you mind me asking why you're so interested in the company Hummer DCI Sparks?'

'I'm just tying up all the loose ends.'

'Of course, well here we are.' He said as they walked down a ramp to an underground car park. 'We always park the Hummer there at the back of the garage.' He pointed and then scoured the garage.

'That's strange.'

'What is it Mr Davis?'

'Well it isn't here. It's always parked over there in that space.' He said as he pointed to an empty space.

'When did you last see it parked here?'

'It was definitely here last Wednesday morning when I did my regular check.'

'Well where could it be? Stolen?'

'I'm sure that there's a simple explanation. Shall we go back to the office?'

'I would like to have a proper look around first.'

On the A40 from Mayfair to Gerrards Cross

Tom and Newsum were finally on their way back to Gerrards Cross having spent what seemed like hours with John Davis trying to solve the mystery of the missing Hummer.

Davis had explained in excruciating detail that he had a very simple system devised to manage the Proteus car fleet, although the use of the word fleet was misleading as there were only three cars.

He had three small lined notebooks, one for each car. It was his responsibility, and that of his secretary in his absence, to ensure that the books were up to date. A car was an expensive item to lose.

Each book recorded the date an employee took the car, the name of the employee, the date it was returned and its new mileage. The books and the keys of the cars not being used were locked in the safe in his office to which he had the only key.

On their return to the Proteus office, John Davis had gone straight to his safe and unlocked it. The book for the Hummer was there along with the keys. John Davis was baffled and just sat at his desk scratching his head and mumbling.

Tom opened the book and discovered that the last time the car had been officially used had been three weeks earlier. The employee who had used the car was Michael Defreitas who had returned it on the Friday before he had disappeared. Yet another blasted coincidence, sighed Tom to himself.

In the circumstances the only course of action was to report it as stolen. One way or another it was likely to turn up at some stage.

Tom let Newsum drive whilst he relaxed in the passenger seat and reflected on the day. It had been a day of surprises, full of tantalising discoveries that provoked more questions than answers.

Who was the mystery blonde: was she really a doctor and was she relevant to the case? Helen flashed through his brain again. She was blonde and a doctor. No, impossible, he would have known. Wouldn't he?

Then, of course there was the Hummer. Tom considered the coincidence of Proteus owning a Hummer that conveniently for them, but most inconveniently for him, was now missing. More questions. He pulled out his notebook and wrote a list. His lists were famous at the station not only because he tended to make lots of them but also for the arrows he drew in front of every item. But he didn't care what others thought, they helped him think, helped him clear his mind. Today's list looked like this:

⇒ Where was the Hummer now?

⇒ Was it the one seen on the night the body was dumped on the common?

⇒ Did Defreitas really return it?

⇒ How had the keys managed to find their way back into the safe? (That might be explained easily – there must have been a spare set of keys. Or if the car really had been stolen then it could have been hot-wired or whatever thieves do to cars these days to steal them.)

Then there was Stewart McMillan. Tom was certain he knew a lot more than he was letting on. He had many questions still for him.

He then thought of Helen yet again and wished he could talk to her about this. Why had she been behaving so strangely? He returned to his earlier thought that she was tall, blonde and a sort of doctor. He told himself to stop being so stupid. Having pulled himself together he went back to thinking about the case.

But Helen invaded his thoughts again as he remembered that strange late night call he had received from her and wondered yet again why it had left him feeling something wasn't right.

He replayed the conversation in his head. Of course! She had mentioned William Thornton's death and in particular the bizarre circumstances. How had she known? Another question.

Too many questions and not enough answers he thought as Newsum negotiated the rush hour.

Wembley

Tooley was uncertain what to do next so he called an end of day meeting. Maybe the team had uncovered something of use. If not they could always do a bit of brainstorming, maybe that would give him some inspiration.

'Right, Porter? Anything interesting to report?'

'Nothing new sir except that we just received a report of a stolen Hummer in the Mayfair area. Strangely it is being dealt with by DCI Sparks of Uxbridge.'

'Thanks. I wonder what old Sparkie is up to investigating stolen cars in Mayfair? I'll give him a quick call.'

Tooley looked at the blank faces in front of him and decided to spare himself a futile attempt to brainstorm. *This lot wouldn't even manage a brain-drizzle!* He thought as he asked hopefully, 'Anything else?'

'No sir.'

Tooley sighed. 'Okay well let's call it a day. See you all tomorrow.'

Tooley returned to his office. He hadn't spoken to Sparkie for ages, years in fact. There was a time when Sparkie had helped them out when he wasn't busy. About three years ago however, the local councils had got together and moved a load of troublemakers and gypsies onto a council estate near Gerrards Cross and onto Sparkie's manor. Sparkie was now inundated with his own crimes, albeit minor, and he hadn't seen him since.

He rang the office of DSI Sparks and was told he wasn't in. He rang his mobile.

'Sparks.'

'Hi Sparkie, guess who?'

'Your voice sounds familiar but I am not speaking to you since I got all your cast-offs. The crime-rate here is now horrific.'

'Oh come on Sparkie you know it was political. Trying to impress voters in a marginal seat.'

'Maybe. Now what can I do for you young Tooley.'

'Well, I think we may have a Hummer in common'

'Really, you looking for one too?'

'Yes, it was seen in the vicinity of a murder last week near Wembley Station.'

'Well, well. Perhaps I am talking to you after all. Shall we compare notes over a beer? I have a driver so I can have a couple. We're in Shepherds Bush at the moment, can be in your neck of the woods within twenty minutes. Ten if we put the lights on.'

'Make it twenty minutes in the Dog and Hedgehog then.'

Thirty-five minutes later they were sitting in front of their first pints.

'So, a murder eh? Mind you murders are quite commonplace in Wembley aren't they?' Tom said before taking a long drink from his much needed and, in his opinion, well-deserved beer.

'Yes we manage at least one a month, usually racially motivated stabbings. They tend to be in the town centre and in full view of our network of CCTV cameras. We like them, they're easy to solve and good for the figures. Tooley stopped momentarily to take a leisurely sip of his beer. Before continuing,

124

'So Sparkie, why are you involved in a car theft in Mayfair?' Long way off your beat.'

Tom gave Tooley a quick summary of what had transpired over the previous week including the murder, the death by masturbation and the missing Hummer.

'Blimey,' Tooley exclaimed and then gave a similarly brief version of his past week and his current investigation. At the end of it Tom was quiet and pensive.

Finally he broke the silence.

'I can't make up my mind whether there is any common ground here or not. You know me and coincidences, there are a lot of coincidences here, too many in fact. What are the chances of two different Hummers being involved in two different murders within fifteen miles and on the same night?'

'I am not so prejudiced towards coincidence as you Sparkie but I do think we need to pool our information. Another pint?'

Tom smiled drained his glass and handed his glass to Tooley in confirmation. Newsum and Porter, the designated drivers, sighed in unison. It threatened to be a long evening.

Gerrards Cross

Until recently, Julian Travers and his family had lived in a rented house in Gerrards Cross for nearly five years. It was a town they loved and they had always aspired to own their house there but had been unable to afford one.

Earlier this year however, using a six-figure bonus he had been paid by Michael, they had finally managed to buy their dream home about a half a mile from the town centre. It might have been on the unfashionable side of the A40 but they loved it.

Julian would usually walk to the station, which he enjoyed, unless it was raining when Kate would give him a lift. He often walked back via the pub that frequently proved too big a temptation to walk past on his return journey in the evening.

Tonight he was home early. He and Kate had a babysitter and were going out for a meal, a curry in fact. It was their weekly ritual: they always went out for a curry on a Tuesday.

Julian was a creature of habit; they always went to the same Indian restaurant and he always ate and drank the same. Two spicy poppadums, four onion bhajis with hot pickle, chicken madras and pilau rice all washed down with the house red.

He was starving and couldn't wait to get going. He had been thinking about his curry all day. Despite his hunger, they always stopped for a quick drink in the pub before they went next door to the Rajpoot. It was such a fun ritual and gave them a chance to have a quiet chat and catch-up.

Tonight he had so much to tell Kate. It had been his first day back at the office since the deaths and work was in total chaos. There were police everywhere.

Also in Gerrards Cross

Getting a job in the kitchen of the Rajpoot had been easy, especially after Zolo had kidnapped and killed two of the kitchen staff, dumping their bodies at the bottom of one of the many disused flooded quarries near High Wycombe.

With his usual thoroughness, before disposing of them, Zolo had made both men write notes to their employer to say that their families were in trouble back home in Mumbai and that they had flown back to help and support them.

Earlier that evening, the owner of the Rajpoot had welcomed Zolo enthusiastically when he had popped in and enquired about the possibility of some casual work. He started Zolo in the kitchen immediately stating that Tuesday night was always a busy night.

Zolo's mixed race, especially his Algerian descendancy, often paid dividends for him and this was the case with the owner of the Rajpoot. He could pose as Portuguese, Spanish or Asian depending upon the scenario. Over the years he had also taken the time to learn many languages and accents and could fit in to most situations without too many problems, usually choosing to be the strong silent type.

He watched the restaurant from the kitchen and waited. Tonight there was some kind of birthday party booked and the tables had been re-arranged to fit a large party. An Indian Elvis impersonator had been booked for entertainment. This worried Zolo slightly in case his target was frightened off by such an absurd idea.

But no, they came in bang on time and seemed to be most intrigued when informed of the scheduled entertainment. He was relieved. His preparations were so thorough that he would have been cross if some idiot entertainer had spoiled his plans. For the twentieth time that evening he put his hand inside his trouser pocket and felt the uncomfortable presence of the syringe.

He turned back to help the chef who was busy preparing the batter for the onion bhajis and volunteered to stir the mixture so the chef could start preparing one of the other dishes. The chef looked relieved and moved off to the other side of the kitchen.

Zolo stirred the mix and looked around him carefully. Everyone was busy and no one was watching him as he removed the syringe from his pocket and squirted its contents into the bhaji mix. His movements were so fast that it happened in the blink of an eye. He looked around again and satisfied himself that he had not been watched. He continued stirring the mix and when he was happy, called the chef over.

As he excused himself from the kitchen for a cigarette break, the chef was putting the onion bhajis into the hot fat. They would be served in about ten minutes. Zolo wondered to himself how many people had ordered the onion bhajis. He knew of at least one, he had checked beforehand.

Zolo didn't smoke, he just wanted to take a little time out to allow the others to do the work. The busier they were the less likely they were to look for any problems, let alone notice them.

Zolo would have liked to have left at that stage but did not want to raise any suspicion. He also wanted to make sure that the onion bhajis had reached their target, so he finished his shift. He had to admit that the Elvis impersonator was not quite as bad as he had feared. It was hard work but eventually he thanked the owner for letting him work, took his wages of £40 in cash and left.

It was midnight and all the diners would be at home. It would take another thirty minutes.

Gerrards Cross

Julian had thoroughly enjoyed his evening. He and Kate always loved their Tuesday night curries although they never ate the same food. Some people liked to share their dishes but Kate found chicken madras too hot and could not eat bhajis due to one of her allergies.

There had been a raucous birthday party at the Rajpoot who had booked an Elvis impersonator for the evening. They had never seen an Indian Elvis before but had to admit afterwards that they had enjoyed his performance and it had made an amusing change from their usual routine.

In fact, they had a great time, so they stayed much later than usual enjoying the performance and a second bottle of the house red.

Kate wasn't much of a drinker and, feeling a bit tipsy, went to bed when they got home. Julian decided to sit downstairs for five minutes to have a quick nightcap and check the news. He flicked from channel to channel but learned nothing new.

Work was chaos, and John Davis was running around like a headless chicken. The discovery that the company Hummer was missing had nearly tipped John over the edge. Julian had decided it was best to keep a low profile at work and would work from home for the next few days. When informed, John had seemed relieved.

His stomach rumbled loudly but then it always felt a bit dodgy after a curry. He was starting to regret that second bottle of wine and decided to pour himself a brandy. *For medicinal purposes only,* he assured himself.

He had to admit that the curry wasn't quite as good as normal as the onion bhajis had a bit of tang to them but he had been so hungry he had just put some extra pickles and sauces with them to cover up the slightly strange taste.

Nearby in Chalfont St. Peter

Meanwhile, Barry Kelly and his mates had left the Rajpoot and retired for a late night drink at The Greyhound in Chalfont St Peter where they were in the process of decimating the inn's supply of Laurent Perrier.

His girlfriend was the first one to be sick and they all took the piss out of her for not being able to hold her drink. Barry was next, followed by most of the others. Within twenty minutes the inn was in chaos and it soon became clear that there was a major problem: too many sick people and not enough toilets.

Ambulances were called and they were carted off to A&E in High Wycombe.

Barry's girlfriend Mandy died on the way and there were signs that she could be the first of many.

During the night all twelve died of food poisoning.

Julian didn't make it to hospital: he died in his downstairs cloakroom in agony. His wife found him at 3am when she woke and realised that he hadn't joined her in bed.

She immediately rang the emergency services who sent an ambulance and a very sleepy Tom Sparks.

His mobile had gone off at just after 3am and he was shattered. He had had a couple of beers in The Apple Tree after the Dog and Hedgehog and was definitely feeling the worse for wear.

When he arrived at the house of Mr and Mrs Julian Travers he was hit by the smell. It was gut wrenching and did nothing for his delicate circumstances. Somehow managing to keep everything down he decided he needed fresh air fast and moved outside to speak to the paramedics.

Sue Noteman had been a paramedic for ten years and was looking as green as her outfit.

'I haven't ever seen anything like that. He was lying with his trousers down in a pool of vomit and shit. He must have been sitting on the toilet and leant forward to be sick and collapsed. Poor sod.'

'I am going to need a statement from you, what time and where would be best for you?'

'I am on call until 8am and then will need to have a sleep. I only live in St Giles so why don't I pop down the station at say 4pm?'

'Excellent, if I am not about I will make sure someone from the team is available, Shouldn't take too long.'

The locals always referred to Chalfont St Peter and Chalfont St Giles without using the Chalfont.

'That'll be good, see you later I hope.' She said giving him a very warm smile. *Pretty little thing* he thought to himself as she climbed aboard the ambulance to go back to High Wycombe. He just couldn't see himself with a paramedic, though.

Breathing deep lungfuls of fresh air, he went back into the house. The situation was chaotic. The wife was with a uniformed woman police constable, or WPC as they were usually known, in the lounge, wailing. The kids were running around the lounge crying, screaming and vomiting.

Tom went over to the other uniform in attendance, Jack Bryant, a long-term PC who Tom had known for years.

'What do you reckon Jack?' Tom whispered.

'Well I understand that they went for a curry last night at the Rajpoot. Apparently it was a regular Tuesday treat for them. Mrs Travers is not in a fit state to be interviewed at the moment. The doctor is on his way.'

Tom's mobile rang.

'Sparks.' He said and listened to the voice at the other end of the phone. It was the emergency operations switchboard.

'What?'

'How many did you say?'

'Another twelve? possibly more? Shit, oops! I mean blimey.'

'God this is going to take some clearing up.' Tom grimaced at his second unintentional pun. 'Okay thanks for letting me know. I will be down first thing in the morning please ring the hospital and ensure that the doctor in charge remains till I have seen him.'

He rang off. Turning to Jack Bryant he made his third unintended pun of the night.

'Looks like the shit has really hit the fan.'

Wednesday 21st October 2009

Tom didn't manage to get back to sleep. He kept thinking about the awful smell and the sight of all the human vomit and excrement. He really hadn't seen anything like it before.

One glimmer of light at the end of the tunnel though was the prospect of further contact with Helen that was the inevitable result of this unfortunate episode.

He finally gave up trying to sleep and showered and dressed. He was at work by 7am which was just as well as all hell had broken loose. Not only was the DCC in the station but she was being lectured to by a tall distinguished looking man in a police uniform, Chief Constable Harry Smith.

Uh-Oh.

'Ah there you are DCI Sparks. About bloody time too.'

He had never heard the Chief Constable swear before, this was not a good sign.

'What the hell is going on Sparks? In the past week we have had one as yet unsolved murder and now thirteen people dead from food poisoning. Gerrards Cross is rapidly becoming the most dangerous place on earth. What do you know so far?'

'Very little sir except that thirteen people had a curry at the Rajpoot and died a few hours later; a further two people are still in intensive care on life support. The prognosis for them is not good. I will be conducting a full investigation immediately and will report back to the DCC by this afternoon.'

'Good and get that place shut down immediately.'

'Yes sir I will send uniform down there straight away to seal it off.'

———

Zolo was in first class on his British Airways flight to Zurich. They had just taken off and the plane was climbing steeply. He looked down at London as they flew over and smiled to himself. He had to admit he liked Gerrards Cross. It was a pity he couldn't have stayed longer really.

After the previous evening's stint in the Rajpoot kitchen he couldn't get the smell of curry out of his nostrils and pores. One thing was sure, he would never touch another onion bhaji as long as he lived.

He couldn't wait to get back to the clean crisp mountain air of Switzerland and a wonderful cleansing shower. He settled back and closed his eyes. He would soon be home.

Gerrards Cross

Tom called the team together and gave his morning briefing.

'Well we have a lot to do today. You will all by now know that there was a major food-poisoning incident last night and tragically at least thirteen people have so far died with two more victims in intensive care. Newsum and I will be going to the path lab first and then will go and question the only diner unaffected by their meal, a Mrs Travers.'

'Bill, Julia, can you go down to A&E in High Wycombe and get as much information as you can from the duty doctor? Newsum and I will want a quick word with him or her at some stage this morning so please make sure they remain at the hospital until we arrive.'

'We've got more information on the Defreitas case following our enquiries yesterday. Interestingly we have discovered that Proteus owns a black Hummer that is usually kept at the company garage in London. It appears to be missing, presumed stolen. We will be working in liaison with DI Tooley of Wembley on this as they have an unsolved murder in which a black Hummer is also connected.' Tom paused slightly and took the chance to look around at his motley crew.

'Okay, time to get moving.'

Tom and Newsum arrived at the pathologists to find Helen in a tizz.

'Oh hi Tom I can imagine why you are here. I can't believe it. Thirteen bloody PM's to do today! Are you interested in any of the deceased in particular?' Tom was completely non-plussed by Helen's sudden friendliness.

'Well we don't have a list of their names yet but I was called out at 3am following the death of Julian Travers so I suppose I would like you to work on Mr Travers first so I can tidy up my paperwork.'

Helen sighed.

'Okay, when the bodies arrive I'll cut him up first.'

'Thanks Helen you are a treasure.' Helen scowled and Tom beat a hasty retreat. *Knew it wouldn't last!*

Next stop was the Travers' house. There were three cars parked in the driveway. A lady in her 50s came to the door.

'Can I help you?'

'Yes ma'am I am Detective Chief Inspector Tom Sparks of Uxbridge CID and this is my colleague Detective Sergeant Jane Newsum. Can we come in?'

'Yes of course. I was worried you were the press. We have already had a couple of telephone calls, god knows how they got the phone number. I am Janet Coombs, Kate's mother.'

Tom looked blankly whilst the penny dropped with a loud clang. 'Oh yes of course, Mrs Travers' mother. Apologies for being a bit slow.'

As they entered the house Tom braced himself for the onslaught of last night's disgusting odour but to his great surprise all he could smell was lemon.

Seemingly reading his mind Janet Coombs ventured, 'I've cleaned everything up now. What a mess, poor old Julian what a terrible, ignominious way to die. My husband James and I will be staying to look after the children and make all the arrangements.'

It was clear to Tom that despite the shock, Mrs Coombs was a very efficient woman who was in her element.

'How is Kate, is she about?' he asked.

'Yes she is. She's feeling a bit groggy but I'm sure she will want to talk to you. I'll go and get her.'

Janet Coombs returned with a younger version of herself in tow. Kate Travers was clearly very upset and in deep shock but far more in control than when Tom had seen her briefly the previous night.

'Please come and sit in the lounge, you will be able to talk in there.' Janet Coombs instructed them, leading the way into a nice lounge with French doors leading on to a small but pretty patio and lawn.

'Thank you.'

Once in the lounge Tom said, 'Mrs Travers, I can only offer my deepest sympathy for your tragic loss. I regret I'm going to have to ask you a few questions but I can assure you I will keep them to an absolute minimum.'

'Thank you Superintendent.'

Tom ignored his demotion and continued.

'I understand that you and your husband regularly went to the Rajpoot on Tuesday nights?'

'Yes it was our weekly treat, we would get a babysitter, walk in to town have a couple of drinks in Wildwood and then have a curry. Julian loved his curry, especially the onion bhajis.' Tom made notes as she spoke. Wildwood was one of these very trendy eateries that seemed to be springing up everywhere. He remembered with some warmth its predecessor, the slightly seedy Packhorse Inn.

'Did he always have the same?'

'Oh yes. I used to tease him and tell him how predictable he was and why didn't he live dangerously.' She paused and half-smiled at the irony.

'Had you been married long?'

'Eleven years. It is so sad. Julian was doing so well at work. Last year he landed a fantastic job in London with an investment fund. Strange that two other people from there died last week. They always say things come in three's don't they?'

Tom turned and stared at Newsum and tried to calm his thought processes down. Finally after what seemed like ages, he turned back to Mrs Travers.

'Who did Julian work for Mrs Travers?'

'Oh an investment fund called Proteus, based in Mayfair.'

Tom and Newsum both froze just long enough to calculate the implications. *Good God!*

'How long had Julian worked there?' Tom continued without indication of the somersaults his mind was doing.

'About seventeen months.'

'What was his role there?'

'He was their IT manager. Why are you asking so many questions about Julian and his work? Do you think his death was suspicious?'

'No, no, not at all it is just we have to ask certain questions in these circumstances that's all.'

'Of course. I am sorry, I should have realised, it's just such a shock.'

'I can imagine, Mrs Travers. We are going to leave you in peace now and any other questions can wait until another time.'

———

Tom and Newsum returned to the car and he just sat there for a couple of minutes before turning on the engine and heading the car towards A&E in High Wycombe.

'Can you believe that Newsum? Another death at Proteus? It is certainly becoming a very dangerous place to work. Even as coincidences go this is probably the tragic exception that proves the rule.'

'Sir, they do say that sometimes the truth is stranger than fiction.'

They arrived at a busy A&E just as two uniformed police were leaving.

'Morning lads, have you been here to discuss the food-poisoning deaths?'

'No sir, Phil here caught his arm on some glass and needed a couple of stitches. It is all going haywire in there. Thirteen deaths last night and two likely this morning. Good luck sir.'

'Thanks lads.'

Tom and Newsum walked into the A&E department and introduced themselves at reception. A rather butch looking lady stared laconically at them and paused before announcing: 'But two of your colleagues only left about half and hour ago.'

'Yes I'm well aware of the visit of my colleagues but the death toll is such that we need to be totally clear as to what has happened I'm sure you can appreciate that.'

'Of course, I just feel sorry for Doctor Davies. He was in charge here last night. He's still in his office waiting for you but I must warn you he's very tired and would like to go home.'

'Don't worry, we won't keep him long.'

'Good, he's down the corridor third door on the right.'

Tom knocked and entered the doctor's room. Doctor Davies was young and obviously exhausted. Tom was starting to feel old. This guy looked as if he should still be at school. How on earth could he be a doctor?

'Sorry to bother you doctor but I'm Detective Chief Inspector Sparks from Uxbridge CID and this is Detective Sergeant Newsum. We are here about the food poisonings.'

'Oh thank God, I was hoping you would be here soon. I'm exhausted but your colleagues insisted I must see you before I clocked off. How can I help?'

'Cause of death?'

Doctor Davies answered, sarcastically, 'Poisoning?'

'Sorry I didn't ask that question very well did I. Any idea what type of poisoning?'

'Food poisoning?'

They all laughed albeit rather sheepishly. Tom liked Doctor Davies.

'Okay Chief Inspector let me make life a bit simpler for you. Last night we had to deal with the deaths of thirteen people and two more are likely to die today. The symptoms are vomiting and incontinence followed swiftly by the heart stopping. Can't say that I am expert on poison but I would say it was some kind of a cardio toxin.'

'Is such food poisoning common?'

'No very, very rare, even in curry houses.'

'Is it likely that the poisoning was deliberate?'

'Isn't that more your area of expertise?'

'Point taken. Anything else you can offer us before we leave you in peace?'

'Afraid not.'

On the way back to GX, Tom pondered on the nagging thought that perhaps someone had been murdered. But who? He went back to his theory of no coincidences. If Travers had been murdered, who murdered him and why? What if he wasn't the murderer's intended victim? How did the murderer get access to poison the food?

'I think we need to go to the Rajpoot Newsum.'

'Yes sir.'

There was a police car parked outside the restaurant when they arrived and the front door was in the process of being taped off by a young uniformed police officer to prevent access.

They approached the constable and introduced themselves.

'Good morning sir, I was warned to expect you.'

'Anyone inside?'

'Yes, PC Walsh and the owner.'

'Thanks.'

They entered the curry house and could see a large uniformed policeman and a small Asian man. The policeman turned and smiled.

'Ah Tom there you are.'

Tom grimaced slightly at the familiarity, Walsh was always a little disrespectful but he and Tom had known one another for years and occasionally went out drinking together when their shifts allowed.

'Good Morning PC Walsh,' he replied very formally.

Catching on, Walsh responded. 'Sir I have the owner, Mr Singh here and was just explaining to him about the problems and that we are going to have close the place down until we have completed our enquiries and are happy that the restaurant is safe to re-open.'

'Thank you constable, Newsum and I will take over from here. Oh, one last thing, has anyone spoken to Health and Safety?'

'Not that I am aware sir, I'll get on to it straight away.'

'Thank you PC Walsh.' Tom smiled inwardly at how smoothly he had dealt with Walsh's earlier indiscipline.

Walsh left to join his younger colleague and Tom turned to Mr Singh and suggested that the three of them sit down. Mr Singh was a smartly dressed man in his fifties. He gestured them into the main restaurant where they took their places in a semi-circular booth. Tom could see the place was immaculate and found it difficult to believe the awful events of the previous evening.

'This shouldn't take too long sir but inevitably I have a number of questions for you. Are you happy to answer them here or would you prefer to answer them down at the station?'

'Here is fine sir.'

'Good, can I have your full name please?'

'It Jeeva Sachin Singh. Can I offer you some refreshment? Some coffee, tea or a cold drink?'

Tom was gasping but had to stop himself.

'Mr Singh I don't think in the circumstances that is a good idea do you?'

'No I suppose not.'

'So Mr Singh, I understand from my enquiries that you have been inspected by Health and Safety on a regular basis and have always passed with flying colours. Any idea what could have caused the poisoning?'

'None at all sir, it is a complete mystery to me.'

'How many people ate here last night?'

'Nineteen in total.'

'Is that a typical night for a Tuesday?'

'Tuesday is a fairly popular evening with our regulars, we always get a few locals in to eat. Last night was slightly better than usual because one of our regulars was holding a birthday party. He even hired our Indian Elvis.'

'Indian Elvis?'

'Yes one of my relatives does an Elvis act, he is very good and they all enjoyed themselves immensely.'

'Well of your nineteen customers last night, fifteen are now either dead or on life support machines.'

'I just can't believe it, we are so, so careful. This is the worst day of my life,' said Mr Singh as he unsuccessfully tried to choke back the tears.

'I know this must be incredibly upsetting for you but I really have to ask these questions, they are important. The fact that four people have been unaffected means that only certain dishes were responsible for the poisonings. We need to isolate the dishes responsible and quickly. Do you have a copy of the orders for each table?'

'Yes sir I will get them for you now.'

He returned very quickly with a sheaf of indecipherable order slips.

'We need a seating plan and details of each table's order.'

'Certainly sir.'

'Mr Singh, how many staff do you employ?'

'Well it used to be eight but two of my staff had to return to India as a matter of great urgency this week.'

'Really? Problems?'

'Yes they have family trouble in Mumbai.'

'That must have left you short-staffed Mr Singh.'

'Yes indeed, I was most grateful for a part-time worker who worked last night.'

'Just the one night?'

'Yes he was passing through and heard we needed help.'

'Can I ask this man's name?'

'No I did not bother to take it. I was desperate and he was only helping out for the night.'

'I see, well what did he look like?'

'He was slim, Asian, black-haired and about five foot nine or ten.'

'How old do you think he was?'

'In his 30s I would say.'

'What work did you give him?'

'He was put to work in the kitchen helping chef.'

'So he had access to the food?'

'Yes of course, surely you don't think that?' His voiced tailed off as he took in the possibilities.

'Just covering all the angles Mr Singh. Okay I will leave you with DS Newsum now.'

Tom left Newsum with the car keys as he decided the half mile walk back to the station would give him a chance to think. He passed Costa and the smell of the coffee was too much. He ordered a latte and sat and mulled things over

Proteus had to be the key. Three deaths there in less than a week were just too much of a coincidence. He realised that only one was definitely a murder at this stage but even so, three deaths? Strange that Travers lived in Gerrards Cross too? What did Travers actually do as IT Manager? If he was murdered, why and who would want him dead?

He decided that the moment Newsum had finished with Mr Singh they would return to Mayfair and try and get to the bottom of this.

———

Mayfair

Tom and Newsum finally set off for Mayfair in mid-afternoon due to the time it took Newsum to finalise with Mr Singh the seating plan and each table's order.

'It looks like the onion bhajis or nan bread are favourites sir; at first we thought it was the poppadums but it turns out everyone ate some of those.'

'Well I've sent forensic down there to check the kitchen and to take samples from all the foods still remaining.'

'I don't think I could eat a curry ever again.' She said screwing her nose up. 'Trouble is my Jason loves a nice ruby and would eat them every night if he could.'

'I am sorry Newsum you have me completely bemused.'

'It's cockney rhyming slang sir, Ruby Murray, curry.'

'Oh.'

It wasn't often that Newsum mentioned her Jason so Tom seized the moment to change the subject by enquiring.

'How is Jason?'

'Oh he's fine, just got promoted at work, he's so excited.'

Jason worked on the counter at the local Travis Perkins in Slough. He was a bright, keen young man and he and Newsum made a nice friendly couple. He sensed wedding bells would be in the offing very soon, followed shortly afterwards no doubt by the patter of tiny feet. He would miss her. Tom realised he was jumping ahead and returned to the present.

'Excellent, well please pass on my congratulations.'

'Course sir.'

They arrived at Mayfair in contemplative silence. Newsum was no doubt thinking about her Jason but Tom was thinking about murder. Tom had phoned ahead and asked Jeremy and Mick to meet him there. They were standing in reception making the place look untidy as he walked in.

'Thanks for meeting me here.'

'Well we had to if only out of curiosity, you sounded so mysterious.'

'Sorry about that, I wanted to spring this information on you face-to-face and gauge your immediate reactions.'

'Well get on with it, stop keeping us in suspense.' Mick said excitedly. Mick had never been one for secrets. Possibly the worst character flaw for a policeman.

'Okay, okay, calm down. I was just wondering how you would react if I informed you that another Proteus member of staff died last night.'

They both gasped in unison.

'Who was it?'

'Julian Travers, the IT Manager.'

'How?'

'When?'

'He died of food-poisoning after going out for a curry in Gerrards Cross. One of fifteen people to die. We've started making preliminary enquiries and there are certainly enough suspicious circumstances to make me think it could be murder.'

146

'One of fifteen? Why murder the other fourteen? That's over-egging the pudding in anyone's book. I think you have been watching too many films Tom,' said Mick.

Tom blushed and had to agree that listening to these two seasoned detectives made his theory seem a bit silly.

'Sorry Mick, you're right. Thing is, it is well known that I don't believe in coincidences and that belief has stood me in very good stead over the years. There are far too many coincidences in this case and it makes me think that the whole thing has been very carefully planned.'

Tom paused, giving them the chance to interrupt. When nothing was forthcoming from the two City detectives, he continued.

'I think we need to know exactly what Julian Travers did here at Proteus before we go any further.'

'Agreed.'

They asked the receptionist if they could see Stewart McMillan and were told he was away on business and wouldn't be returning until the next day. They settled for the next best option, John Davis.

'Mr Davis, thank you for seeing us unannounced but we have some questions to ask you about Julian Travers.'

'Julian?'

'Yes. I trust you have heard about him.'

'I know he isn't in work today, but he's on the rota to be working from home. Has something happened?'

'Mr Davis I am sorry to be the bearer of bad news but Julian Travers died last night of food-poisoning.'

John Davis collapsed back in his chair.

'Oh my God. How awful.'

'Yes it was particularly unpleasant, I was called to his house in the early hours. He was one of 15 who died after eating at a curry house in Gerrards Cross. I realise that this has probably come as a huge shock to you but can I just ask you a few questions about Mr Travers and his role here at Proteus?'

'Well he was employed by Michael to completely overhaul and re-design our IT system. He was a bit of an IT whizz-kid and Michael wanted a state of the art system.'

'How was he getting on?'

'Not too well really, to be honest he came across to me as being a bit thick. But Michael and he used to spend hours closeted in Michael's office so Michael must have been happy with his work.'

'Did he have a laptop?'

'Yes but it is unlikely to be here. Julian took his laptop everywhere with him.'

'Can we have a quick look round Julian's office?'

'Yes of course. Please come with me.'

'Just one last question. Did Julian ever use the company Hummer?'

'Not to my knowledge.'

A long painstaking search of Julian's office yielded nothing of any consequence. A photo of the family on his desk. A diary with a few entries, mainly meetings with Michael or holidays.

Tom was a disappointed and frustrated detective when he and Newsum returned to GX. He put in a call to Helen but she was too busy to talk to him. He sent her a text.

'Drink later?'

He swiftly got one back.

'No.'

He thought of going to the path lab and decided tomorrow would be better. He decided to have a quick beer in The Apple Tree and call it a night.

Refreshed after a good night's sleep, Zolo went online and checked his bank account. Two separate payments of one million euros had been deposited into his account in the past 24 hours, signs of a happy client and a job well done.

It was another wonderful autumnal day and he had to admit to feeling rather pleased with himself. He decided to have a lazy day and after a shortened workout, he prepared a salad for lunch and ate on the balcony.

The great thing about hiring Zolo was the total anonymity. No one knew who he was and he never knew the identity of his clients. This discretion allied to his 100 per cent success rate enabled him to charge very high fees.

He had never had one complaint.

Zolo was however becoming increasingly wracked with doubt. He had been in the profession for too long. He was getting older as, of course, was his mind and body. The law of averages said that one day he would make a misjudgement and either fail or be caught. He knew he couldn't last forever, however well he looked after himself.

Every time he received a new job he wondered whether this would be the one that would be his last. He could afford to retire but life would be too predictable and mundane. He needed the thrill of the kill.

His phone bleeped, another mission. He smiled and put on his bicycle clips.

Thursday 22nd/Friday 23rd October 2009

Tom returned to the Travers house early the next morning and found Mrs Travers still deep in shock and looking completely out of it. He could see no point in asking her any more questions so he decided to have a chat with her mother to try and find out what he could from her instead. After all, her mother seemed to be the nosy type who tended to know everything and what she didn't know she made sure she found out.

Janet Coombs made him a mug of tea and they sat in the conservatory and chatted. After some words of sympathy and concerned enquiries about Kate, Tom quickly brought the subject round to Julian.

'I hear Julian was a bit of a whizz with computers Mrs Coombs.'

'Apparently, but God knows how, I always thought he was as thick as two short planks.'

No love lost there, Tom thought.

'Where did he work before Proteus?'

'Oh he flitted from job to job until he finally went to night school and studied IT. He then got a job with an insurance company before Michael Defreitas offered him a job at Proteus.'

'Did he know Michael before he joined?'

'Oh yes they used to go out drinking together. In fact, Julian had been doing the odd bit of freelance work for him before he joined Proteus. Used to do it from home. It paid handsomely I understand.'

'Any idea what the work entailed?'

'Oh he was very secretive and he often joked that if he told us he would have to kill us.' She paused and looked tearful as the full irony of her comment sank in. 'I expect it is all on his laptop somewhere.'

'Do you know where his laptop is?'

'Yes of course, it is on his desk in his study. Saw it there this morning. Would you like to see it?'

'Very much.'

Janet Coombs led Tom into a small reception room where the curtains were still half closed. The room was pristine and sparsely furnished, in fact very similar to his London office. Tom immediately spotted the laptop sitting in the centre of the desk.

'I hope you don't mind Mrs Coombs, but I will need to borrow the laptop.'

'Of course although I must say I don't understand what a laptop could possibly have to do with food-poisoning.'

'Probably nothing at all, but it is best to be thorough.'

'Chief Inspector, do you suspect foul-play?'

Tom realised that this lady was not stupid and that he would have to feed her a half-truth. 'Not as such, no, but I'm suspicious that there have been so many deaths at Proteus in such a short time.'

'I'm sure you know what you're doing Inspector. Feel free to take the laptop, I'll warn Kate you've borrowed it.'

Tom gratefully took the laptop and placed it under his arm. Now all he had to do was find out what was on there.

Half an hour later Tom was at his desk and bemused. On his return he had opened the laptop in great anticipation of finding something that would break the case. Unfortunately all he'd managed to generate was a message informing him that a password was required for access. He was worried that it might self-destruct if he put in the wrong one.

Staring out of the window in frustration, Tom had a brainwave. He picked up his mobile and punched in a number. The phone rang twice and then was answered.

'Tooley'

'Hi Tooley, it's Sparkie here.'

'Oh hi mate how are you, hear you are up to your neck in shit and vomit up there.'

'Tell me about it! Look I need a favour. Can you put me in touch with your computer hacker?'

'Yes of course, anything to do with my murder?'

'Not sure yet. One of the people poisoned worked for Proteus in the IT Section. I need to break into his laptop.'

'Course, no problem. Her name is Margaret. We all call her Mog. I'll text you over her number. She's brilliant.'

'Thanks Tooley, you're a star.'

The text duly arrived and Tom rang Margaret.

'Hello.'

'Hi Margaret or do I call you Mog? This is Detective Chief Inspector Tom Sparks I am a colleague of Detective Inspector Tooley. He has recommended you.'

'Mog is fine if you're a mate of Tools.' Sparks smiled, as Mog continued, 'computer problems eh?'

'Indeed.'

'Okay where are you and when do you want me to come over?'

'Well I am with the Uxbridge CID but based in Gerrards Cross and would be grateful if you could come here as soon as possible.'

'Can't do it now just getting ready to go out on a hen night, how about 12 noon tomorrow?'

'Yes that would be fine.'

'Okay see you at GX Station at noon and please make sure I have a quiet office somewhere where I can do my stuff.'

'Yes of course, do you know where the station is?'

'Course, see you tomorrow.' Then she was gone.

Tom decided the only course of action now was a thorough review of the case over a nice pint at The Apple Tree. He was relieved to find it quiet and managed to find himself a table in an alcove where he could sit undisturbed.

———

The following morning Tom got to work at his usual time and after updating his team, started looking at the list of questions he had compiled over a pint the previous night.

This time his list was long and bulleted. Tom loved to doodle arrows on his lists, had done since he was at school:

⇒   Where is the Hummer?

⇒   Who is the mystery blonde?

⇒   Where was Michael's body kept before it was found?

⇒   What happened to the head?

⇒   Was Shirley's death connected to Defreitas and Proteus?

⇒   Did the Rajpoot workers really return to Mumbai?

⇒   Was Julian Travers murdered?

⇒   What had happened to Tomas & is there a connection?

⇒   Where is Adam Batstone?

⇒   Why was Defreitas's car near the scene of the burglaries?

His train of thought was interrupted by the arrival of a stunningly attractive black haired girl who looked no more than 20. She had the body of an athlete and warm, inviting green eyes that made him feel all shaky.

'Chief Inspector Sparks?' she asked.

'Y-yes,' he stuttered.

'Oh good I am in the right place then. I'm Mog.'

Slightly disappointed she was only there on business Tom snapped back into work mode.

'Ah good, yes I have a laptop that needs hacking into and Tooley says you are the best.'

'Yes, of course to both. Where is it?'

'Over here.'

'Ah, Sony Vaio, easy peasy lemon squeezy. I'll need a couple of hours, where do you want me?' She said with an outrageous wink.

Tom blushed and quickly headed for the door.

'Yes of course, please follow me.'

He left Mog in a nearby office and went back to his list. He was distracted now though. God she was attractive, Tooley could have warned him! Tom was increasingly imagining having sex with women he was coming into contact with and realised he was going to have to get laid soon. He just felt so tired and lethargic outside work. He put it down to PHS, Post-Helen Syndrome.

At this moment Newsum walked in and excitedly announced that she had found out some important information.

'We know what car she drives sir!'

'Who?'

'Ooops sorry sir, the mystery blonde. We know what car she drives!'

'Which is?'

'A silver Audi sir.'

'Thanks Newsum – do you have a registration number for the car?'

'No fraid not.' Newsum replied looking a bit crest-fallen.

'So, do tell how GX's finest came across this information.'

'Well as instructed, the team have been interviewing all the other residents in the block of flats where Defreitas lived.

'Yesterday, Mel met a neighbour called Mr Ross who was very helpful. He described the car but when asked about the registration number commented that was the height of nosiness. He did however confirm it was a 57 plate, he thought.'

'So how did he come to have this information?'

'Well, apparently the mystery blonde used to call regularly, late at night and leave early in the morning. Mr Ross has trouble sleeping and often sits at the window and counts the cars on the road as a way of trying to get to sleep.'

'Well done Newsum good work, that certainly narrows it down a bit. Did Mr Ross say what type of Audi it was?'

Newsum confirmed Tom's worse fears.

'Yes, he said it was a sporty convertible.'

'Thanks Newsum, leave it with me.' Tom said dismissively and returned to his notebook and the list.

He gave up after twenty minutes of non-productive head scratching. No point delaying it. Get it over with he told himself.

He picked up the phone.

'Path lab. Doctor James speaking.'

'Helen, Tom here.'

'Yes Tom," she said brusquely.

'Helen we need to talk. What time shall I come round?'

'Sorry Tom I'm up to my eyes in it. I'm still dealing with the PM's on all the victims of the food poisoning.'

'Helen, I'm afraid this is official and must be done today. We can do it the easy way by me popping around at an agreed time or the hard way in which case I'll come by with another officer and bring you back to the station for questioning. The choice is yours.'

'Okay come here at six.' Her voice sounded hollow and sad.

It was early afternoon and Tom knew the time would drag and he was grateful when Mog poked her lovely head around the door.

'Chief Inspector, you really must come and look at this, I think you're going to be very pleased with what I have to show you.' She followed this with another outrageous wink.

'Oh I do hope so.' Tom replied, enjoying he banter.

He followed Mog into the adjoining office. She was beaming.

'Well you certainly set me a tough challenge didn't you Inspector? It's always difficult trying to break into a fellow expert's laptop or PC. Good job I am the best.'

This woman certainly doesn't lack self-confidence Tom thought in admiration.

'Find anything interesting?' Tom asked.

'Difficult to say, I think so. Julian's laptop was used to build a set of complicated accounts for an investment fund. But the really interesting thing was that it was set to automatically increase daily at a certain rate. Do you have any idea where the main PC is for a company called Proteus?'

'Yes, it's in Mayfair, in London.'

'Chief Inspector I know where Mayfair is, I do play Monopoly you know!'

Tom looked at Mog in admiration and wanted to say something but his mind had gone totally blank. In the end Mog broke the silence.

'Anyway I need to see it and confirm my suspicions.'

'Shall we go there in the morning?'

'Fraid not I've a lecture tomorrow. Can we go now?'

Tom looked at his watch and realised he would be late to see Helen – but this was important so he nodded his head and off they went.

The drive, which Tom spent mainly taking furtive glances at Mog's thighs, went by in a flash. On arrival at the Proteus offices in Mayfair, Tom introduced Mog to John Davis and she was given the freedom of the Proteus main computer.

Tom decided to have a chat with John Davis while he waited but found it very uninspiring. The man was a typical accountant. Grey, grey and more grey!

After forty minutes Mog was back. 'Okay Chief Inspector, I'm ready to go back now, or shall I call you Sparkie?'

'Chief Inspector will do fine."

Once in the car Tom asked 'Were your suspicions confirmed?'

'Oh yes they were indeed.'

'Are you going to share your suspicions with me?'

'Oh of course Tom, oops I mean Chief Inspector. Basically, Julian Travers had written a clever program that provided a dummy set of accounts for Proteus that factored in automatic daily increases to the fund valuation. He had also set up the main computer at Proteus to re-direct to this set of accounts whenever anyone logged in to look at them.'

'Margaret, I am afraid I am not very good at this high-tech stuff but as I understand it you are saying that Julian Travers set up a computer programme on the main Proteus computer system that ensured that anyone who logged in to check the Proteus performance and financials was diverted to the artificial set of figures on his laptop 24/7.'

'You catch on fast guv, except the bit about calling me Margaret.'

'Good grief, is the automatic divert still on?'

'As of now, yes. I thought I better check with you before I switched it off. Clever bugger Julian Travers.'

'Let's leave it as it is for now. I need to give this some thought. I might need you to delve a bit deeper.'

'No problem guv, you're the boss. We need to talk about dosh though.'

'Dosh?'

'That's the trouble with you posh blokes, you all swallow a dictionary before puberty. Remuneration?'

'Oh of course, what is your rate?'

'Twenty quid an hour okay with you?'

'Sure. Let me have your invoice.'

Tom fell into a pensive silence that not even the sight of Mog's thighs could lighten. They had reached Uxbridge High Street when Mog broke the silence.

'This will do fine Tom.'

Tom returned to the present and quickly responded.

'Oh okay, excellent. Well thank you for today. Don't forget to let me have your invoice.'

'Always happy to oblige.' She said as she walked off. 'And cheer up, it may never happen!'

It already has, Tom thought.

Gerrards Cross

Tom was dreading seeing Helen and this feeling of dread increased when he saw the expression on her face as he walked through the door to her office.

'About fucking time too! This is so typical of you. You never think of anyone except yourself you selfish bastard.'

At this point she stood up and went to slap him, he caught her arm in mid-slap.

'Helen just calm down I did phone you and warn you I was running late. Big break in the Proteus case.'

At the mention of Proteus, Helen immediately stopped her attack and asked. 'How big a break?'

'Not sure yet but it is what we've been waiting for I think.'

'Do you know who killed Michael?'

'Not that big a break but it's a start.' Tom noticed her use of the name Michael and thought well it is now or never. 'Talking of Michael, how did you meet him?'

'Michael? We met at a wine-tasting at The Bull Hotel. Seems we share, sorry shared, the same wine supplier.'

'When did you start going out with him?'

'You really want to know when I started shagging him don't you Tom? Well that day, we went back to his flat and he fucked the arse off me. It was the best sex of my life.'

Tom felt like he had been shot through the heart. A tidal wave of sheer sadness ripped through his body as he tried to keep steady and calm. In the end he just stared at her and said. 'Doctor Helen James, you leave me with no alternative but to ask you to accompany me to Gerrards Cross Police Station to help us with our enquiries into the murder of Michael Defreitas.'

'You really are a petty bastard aren't you Tom? Hiding behind your job and power because you feel insulted. I can't help you with your enquiries into his murder. Okay I shagged him about three times a week but I am sure he never regarded himself as being exclusive to me. If you want to ask me more about our relationship just do so. I have been totally honest with you up until now.'

'When was the wine tasting?'

'It was about six months ago and yes it was whilst you and I were still seeing each other.'

Tom thought about the words *seeing each other* and thought about what a strange phrase it was. He realised he was trying to divert his thoughts from the hurt of Helen's infidelity but it helped.

Helen was glaring at him as he fumbled for his next question. 'Did Michael give you any indication that he was being threatened or that he was in danger?'

'No, not at all. In fact quite the opposite, he thought everyone loved him.'

'Well you obviously did,' he said and bitterly regretted saying it immediately. She smiled at him and wound him up further.

'Awww has the boy with the little cock had his nose put out of joint by the rich man with the big cock?'

Tom realised that he was getting nowhere.

He turned and left without another word. He reached his car and felt a massive urge to be sick. He vomited in the car park and immediately felt much better, albeit shaky.

God, he hated women, they always knew the best way to hurt you. He wondered whether they gave lessons to them at school and then realised that such lessons weren't necessary because deep down they were all bitches.

Snakes with tits. That's what one of his friends called them. Another of his sayings was *Life's a bitch and then you marry* Unsurprisingly he was as unsuccessful as Tom on the romance front.

God he needed a drink badly. He drove straight to The Apple Tree and bought himself a pint and found a nice table in the garden.

Geneva

Zolo was a happy man. Not only was he rich and fit but he was going to Spain, in fact Marbella. He loved Spain, especially the Costa Del Sol, at this time of year. So much nicer than The Algarve, less windy. He was leaving for the airport in two hours. Time to pack.

Happy days!

Marbella

Pete and family strolled out of Malaga airport and into the Spanish sunshine and immediately donned their sunglasses in unison. They had arrived without a hitch and were looking forward to a wonderful fortnight of sunbathing, eating and drinking, especially drinking.

They hailed a taxi and were on their way to the villa that they hoped would be as wonderful as it had looked in the photos.

At exactly the same time, Zolo was being waved through passport control on the other side of the airport.

Gerrards Cross

Meanwhile back in Gerrards Cross things were hotting up in every way except the weather which had turned damp and gloomy, matching the mood of Detective Chief Inspector

Thomas Algernon Frederick Sparks. Tom tried to avoid telling people his middle names, especially Algernon.

The previous night over what must have been either his fourth or fifth pint, Tom decided that the time had come for the three different CID's to get together to compare notes on the Michael Defreitas/Proteus situation and to plan a way forward. The City boys were a bit reluctant to go off piste but finally, reluctantly agreed to meet at Wembley which was about half way between Mayfair and Gerrards Cross.

Tom started by introducing everyone to each other and then quickly got down to business.

'Thanks for coming, we're all busy but I think it is important at this stage that we establish what we know so far and plan a way forward.'

He glanced round the table at the other five, A very fat DS Porter who seemed to be falling out of his chair in slow motion, DI Tooley looking grim and worried, DI Ward looked as handsome as ever, DS Newsum, who had somehow managed to get herself seated next to Ward and last but not least his old mate DS Mick Brunton who looked as though he hadn't slept for a month. No wonder his wife was looking elsewhere.

'From my point of view the current situation is that we found a mutilated body on West Common that has been identified as Michael Defreitas, the co-founder of an investment fund based in Mayfair called Proteus. The body was headless and identification could only be made by blood type and the belongings on the body.'

Tom paused to let this information sink in.

'The pathologist has confirmed that the murder took place elsewhere and that the decapitated body was dumped on West Common shortly before its discovery. We have little information about this murder although the one lead we do have is the sighting of a black Hummer nearby just hours before the body was found.'

'Two other Proteus employees have since died one of which, Julian Travers, also lived in GX. Mr Travers, died on Tuesday night of food poisoning. I strongly believe the two deaths are connected but have no proof at this stage just a gut instinct. I will rely on Jeremy to update us on the other death, a gentleman by the name of William Thornton.'

'We've managed to locate and open Travers's laptop which contained some very interesting information. Travers had created a false set of accounts and figures for Proteus and installed some kind of program on the main computer system that automatically re-directs any enquiry to these accounts not the true ones. Travers was thick with Defreitas and we can only assume that Defreitas was behind the deception.'

Jeremy Ward looked puzzled.

'Why would they do that Tom?'

'I believe that there was something that needed to be hidden from view and this was the best way to do it.'

'Have you seen the real accounts and figures?'

'No not yet, we're trying to locate them. We think they're on Michael's laptop. But we can't find that anywhere. We think the murderer or murderers have got it and may even have killed him for it.'

'A black Hummer was seen at the scene of two, as yet, unconnected murders on the same night. Coincidentally Proteus owns a black Hummer that is missing. And you all know I don't . . .'

'Believe in coincidences,' they all interrupted in unison to much laughter.

'Maybe the two supposedly unconnected murders are, in fact, connected in some way?' Newsum chipped in.

'Good point Newsum. Brian have you any more information on your murder?'

'Not really Tom, whoever did it seems to have vanished without a trace and left little, if any, clues behind. We've gone through Shirley's PC with a fine toothcomb but haven't found anything yet except a very suspicious weekly payment from the Cayman Islands.'

'Any sign of the missing Czech?'

'No, he has vanished.'

'Think he did it in a fit of anger because she wasn't what he expected?'

'No Tom, personally I doubt he was the man at Marylebone as he went missing on the Sunday and was more likely to be in a river somewhere by the time the meeting took place.'

Tom thought about this briefly and then continued.

'Interesting, so Tomas is missing, probably dead, yet Shirley still turned up at the appointed time and place for their liaison and definitely met and left with a man who she thought was Tomas.'

He turned to Tooley.

'I know Shirley's murder is not my case but the Hummer intrigues me and I am convinced our murders are connected Brian. There is so much I need to know. Really all of Rudyard's honest working men apply here.'

The others looked at Tom as though he was mad. Tom realised that Kipling clearly only supplied them with cakes and not literary inspiration.

Tom sighed before continuing his questions in staccato style.

'What was the motive for killing Shirley?'

'Why was Tomas brought over to the UK and then killed?'

'When was the last contact between Shirley and Tomas? Internet or otherwise?'

'How did the murderer know about the meeting at Marylebone?'

'Where is Tomas?'

'Who is behind this?'

'Brian I am really interested in knowing more about your murder. Do you mind keeping me in the loop and perhaps letting me attend the odd meeting with your team?'

'No problem Tom, we can only benefit from your great experience and of course more cultured approach to crime.' Tom knew Tooley was winding him up and ignored him by turning to Jeremy Ward.

'How have you been getting on Jeremy?'

'Not much better really Tom, uniform are dealing with the missing Hummer but don't hold out much hope. That leaves us with a death by misadventure.'

'Or masturbation!' Tooley chortled before blushing. 'Oops sorry Jane, bit of lads' humour.'

Tom came to Tooley's rescue.

'I hear from David Browne that you had a hacker in to open the Proteus main PC, shame he didn't spot the duplicate program they were running.' Jeremy felt himself starting to blush as Tom looked at him in a very enquiring kind of way. He sought to quickly nip this line of conversation in the bud.

'He was a friend of a friend and to be honest I only asked him to open the locked files which he did.'

'So any ideas going forward?' Tom asked the group in general. Tooley was first to respond.

'Have you got any nearer to finding out who Defreitas's mystery blonde girlfriend is?'

Newsum immediately responded. 'Well we know what car she drives now.'

'Yes,' Tom said. 'We know she drives a silver Audi convertible which narrows it down a bit but we don't have a registration number.'

Tom felt a bit guilty about misleading his fellow officers but he had no choice. He didn't want to taint Helen's reputation until he knew for certain the degree of her involvement.

They were, of course, all busy and the meeting was quickly concluded. It had achieved two things from Tom's point of view.

They were now working more as a team which was important if he was to establish any link between the three cases and he had managed from a personal point of view to manoeuvre himself into a position of leadership. This was key for him because he wanted to make sure that as much information flowed through him as possible.

And he had a concern over Jeremy Ward. He didn't trust him. He would have to keep an eye on him.

Marbella

It was another lovely day in Marbella, bright sunshine and a lovely cool breeze blowing inland from the ocean. Despite this, Pete and his family were yet to venture from their villa.

They were suffering from their considerable indulgences the previous night in Puerto Banus. Too much bloody sangria and sambucca, thought Pete. It had been such good fun at the time but now they were really paying for it.

There was a loud knocking at the door. Pete opened it to be greeted by a local in a sweat stained cap and wearing dirty overalls. He could see the man's van on the driveway, it was small and white and, like its driver, had seen better days.

'Buenas dias, Senor.'

'Oh hi, how can I help?'

'Ingleeeesh?'

'Oh yes. You speak English?'

'A beet. I boiler man. I see boiler?'

'Oh yes of course. I boiler man too, back in England. Wouldn't have a clue how Spanish boilers work though. We had the heating on last night as it was very chilly. I thought this place was supposed to be hot.'

'Ke?'

'Doesn't matter, please feel free to have a look at the boiler.'

Fifteen minutes later after a series of nonsensical attempts to hold a conversation with the local boiler man Pete gave up and went and sat by the pool.

Ten minutes later the boiler man re-appeared.

'I feeneesh, it okay now.'

'Excellent, have a nice day.' Pete said as he gave him a couple of euro coins.

Zolo, in his sweaty cap and stained overalls, returned to the dirty, decrepit white van throwing the coins over the garden wall. He drove the van to the nearest car park where he left it. He wiped the van clean out of habit and then returned to his hotel to change, pack his things and checkout.

Three hours later he was on his way home hoping the weather forecast of another cold night in Marbella was correct. The Swissair flight was on time, as usual, and he would get home in time to enjoy a glass of chilled fruit juice on the terrace watching the sun go down over Lake Geneva.

Clerkenwell

Tony Marciano was a worried man, Andy had rung him after his visit to Proteus and reported back to him that there was something very dodgy going on. He had spotted a strange program on the main PC which automatically diverted all accounting enquiries to another computer. As yet though he had been unable to find the location of the divert which had been very cleverly hidden.

The news that Tony's initial concerns were justified did nothing to alleviate his worries.

Tony had been the main money man for the organisation for the past 22 years. During this period he had successfully legitimised many millions, if not billions, through Proteus. This success had enabled him to establish himself with the organisation and he was now considered one of their most trusted.

The problem Tony had was that the organisation still had over £2bn invested in the Proteus fund. Any fraudulent or illegal actions by Proteus would inevitably lead to a thorough investigation and in turn lead to him being asked questions that he did not wish to answer.

Tony pondered his next move. He needed time to think but he knew time was running out.

Gerrards Cross

Following the group meeting, Tom and Tooley adjourned to the Apple Tree. Tooley had a quick pint and then left, promising to ring Tom the following day. Tom was glad of the respite; he liked Tooley but he needed time to himself to reflect on things, especially the Helen situation.

He found a table in the corner and settled down to his second pint. Tom spent the first fifteen minutes thinking about what a bitch Helen had been and feeling sorry for himself. Gradually, though, his thoughts returned to the job in hand and what he was going to do about her.

Helen had admitted to being Defreitas's girlfriend and this explained her recent weird behaviour. What he couldn't understand, though, was her failure to disclose her conflict of interest. He would have thought Helen would have used any excuse to avoid conducting the post mortem but it was quite the opposite.

Why?

Tom decided that his next move was to have a quiet off the record chat with DCC Protheroe.

He felt sad and empty. He had loved Helen very much and still did. He decided that for the purposes of self-preservation, the best way forward for him was to bury himself in the case. He purchased another pint and started to relax. He put Helen to the back of his mind and started to concentrate on the case. He needed clear perspective on which direction his enquiries should take.

Up until now he had really concentrated on Michael Defreitas and Proteus. Something told him that perhaps it was time he looked at the periphery of the case – specifically at the murder of Shirley and the disappearances of Tomas and Adam Batstone.

He phoned Tooley on his mobile.

'Sorry to ring so late but I was just having a beer and thinking about the case. Would you mind if I spend some time at your station tomorrow to go through the murders with you? I know you're up to your eyes in it but maybe between us we can make a big impression on your case as well as mine.'

'I think it's a great idea Tom. Always good to have a fresh pair of eyes. I can arrange to be free in the morning, what time shall I expect you?'

'At nine,, with Newsum'

'Excellent, see you then.'

Wembley

It was actually 9.03am when Tom and Newsum walked though the front doors of the Wembley police station. Tooley took them to the incident room.

'Coffee?'

'Yes please, two, both white with one sugar.' Newsum responded.

'Sure, take a seat, here's the paperwork we have so far.' Tooley gesticulated to a couple of files on a nearby table before rushing off in the direction of the coffee machine.

Tooley's paperwork was surprisingly well organised and definitely made Tom feel embarrassed at his own inadequacies. Tom and Newsum took a file each and starting working their way through them.

The file on Shirley was thick and consisted mainly of the numerous print-outs of emails. The print-outs had been sorted into sections which made life much easier. Tom started reviewing the communications with Husky23. Disappointingly it told him very little he didn't already know. He opened his notebook and jotted down some more questions.:

⇒ Who is Husky23?

⇒ Did he have enough information to find out?

⇒ Maybe the money was the key, who was paying?

⇒ Is it traceable?

Moving on, he read through a couple of other sections before turning to the communications between Shirley and Tomas. He was embarrassed by some of the language and shook his head in amazement. He was starting to realise that his life was comparatively mundane and took it as a sign he was getting old and maybe even out of touch. What was clear from the communications is that Tomas did not come across as a murderer.

Tom realised that the last email exchange between them had taken place over a week before Shirley was murdered. That made sense as it would have coincided with Tomas leaving Prague. Tomas obviously had Shirley's phone number by then. That solved one mystery.

Tom realised he had missed something. He returned to the Husky23 section. He found what he was looking for. On skimming through the first time, he had been concentrating on looking for clues to identify him. He had missed the email he was now staring at.

It was from Shirley to Husky23 and read.

Tomas arriving in the UK on Monday, he has booked himself into lodgings in Harrow. His number there is 02086735901. I am meeting him at Marylebone on Wednesday week at 8pm, under the clock. I will be wearing a bright pink coat so he can't miss me!

We have agreed a code for our first conversation which is as follows:

'Good evening my English beauty, are you waiting for someone?'

'Yes dear sir, I am an English rose waiting to be plucked and appreciated.'

Tom felt a rush of adrenalin and having gleaned as much as he could, he swapped files with Newsum and started reading the very thin file on Tomas.

Again he scribbled questions as he wrote, this time:

⇒ Was it Husky23 who rang Tomas?

⇒ Where did he go on that Sunday after the phone call?

⇒ Who saw him last?

⇒ Was it Tomas who met Shirley? If not, was it Husky23?

Tooley was in his office and Tom strolled over and asked whether he could have a copy of the files. Tooley said he would send it over. Tooley then asked Tom.

'Find anything we missed?' A loaded question Tom thought.

'I doubt it. I am interested in this Husky23 character though. £200 a day is a lot and let's face it the cover story about recruiting for a porn film is a bit thin. He also knew all about the meeting at Marylebone.'

'He did?' Tooley asked and then realising his mistake said, 'yes of course he did. I was going to discuss that with you.'

Tom let Tooley get away with his slip and continued.

'Okay so lets assume that the cover story is a load of rubbish, what do we have?'

'Well we have this Husky23 looking to find a six foot black-haired Eastern European.'

'Indeed. Guess how tall Defreitas was?'

'Not six foot by any chance?'

'Well it is impossible to be exact without his head but the pathologist says he was six-foot tall give or take an inch.'

'Probably just a coincidence!' Tooley said, winking.

Tom smiled and continued.

'We need to find out who Husky23 is.'

'Yes I think you are right. What do we do next?'

'Can you get hold of Mog and ask her to come in and see us? Maybe she can find a way of finding out who Husky23 actually is.'

'Good idea,' said Tooley reaching for the phone.

Mog wasn't too pleased to hear from Tooley as she was busy cramming for an exam. Her attitude adjusted instantly when Tooley told her that Tom was with him. She agreed to come over immediately. Tooley was starting to wonder whether she fancied Tom. He would be very envious if she did.

Mog arrived breathlessly a few minutes later looking a bit flushed and struggling to breathe due to the tightness of her top and jeans that must have been sprayed on. Tom recovered his composure quickly and explained what they needed.

'So you want me to find Husky23 eh? The good news is that he was with AOL. They're one of the better companies for finding out information about account holders. Well let's see what AOL can tell us about him.'

She started tapping away on the keyboard of her laptop until she said. 'Interesting, Husky23 is no longer a current name.'

'Oh typical, another dead end.' Tom sighed. 'Not necessarily.'

She continued tapping away before a look of triumph replaced her previous studious demeanour.

'Gotcha!' She said excitedly.

'Well?' Tom asked.

'Husky23 was a screen name that someone used briefly and then discarded. Unlike most internet providers however, AOL keeps discarded screen names for six months before they can be taken by anyone else. They also very helpfully store the unwanted names on a subscriber's profile alongside any current screen names still being used.'

'Our man has four other screen names.'

Wembley

Mog printed off the list of screen names and Tom looked at the list again and again looking for some kind of a clue. God he was shit at puzzles, all types, crosswords especially and as for Sudoku well God knows what that was all about. He decided to look at each name individually whilst Mog continued to tap away at the PC keyboard.

Bigboy4u. Tom looked at the name and thought. He is trying to attract women by tempting them with the size of his old chap.

Cool007. Whoever he was he was clearly a pratt.

Mad250871. So what did this tell him? Well that the man liked to think he was maybe eccentric and thought it was clever. But what were the numbers? Date of birth! Tom was on a roll now. Just then his thought processes were interrupted by Mog shouting excitedly.

'His name is Michael!'

'How could you possibly know that?'

'I hacked into his email accounts and there is one to a screen name called Pathlady arranging to meet. It is signed *Love Michael.*'

A light bulb exploded in Tom's head.

'Of course, of course! God I would kiss you if I wasn't on duty!'

'And I would let you if you weren't on duty!' Mog replied in a jokey way that got Tooley thinking further and made him even more jealous.

Tom felt his face getting hotter and hotter and changed the subject.

'It's Michael Defreitas!' He said. 'MAD are his initials and I bet his date of birth is 25th August 1971. Newsum, ring GX and check.'

Five minutes later Newsum returned and Tom's theory was confirmed. Tom felt a flush of achievement that made him realise why he loved the job so much. He needed time to collect his thoughts. Tom turned to Tooley saying, 'I need some fresh air and a walk – see you in 30 minutes or so.'

Tom found a Costa in the high street and pulled out his notebook. He always found it easier to think while he scribbled.

So Michael Defreitas hired Shirley and paid her to find a man who was a similar height and build to him. Why?

His notebook forgotten for a moment, Tom stirred his latte absent-mindedly whilst he went through the various scenarios in his head. Defreitas obviously intended to use Tomas in some way shape or form and as he was Czechoslovakian it must have been in a non-speaking role.

A startling thought came into Tom's mind and kept swirling round and round getting bigger and bigger. Ridiculous, he told himself, but still the idea gathered momentum until he could hold it back no longer. It was so obvious. The body on the common was not Defreitas at all. It had to be Tomas!

The call Tomas had received was from Defreitas, Husky or whatever name Tomas had known him as. He had arranged to meet Tomas promising him work on his film and probably new digs as well. But Defreitas had taken him somewhere and tied him up before returning on Monday afternoon to murder him.

He then chopped his head off, before dumping Tomas on West Common in the early hours of Friday morning. Defreitas had in the meantime found time to meet Shirley and murdered her. After all, she knew his identity and had to be silenced.

He returned to his notebook and scribbled excitedly:

⇒ Where is Michael now?

⇒ Does Helen know where he is?

⇒ Stewart McMillan knew more than he was telling them.

Uxbridge

'I knew you would be back. It doesn't matter how badly I treat you, you always come back for more, don't you Tom?'

'Oh I can assure you that this is purely professional Helen. Or shall I call you Pathlady?'

'What the . . . ?' Helen had paled visibly. She hesitated and then whispered, 'You better come into my office.'

She closed the door behind them and stood hands on hips, 100 per cent aggression.

'What is this all about Tom?'

'It is all about Michael Defreitas, or should I say a Czech called Tomas.'

'I don't understand.'

'Helen I don't think Michael Defreitas is dead. I think the body found on West Common was in fact that of Tomas from Prague who Defreitas enticed over to this country and then murdered because of their physical similarities.'

'That is incredibly far-fetched Tom.'

'Thing is, Helen, you were Defreitas's lover and I assume that you knew him very well physically. What I don't understand is how you could make a mistake like that?'

'A mistake like what? Choosing him instead of you? That wasn't a mistake Tom.'

'No Helen, the mistake I am referring to is the mistake of compromising yourself and your professional reputation by lying.'

'Tom this is ridiculous. I would never do such a thing.'

'Ridiculous is it? Hardly. Helen this is your final opportunity to come clean or I will have no alternative but to . . .'

'To what Tom?'

'Arrest you.'

'On what charge? Sleeping with someone you don't approve of?'

That was it.

'Doctor Helen James, I am arresting you on the suspicion of deception and attempting to divert the course of justice. I must also advise you that . . .'

Tom looked at Helen and saw nothing but bitter hatred and then she started to sob, gently at first and then increasing to a full blown wail.

'You don't understand Tom. I love him and he made me promise that I would identify the body as his.'

'So I am right then. It isn't Michael Defreitas.'

'No, I don't know who it is, but I can assure you it isn't Michael – for a start, Michael was far better endowed than the victim.'

'Better endowed? Is that what they teach you when you become a pathologist? Compare the guys' dicks? Surely there are other signs that it isn't Michael?'

'He is so clever, he chose his victim so carefully. I can't see any other difference between the corpse and Michael.'

Tom let her get her composure back before continuing.

'When did you last speak to Michael?' He asked gently.

'Well over a week ago, it was the weekend before the body was found. We were supposed to be going to Paris for the weekend. He cancelled saying something had cropped up at work. I haven't heard from him since.'

'Is it usual for him to drop out of your life in this manner?' Tom tried not to ask the question in a smug, told you so, tone.

'No he has always been very attentive. I must confess I am getting a bit worried about him.'

'Do you think he killed whoever we found on the common?'

'I am still coming to terms with this Tom. Michael is not the murdering type. He would be more likely to hire someone than do it himself.

'What are you going to do about me, Tom?'

'Nothing Helen; you made a mistake. I do think you need to come forward and make a full statement once I have managed to speak to the DCC. And thank you for coming clean in the end, Helen.'

'Thank you Tom. I don't deserve it.'

No you don't deserve it, Tom thought as he left the building and finally started what threatened to be a miserable weekend.

Marbella

Pete's daughter awoke to a feeling akin to having her eyes pierced by a laser beam whilst her head was stuck in a vice. What time was it and what was she doing on a sun-lounger on the patio?

Then it all started to come flooding back.

She had gone down to the port on her own and got pissed in one of the local clubs, finally staggering home in the early hours to find herself locked out of the villa. Ten minutes of knocking had no effect. The rest of her family were clearly all fast asleep and she wasn't going to be able to wake them. Feeling the effects of the drink, she had laid down on a sun lounger while she decided what to do. She had obviously passed out.

She glanced at her watch and realised that it was after 1pm. She shook her wrist, listened to her watch and checked the time again. It was still just after 1pm and the watch was ticking and definitely working.

This was weird. How come no one was up? Her dad always woke at 6am wherever he was and whatever his activities the night before.

She walked round the outside of the villa but couldn't see in because all the curtains were still drawn. She went round to the front and rang the doorbell again and again. No answer. She rang her dad's mobile. It rang, but no answer. She rang her mum's mobile, same thing. Then her sister's, again no one answered. She started crying. She ran, crying, down to the nearest villa, knocking loudly on the door, but there was no one in.

Finally she saw two men walking up the hill towards her and she stopped them. They were local workmen of some kind, big and beefy. They realised she was in distress and though they didn't speak much English they followed her to the villa, shoulder-charging the front door. What they saw was extraordinary.

Her parents and sister were all seemingly fast asleep in their beds. But they were not asleep, they were dead. The workmen, on realising what had happened, immediately opened all the doors and windows and started searching the villa. They stopped their search when they got to the boiler and turned it off. One of them got onto his mobile and spoke very quickly. The only words Andrea recognised were carbon monoxide.

Monday 26th October 2009

After a weekend of sulking about Helen and somehow failing again to venture into the garden, Tom decided that although it was Monday morning he was going to take a little bit of time out. He was normally at his desk by 8am but this morning he decided to sit in the neglected garden and relax with a cup of coffee whilst he planned his next move.

With the ubiquitous notepad on his lap, he started to think and scribble. As usual he asked himself a number of questions, some old, some new.

⇒ Where is Michael?

⇒ If the body was Tomas, how did Michael persuade Shirley he was Tomas?

⇒ Where is the head?

⇒ Why would Michael fake his own death? Financial?

⇒ What should he do about Helen?

He then thought about each question in more detail and waited for inspiration that, sadly, was not forthcoming.

Arriving at the station half an hour later Tom was pleased to discover that the DCC was in her office and available. He knocked on the door and was summoned inside. The ever-pristine Jane Protheroe offered him a coffee which he declined.

'Well Tom, what do you have for me this morning?'

'Well last week was an extraordinary week which ended with us wondering whether Michael Defreitas is in fact still alive.'

'What? You can't be serious Tom.'

'Ma'am can we have this conversation out of the office and off the record?'

'Are you asking me out?' She said with a twinkle in her eye.

Tom blushed and coyly responded. 'In a way I suppose I am ma'am.'

They left in her car and found a park bench on the nearby common. Fortunately it was a very warm sunny morning with hardly a breath of wind.

'Okay what's this all about Tom?'

'The reasons for these measures will shortly become clear ma'am.'

'Why don't we drop the ma'am and you call me Jane, as this is out of the office.' 'Yes ma'am – err – Jane.' Tom felt uncomfortable; it didn't feel right calling the DCC by her first name.

'Well during our enquiries into Defreitas, we spent considerable time and effort trying to find his girlfriend. A combination of good police work from DS Newsum and some good old fashioned intuition have finally established her identity.'

'Helen James?' The DCC interceded.

'You knew?'

'Only last night, Helen came to see me and made a complete confession. She has been very silly. I must confess that I am impressed by the way you are handling this. Are you still in love with her?'

Tom paused, desperately trying to control his embarrassment and hoping the DCC hadn't noticed the heat rising in his face. He fudged his answer.

'The honest answer is that I don't know.'

'So what is the next step?'

'The first and most important thing is to establish the identity of the dead body.'

'Helen is adamant that Michael was too well endowed for the body to be him.'

Jane Protheroe smiled because she knew she had Tom. 'There is that to take into account, but we can hardly base the direction of our investigation on the size of a man's erm . . .'

Tom paused as he sought a polite word to use. The DCC sensed his embarrassment and quickly interrupted.

'A lot of men consider the size of their manhood to be of major importance I believe.' She sighed wistfully and continued. 'Who provided the initial identification of the body?'

'I have to confess I have yet to have the body identified. I was hoping to spare Mrs Defreitas further distress. I was going to ask his business partner Stewart McMillan as I was interested to see what his reaction would be to the body.'

'You haven't had the body formally identified yet?'

'Well, the body being headless makes things very difficult and formal identification in these circumstances might not stand up in court anyway. Our identification was based more on the medical records especially the blood results and the personal effects found on the body, such as his wallet.'

'I am sure you now realise Tom that maybe you should have a bit more thorough.' She sighed before continuing. 'It might have avoided this potentially embarrassing mis-identification we now face. The media are going to have a field day. God knows what Harry Smith will say.'

Tom shifted on the bench uncomfortably and decided that not saying anything was probably the wisest course of action. He didn't have to wait long as the DCC soon broke the pregnant pause.

'Have you spoken to Mrs Defreitas?'

'Not since a few days ago. She is going to be very disappointed. She seemed quite relieved to have become a widow and was already planning on how to spend the life insurance pay-out.'

'Well I think you need to have a second PM done out of area to establish if there is anything concrete to make a positive identification. Helen's report is clearly unreliable.'

'What are we going to do about Helen?'

'Leave that one to me. For now let's just find out who the dead man is and then move forward from there.'

'Thank you ma'am – err – Jane . . .'

'No, thank you Tom, for being so charming and gentlemanly on our first date!'

Tom rang Tooley first.

Gerrards Cross

'Hi Tooley, Tom here. Look I don't want to say too much at this stage but I am starting to have suspicions about whether the body found on the common was Defreitas. I really need to have a second PM done. What is the name of your man?'

'Oh you mean Townsend. Doctor Roger Townsend. Grumpy old bugger, hates not being called doctor. Good pathologist though.'

Tooley gave Tom Dr Townsend's contact details and Tom thanked him and rang off.

Tom was fortunate enough to get Dr Townsend first time.

'Good Morning Doctor Townsend, DCI Sparks from Uxbridge CID. I hope you don't mind me ringing you. I was given your number by DI Tooley.'

'I see. Aren't you the poor sod who lived with Helen James before she dumped you?'

Tom was starting to understand the accuracy of Tooley's description of this man. Townsend continued.

'I hear you are inundated with dead bodies over there at the moment. How can I help you Inspector?'

'Well, I have a body which I would like a second opinion on.'

'Mmm, you want me to check up on your ex, the great Helen James, the self-proclaimed best pathologist in the country?'

God this man is vicious, Tom thought as he replied.

'I wouldn't call it checking up Doctor more a case of getting a fresh pair of eyes to look at things.'

'I see.'

It was clear to Tom that Dr Townsend didn't really believe him.

'I will be more than happy to help. When can you get the body over to me?'

'The body is currently under the jurisdiction of the coroner's office while we search for the head but it won't take me long to get it released. Should be with you by the end of the day.'

'I am sorry, did you say you were still searching for the head?'

'Yes, pretty gruesome, but I expect you see some pretty awful sights doing your job.'

'All in a day's work Chief Inspector. Fortunately I am relatively free at the moment, so why don't you send the body over and I'll have the results you need by tomorrow.'

'Excellent, thank you Dr Townsend.'

Tom made the arrangements with the Coroner's office and popped in there to sign the necessary papers to re-assign the body. He just hoped Helen didn't find out too quickly.

Tom was becoming increasingly certain in his own mind that the body was Tomas, and decided to continue his investigation as though that were the case.

He rang Tooley back.

'What's this all about Sparkie?'

'Well I think we may have found your missing Czech. Do you want to come over to see me and I will go through things in detail?'

'Yes, of course, where did you find him?'

'He was here in GX all along. It's a long story. I will give you

chapter and verse when you get here. I'm calling Jeremy now, shall we meet in an hour?'

'Sounds intriguing, see you then.'

Tom then rang Jeremy and had a similarly cryptic conversation with him. Jeremy didn't seem quite so keen to come over but in the end agreed.

So, the now gang of six were again gathered in the incident room. Tom again took the lead.

'Thanks again for coming over to see me here. It seemed the best place to hold the meeting.'

'You were very economical over the phone. What gives?' Jeremy asked grumpily.

'Well we may have made a bit of a breakthrough last night. We discovered that the body which we identified as Michael Defreitas may not be him at all.'

'What?'

'How?'

'What on earth?'

They all chimed together. Tom brought silence by raising his hand.

'I think it's best if I just give you the story and then we can discuss things afterwards. Certain information came into our possession late last week which calls into question our identification of the body.'

The look on Newsum's face was a picture although she quickly regained her composure.

'It is however clear that great efforts have been made to make the body appear to be that of Defreitas. Any questions so far?'

'Whose body do you think it is?' Porter was quick to ask.

'I think it is your Czech friend Tomas.'

'But if that's the case then who killed Shirley?'

'I think Defreitas recruited Shirley specifically to find someone who could be mistaken for him. This person turned out to be Tomas who Defreitas lured to the UK through Shirley with the promise of well paid employment.'

Tom paused before continuing.

'He then kidnapped Tomas, held him hostage whilst he obtained all his medical information such as blood type, dental details and any identifying marks. He then broke into doctor's and dental surgeries in Gerrards Cross and altered his own records. So when the checks were made it appeared that Tomas was indeed Defreitas.'

'But I don't understand.' Newsum interrupted. 'If the dental records had been changed why chop the body's head off before dumping it?'

'Good point which I think will be clarified when we re-investigate the break-in at the dental surgery.'

= 'How on earth would he have the expertise to alter computerised records?' asked Tooley.

'That's something I'm still working on.' Actually, Tom had a pretty good idea who had the IT expertise to have helped Defreitas.

Jeremy now broke his silence.

'Wow,' he said. 'Let me get this straight, are you saying that Michael Defreitas kidnapped and murdered Tomas before chopping off his head and dressed the body up in his clothes before dumping it on the common? With Tomas out of the way he then met Shirley at Marylebone and kidnapped and killed her too?'

'Yes, that is pretty much what I think happened.'

'But why choose the same night to dump the body and murder Shirley?'

'Must admit that crossed my mind but I think the timing was crucial because Defreitas was leaving the country the following day and needed to cover his tracks.'

'Surely he had to have help, it is a hell of a lot to do on your own. For a start Shirley was over 19 stone,' Porter pointed out.

'Good point Porter, Shirley was a big girl and very heavy. Defreitas must have had an accomplice. I believe that he hired an assassin to help him and to mop up behind by murdering Julian Travers and probably William Thornton.'

'Wow, it is a lot to take in but it would certainly help to solve the conundrum of the Hummer.'

'Yes it would clear up a lot of question marks although it is imperative we find the missing vehicle as soon as possible as there are still a lot of unanswered questions remaining. We also still need to find out whether the deaths of Julian Travers and William Thornton were in fact murder. There is also the strange disappearance of Adam Batstone, an accountant from Wolverhampton. He was due to have an interview at Proteus over a month ago and never arrived. He hasn't been seen since.'

Newsum cleared her throat.

'I doubt whether it is connected sir but we had a report this morning confirming the death of Peter Panton, his wife and one of his children in Marbella.'

'Panton is known to us as being a petty thief and burglar.' Tom explained to the others. 'Although I am not sure how he could be connected to all this.'

'Well sir I was thinking about the break-ins at the surgeries.'

'Interesting logic Newsum, I like it. How did they die?'

'It was a tragic accident sir, they died of carbon monoxide poisoning from a faulty boiler in the villa they were renting.'

Tom considered this new information and wondered indeed whether there was a connection.

'Well, well, another tragic accident and yet another coincidence. The number of coincidences is rising almost as quickly as the death toll. Must say I wouldn't of thought that Marbella was really Panton's style. I would have seen him more as a Benidorm sort of chap. Wonder how he could afford a villa in Marbella? I think I can feel a trip to the Costa Del Sol coming on.'

'So we have one definite murder and a number of suspicious deaths some of which appear to have been accidents.' Tooley suggested.

'Or made to appear like accidents!' Tom interjected. 'Proteus is connected to the West Common murder, the food poisoning incident, the death of their finance director and also the disappearance of a potential employee who went missing on his way to an interview there. Our next step has to be to take the offices of Proteus apart piece by piece until we find out why Defreitas would fake his own death. I suspect it is all down to money.'

Tom suddenly remembered something.

'Jeremy, Mick, you were going to check up on that chap Marciano for me. What have you got?' Tom was not entirely surprised by the resultant silence. He snapped: 'Don't worry I will speak to the Met myself.'

Jeremy looked uncomfortable as he said.

'Tom I am so sorry. My fault. Been so busy it slipped through the net. I will get onto it first thing.'

'Okay Jeremy, sorry for hassling you.'

The meeting finally ended an hour later by which time it had been agreed that Tom would run the whole investigation from the Gerrards Cross incident room despite resistance to this suggestion from Jeremy.

In the end Tom pulled rank on Jeremy and it was agreed that Tom would keep the others in the loop and call on them as and when they were needed. Tooley was relieved – another case off his workload.

Jeremy was not at all relieved. The moment he got back to Mayfair he made his excuses and left Mick to do some paperwork. He walked to Hyde Park and punched the numbers on his mobile. The call was answered on the second ring.

'Tony. It's me.'

'Hi Jeremy, I was starting to think you had forgotten me.'

As if, thought Jeremy.

'There has been a big break in the Defreitas case. Apparently DCI Sparks thinks he faked his own death.'

'We need to meet. One hour, usual place.'

Tony Marciano rang off and sat back to think about the implications of the bombshell Jeremy had just dropped. He didn't know what he was going to do but one thing he did know was that if Jeremy was right he was in big trouble.

Hyde Park

Jeremy hated meeting Tony Marciano. He always felt so vulnerable. It wasn't so much the prospect of being seen with Tony that scared Jeremy so much as being seized and killed by him. He usually managed to calm himself down at times like this by convincing himself that he was far too useful to Tony to be dispensed with. He did however know that one day his usefulness would run out and that he needed an exit strategy.

Tony Marciano was on time as usual. His black Rolls-Royce cruised to a halt by the bench where Jeremy was perched uncomfortably. The window of the Roller slid down and released the unpleasant odour of very expensive cigars and stale garlic.

'Get in.' Tony rasped as he kept his teeth tightly clamped on the main culprit of the odour. Jeremy opened the door and climbed inside. The car glided off while Jeremy nervously took Tony through everything he knew.

'So our Michael might not be dead after all?'

'That appears to be the case although as yet we can't prove it.'

'So let me get this straight. As I understand it, he stages his own death and disappears. Wonder why?'

'That's what we are trying to find out. He seems to have had a very complicated private life and was facing a messy divorce but we think the motive is almost certainly money.'

'He was obviously cooking the books of that fund of his and knew he was about to be caught out.'

'That's our assumption and we're working hard to prove it. The death of the finance director and the IT manager haven't helped us. Still the fraud squad will no doubt get to the bottom of it.'

'In my experience the fraud squad are about as useful as a chocolate teapot. They rarely get a case to court and even when they do the judge eventually throws the case out.' He sneered. 'Who are Tomas and Shirley and what did they have to do with Michael?'

'The theory is that Shirley was hired by Defreitas to find and lure someone who had Defreitas's physical attributes, height, size and black hair. Tomas was the man she lured.'

'Any idea where Michael is?'

'None at the moment but we've given his information to Interpol. He won't get far.'

'He already has! He has a week's start on you guys and probably a truckload of cash that he has stolen from the fund. What is McMillan up to?'

'He is being particularly unhelpful at the moment'

'Well make sure you keep me in the loop.'

'Of course Tony.'

The car stopped and Jeremy was alone again in Hyde Park watching the elegant car silently disappear.

Tony Marciano sat back and closed his eyes.

Problems, problems, problems.

He had a lot of clearing up to do on this one. First thing though was to find Michael Defreitas and he knew just how to do it.

———

Tom sat in his office and stared out the window. What a couple of days! He felt tired again. He closed his eyes briefly and could feel himself drifting off.

He decided to do something positive. But what?

He settled for making a list of things he needed to do. This required a shiny new notepad and another arrowed list:

⇒ Establish true identity of the body

⇒ Check if any new evidence results from Townsend's PM

⇒ Make sure that Helen's PM report matches Townsends so she is cleared of suspicion *Tom's gut knots writing this one.*

⇒ If it isn't Michael Defreitas then they had to find him

⇒ Investigate the finances of Proteus

⇒ Find the cause of the food poisoning

⇒ Investigate the disappearance of Adam Batstone

⇒ Find out what happened in the Costa Del Sol

⇒ Find the Hummer

At this point he stopped his list feeling that there was a week's work there at least. He was going to need help. He called Tooley but he was up to his eyes investigating a gang feud in which three people had so far been stabbed and killed in the past 24 hours.

Tom's distrust of Jeremy had, if anything, increased. There was something about him, a kind of shadow, as if he was hiding a dark secret. Tom realised he would simply have to crack on with his small team. He called Newsum and told her to get the team together in thirty minutes.

Half and hour later he stood in the incident room and gazed over the familiar faces of his team.

'Right ladies and gentlemen!' he started.

'We have a bit of a mystery on our hands. I think it best if I go through everything we've got so far. So, if you are sitting comfortably, I'll begin.'

Judging by the looks on their faces, Andy Pandy, it seemed, was wasted on them.

Tom paused for effect and to make sure everyone was listening. He opened his shiny new notebook and began.

'Over the past few days and working closely with the Met and Wembley CID, I now have an update for you. Apologies for going over old ground to start with but I want to be as thorough as possible so please bear with me.'

Tom paused again.

'Michael Defreitas is a very successful and wealthy investment banker who is a bit of a local celebrity, especially with the ladies. He was originally and, I believe, incorrectly declared murdered after a headless body was discovered on West Common. We now believe that the murderer, or possibly murderers, deliberately set out to mislead us into thinking that the body was that of Defreitas but that it was in fact a man called Tomas from Prague.'

There was a sharp intake of breath from his audience as he continued.

'Tomas had a lady friend who he was due to meet at Marylebone station last Wednesday evening. Her name was Shirley and she lived in Leeds. They had met on the internet and that night they were due to meet in person for the first time. Tomas had however disappeared from his lodgings four days earlier and we believe was already dead.'

Tom took a drink of water before continuing. You could hear a pin drop.

'Shirley left Marylebone in the company of a man of Tomas's size and description and was later found strangled near Wembley Station. We have every reason to assume that the man she went off with was in fact Defreitas and that he then murdered her and dumped her body on the embankment by Wembley Station.'

'Sorry to interrupt sir but this Shirley was a big girl to say the least. Is it practical to think that Defreitas could have done all this on his own?' Mel interjected.

'Good point Mel.'

Tom returned to his notes and continued. 'You will all be aware of the tragic food poisoning at the Rajpoot the other night when 15 people died. One of those who died was a man called Julian Travers who worked as an IT expert at Proteus. We have since discovered that Travers had created a very clever programme within the Proteus main system which automatically diverted any enquiry to a totally different set of fund performance figures to the real ones. Travers was very friendly with Defreitas and was clearly acting on his instructions. It is also my belief that Travers may have had a part in the surgery break-ins, albeit possibly unwittingly.'

Tom paused again checking his notebook to ensure he missed nothing out.

'In addition to these two local Proteus deaths, we have the apparently accidental death of William Thornton who died during a bizarre masturbation ritual.'

'There is also the disappearance of Adam Batstone. He left his home in Wolverhampton to attend an interview at Proteus but never turned up and hasn't been seen since.'

'Finally, to complete the carnage we have the deaths of three St Peter residents in the Costa Del Sol, one of whom was Pete the Plumber whose MO fitted the GX surgery break-ins. I believe that Pete had an accomplice for those break-ins, either Travers or Defreitas, and it was their job to hack into the computer systems and change the medical and dental records of Michael Defreitas.'

'So to summarise, so far we have two Proteus employees dead, a potential Proteus employee missing and one who appears to have faked his own death.

'I know I keep going on about coincidences but there really are too many.'

Tom turned to Jez saying,

'Right, Jez, I know you have been making background enquiries into Proteus, it is time to deliver. I want chapter and verse on Proteus and the real position of its finances. Fund performance, bank statements, anything you can dig up, however trivial. David Browne of the fraud squad is currently investigating and I want you to go and give him some assistance."

Jez looked as pleased as punch.

'Bill, want you to check into the Costa Del Sol deaths. Can you please go over there and establish exactly what happened.'

'Julia find out all you can about Adam Batstone and if you have time, masturbation techniques.'

There were stifled giggles from all and even Tom could see the funny side of things. He decided not to dig the hole any deeper.

'Finally, Mel, I want you to check into the Rajpoot incident. Good luck everyone tomorrow is going to be a very busy day.'

Tuesday 27th October 2009

Tom had decided that he and Newsum would concentrate on establishing the true identity of the body and, assuming his theory was correct about it being Tomas, set about finding Defreitas. The problem was where to start.

Tom thought he had to be abroad, but where? The world was a big place. Time for another list.

He drew up a list of the things that Defreitas would need:

⇒   A new identity

⇒   Somewhere safe

⇒   Money and a fair bit of it

Tom thought the money was the place to start and for that he needed the help of Mog. While he and Newsum were making their way yet again to the Proteus office, he arranged for a car to pick up Mog so she could meet them there.

The two of them entered reception where a very strained looking John Davis was waiting.

'Morning Mr Davis. I hope you don't mind but I really need some more of your time and a bit more information about Proteus. I promise we won't get in your way. Is Mr McMillan in?'

'Stewart is visiting clients this morning – all the bad news is making our investors nervous. He is then due to see the FSA inspector who oversees our funds.'

'FSA?'

'Financial Services Authority, the financial regulator.'

'Ah I see, well if he rings in can you please tell him I would like to talk to him as a matter of urgency. Would you mind if I use Mr Defreitas's office?'

'No that will be fine and please let me know of anything you need.'

'Thanks I will, two coffees would be a great start. I will get you a list of the information we need.'

Tom made his way to Defreitas's office and settled down in the soft leather chair behind the huge leather inlaid oak desk and took out his pad. At that moment Mog poked her head round the door of the office looking gorgeous as always.

'Morning guv,' she said in a mock East End voice.

'Morning Mog. Thanks for coming down here. I have a bit of work for you. I am afraid it might be quite time consuming as I want chapter and verse on anything and everything."

'Can you be slightly more specific?' She grinned.

'Of course, I would particularly like you to investigate all Michael Defreitas's email addresses both private and business and all his private and business bank accounts. I want as much information on the bastard as possible.'

'Chief Inspector you really shouldn't speak ill of the dead like that,' Mog berated him mockingly.

'Oh, of course, you haven't heard the news. We think that Defreitas is very much alive and that he faked his own death, murdering at least two people in the process.'

'Blimey. Right, well I'll get on it straight away.'

'Thanks, can you access his email accounts from here?' Tom pointed to the PC sitting on the desk in front of him.

'Yes of course.'

Mog started up the PC and was soon tapping the keys in rapid succession. The screen went bright and very quickly she was scrolling down a list of emails.

'There you go guv.'

Tom grimaced at being called guv. He knew however that if he complained it would only encourage Mog to use the term more often. He took over control of the keyboard and suggested to Mog that she found herself an office somewhere and got to work.

He looked down the list of emails as Newsum returned with their coffees.

'Newsum, can you go and ask John Davis for a list of business trips that Defreitas went on during the past 18 months and ask him for the details of all the Proteus bank accounts both here and abroad. You can let me have the list of business trips but pass the bank account details to Mog please.'

'Yes sir.'

Returning to the list of emails Tom continued the laborious process of going through each one in turn. He wasn't expecting anything earth shattering to appear and therefore wasn't too disappointed when he found nothing. He realised that Defreitas would have covered his tracks thoroughly.

But, and there was always a but.

Malaga

William Dean was no longer in agonising pain but he was very sore and unstable on his remaining foot. This was accentuated by the fact that from time to time he would forget that he now only had one, lapses that would cause painful falls. He was gradually getting used to using the crutches but it was taking time.

His days were made up of taking pills, having meals and reading the papers. The chief of the clinic had managed to find a source for the papers of his country although there was always at least one day's delay before they reached him.

Today was a very important day. It was the day he got the first proper view of his new face. They had been keen to keep it bandaged up whilst the main wounds healed and now it was time for the bandages to come off.

The doctor returned and with the nurse they gently removed the bandages. It was strange feeling the air brush against his face. He wondered what he looked like.

Obviously reading his mind, the nurse guided him to a mirror. The face he saw was hideous. It was so bruised it was black and blue and very swollen. He grimaced and looked away. The doctor was quick to reassure him.

"Meester Dean you okay, I promeese, the operation was great success and in two weeks you good as new, no, you better than new." He laughed and left leaving Dean feeling a bit like the elephant man.

Oh well at least he had the first fitting for his prosthetic leg that afternoon. He was of course going for the best that money could buy and had been assured that he would not notice any reduction in mobility whatsoever. In fact the doctor, a keen golfer, was continually waxing lyrical about having a more stable left side to hit against. William, a non-golfer, didn't know what the hell he was talking about.

———

Mayfair

Mog had set up in a separate office and gone to work. About an hour later she returned to update Tom on her progress.

'Hi Tom.' Tom felt relieved not to be called Guv for once. 'How are you getting on?'

'Made good progress already. Want to come and have a look?'

She winked at him mischievously as she said it. Tom tried to brush off the inevitable blush that he could feel spreading across his face. He seemed to spend his whole time in a state of embarrassment these days.

'I would be delighted. What have you found?'

'I can't make sense of a lot of it but there are loads and loads of bank accounts, all set up in the names of various companies and individuals. Could be nearly a thousand at a guess. I am in the process of making a list.' Mog handed him a pile of print-outs.

'Where are the accounts based?'

'All over the world, especially the Channel Islands, Gibraltar, British Virgin Islands, Switzerland, Spain and the Cayman Islands.'

'Interesting.' *Especially the ones in the Cayman Islands* he thought to himself.

He was given the first few sheets and read down the long list of account names, numbers, which bank, branch and country and the account balances. It was mind-boggling. This would take him hours, if not days, to check.

Clearly, like all top criminals, Michael Defreitas had gone to great lengths to firstly avoid suspicion and secondly to make it very complicated and very difficult to track any fraud.

'Is there any way of knowing how much money there is in these accounts in total?'

'Yes I thought you might want to know that. The total is £25,315,827.49.' She replied, reading from a post-it note stuck to the PC screen.

'Any idea how much should be in these accounts?'

'Well,' she said smugly, 'there is no legal requirement at the moment but I have been researching Proteus and the promises that they make their investors. They go to great lengths to publicise the conservative nature of their investment strategies and they assure their investors that they always have at least a quarter of the fund invested in cash.'

Tom was impressed with Mog's knowledge of financial regulation and shot her a surprised look that provoked a sharp reaction.

'Inspector, don't look so shocked, I am studying for a business degree, you know.' Tom decided to show his own particular knowledge.

'Proteus currently has over £7.95 billion invested according to its published accounts. My math isn't very good but are you telling me that instead of holding just over £25 million in cash, they should actually be holding £2 billion?'

'Yes Tom.'

'Strewth! Got any suggestions where the rest is or how we can find it?'

'I am working on it.'

'Thanks Mog, you are a diamond. After that can you get me a list of all the Proteus investments?'

'Sure, tell you what, why don't you shove a broomstick up my bum and I will sweep the floor at the same time . . .'

Tom ignored her sarcasm which be had to admit was deserved. Time to go and see the office manager.

John Davis was sitting behind his desk when Tom entered his office without knocking.

'Ah there you are Mr Davis, mind if I ask you some questions?'

'Not at all, anything to help.'

'I asked you before about Adam Batstone and whether there was a file for him?'

'Adam Batstone? Who the hell is . . .' He paused and something seemed to click in his memory as he then went on: 'Oh yes of course, the young lad who missed his interview. In the turmoil I forgot all about it. I believe there is a small file. Let me get it for you.'

John Davis returned quickly with the file and handed it to Tom. Tom flicked through it. There were a number of items of correspondence including Adam's initial application letter and CV, a response from Proteus and a completed job application form and attached photograph. Tom was surprised to see that there was also a medical report on Adam.

'Why the medical report? Is it usual for applicants to have a medical before an interview?'

'It was an innovative scheme that Stewart introduced recently to speed up the employment process. Personally I thought it was a waste of money but Stewart told me to be patient and to give it time and that besides the company could afford it.'

'How many other candidates had a medical prior to their interview?'

'Actually none, when Adam Batstone didn't turn up, the experiment was abandoned.'

'I see. I hope you don't mind if I keep the file?'

'Not at all.' Davis said handing over the file. Tom cleared his throat.

'Mr Davis I understand that your funds promise in all the literature to keep at least 25 per cent of investments in cash?'

'Yes that is correct. We are very proud of our conservative approach to investment and having a large proportion of the fund in cash is very reassuring to our investors.'

'Where is the money kept?'

'Oh it varies according to the client and their instructions. But it will normally be kept in client accounts all over the world wherever we can get the best returns for cash on deposit.'

'How much is the fund currently holding in cash?'

'Let me see' He took his calculator from the desk and tapped away for about 30 seconds.

'You have to realise, Chief Inspector, that this is not really my field but I would expect us to be holding Just over £2 billion.'

'I would like a list please of all the accounts and their balances.'

'But I thought . . .' Then it seemed to dawn on him like a light bulb going off. 'You don't think . . . ?'

There was a deathly hush before John Davis continued.

'You do, don't you?'

'I don't think anything Mr Davis, I am just doing my job as thoroughly as I can.'

'I am afraid that if you want a list of that nature you will have to ask Stewart McMillan.'

'I see, did you manage to get hold of Mr McMillan?'

'Yes he is returning late tonight, probably about 7pm.'

Tom glanced at his watch. It was already after four. He didn't really fancy staying there until seven, though.

'Mr Davis do you have the personnel files for William Thornton, Michael Defreitas and Julian Travers?'

'Yes I suppose there won't be any harm in releasing them as they are all dead.'

'All dead?' Tom embellished his look of surprise.

'Yes, all three them are dead, aren't they?' John Davis looked bemused.

'Oh I didn't tell you did I? We think Michael Defreitas is still alive. I do apologise for not letting you know earlier but we believe that he faked his own death and in doing so was responsible for the murder of at least two people, possibly more.'

John Davis slumped in his chair and just stared at Tom.

'Michael not dead? But how can that be?'

'Quite easily really Mr Davis, he faked his own death by murdering someone with a very close physical likeness to him and then chopping his head off.'

'But you said you think Michael was responsible for two murders, Chief Inspector. I don't understand.'

'Well spotted, it is our suspicion that in addition to the original victim, he also murdered the man's girlfriend. There are also the deaths of Julian Travers and William Thornton to investigate, not to mention the disappearance of Adam Batstone.'

'But surely Michael wouldn't have, couldn't have?' He stopped in mid-sentence. 'I have known him for years.'

His sentence tailed off again and he sat there looking like a totally disillusioned man.

Tom waited to see if John Davis would offer anything else but eventually asked. 'Now if I could have the files please Mr Davis.'

'Oh yes of course.' He went to his filing cabinet and took three manila coloured files from the top drawer.

'There you go Inspector. Do you have any idea why Michael did the things you are alleging?'

'I can't really divulge any more information at this stage but let's put it this way, things are rapidly clicking into place. I intend to find out everything there is to know and of course find and arrest Mr Defreitas.'

Tom paused.

'I would warn you that if you are hiding anything now is the time to come clean with me Mr Davis.'

'I-I-I don't know anything.' John Davis stammered. 'I am just the office manager. I deal with the office admin and staff matters but I don't nor have I ever got involved in the money side of the business.'

'So Mr Davis, you think this is all to do with money do you?'

'Well I am basing this on the questions you asked me earlier that's all.'

'Okay Mr Davis, it has been long day for both of us and perhaps a bit of a shock. Thanks for the files and the help.'

Tom returned to Mog who was concentrating so hard she didn't realise he had come in. God she is gorgeous Tom thought, if only he was 15 years younger. He tried to pull himself together. He had to stop fantasising about this girl who was half his age. Tom cleared his throat and she jumped.

'Blimey Tom you nearly gave me a heart attack standing there like that. Come for a progress report?'

'Well yes.'

'I'm currently printing off a list of the funds, shareholdings and the transactions for the past 18 months. I managed to access most of the bank accounts and have printed off a statement of those I have accessed so far. There are rather a lot.' She said rolling her eyes as she pointed towards the huge pile of paperwork on the table beside her.

Tom called Newsum in and instructed her to load up the car with the pile of print-outs.

'That lot should keep Mel nice and busy.' He said.

'Oh sir you can be so horrible to Mel at times.'

'Oh rubbish Newsum she loves it, makes her feel wanted. Now let's get home shall we? Radio ahead and we will have an end of the day debrief.'

Tom and Newsum suffered the joys of the rush hour on their return journey and yet again Tom realised how fortunate he was not to have to go through the daily commuting grind like so many of the high earners in GX. The drive took them nearly two hours which, despite Newsum's sunny disposition, dragged horrendously once Tom had caught up with his phone calls.

Finally arriving back at the station, Tom felt as though he had jetlag and was relieved he had already postponed the debrief until the following morning, much to the relief of most of his team.

Mel as always was still there though, and Tom saw her eyes light up at the prospect of days if not weeks trawling through the print outs.

'There you go Mel an early Christmas pressie.'

'Thanks Sir. I will make a start now if you don't mind. My mum is feeding the cat tonight.'

'Excellent.'

Tom left and went for a pint.

Thursday 28th October 2009

Tony Marciano had not slept well. He had tossed and turned all night worrying about Michael Defreitas, Proteus and in particular the organisation's money. Jeremy Ward's warning that the police were convinced that Michael Defreitas was still alive and had faked his own death had startled him. Tony knew there was only one reason why Michael would have done that.

Money.

He had stolen money from the fund. Their money. No one stole money from the organisation and lived and he was stuck right in the middle of it. He wondered how much was involved?

It had been whilst talking to Jeremy that Tony had worked it all out.

Michael knew he was in trouble and the only way to escape was for everyone to think he was dead. Clever, but his plan had back-fired, he got found out. One thing was certain: to take such desperate measures the amount of money must be considerable.

The organisation would hunt Michael down and kill him. Tony would have some very difficult questions to answer and was also in real danger. He knew he had to find Michael and fast. He rang Rocco an old friend from the neighbourhood.

'Eh Rocco, how you doing?'

'Good thanks Tony, what can I do for you?'

'Rocco, I have a very special job for you. I want you to find someone for me. Can you meet me at Mario's at 12.30. You can buy me lunch.'

'Yeah sure Tony.'

Mario's was a small Italian Restaurant on the outskirts of Clerkenwell. It was Tony Marciano's favourite place to have lunch and he could be found there most days holding court. He wasn't particularly good for business but Mario the owner had little alternative but to accommodate him especially since Tony was holding Mario's marker following a spot of trouble Mario had got into the previous summer. Tony had of course sorted everything out but now Mario was in Tony's debt.

Rocco turned up bang on 12.30. He was a huge man built like the proverbial brick outhouse. He looked distinctly uncomfortable in his dark suit. He smiled and shook Tony's hand vigorously.

Rocco knew that lunch didn't really mean lunch. Tony was a very dangerous man and Rocco always seemed to lose his appetite when he was with Tony. Rocco could tell immediately that Tony was troubled and this made him more nervous that normal which was saying something. He wanted to get out of there as quickly as possible.

'Hey Tony it has been too long, you are like a stranger.'

'I know, but you know how things are. Business, business and more business!'

'Okay so tell me what you want me to do?'

'I have a folder here which gives you all the details of the man I want you to find.'

'No problem. Do you want me to kill him?'

'Not immediately, I want you to find him and bring him to me.'

'Of course Tony.'

Gerrards Cross

Tom had had a reasonable morning for a change. It had started with a meeting with DCC Jane Protheroe at 8am. He had updated her on his progress and explained how he needed some additional help with the investigation into the finances of Proteus.

She suggested David Browne who seemed ideal to Tom. He had accepted and David was already on his way to Mayfair to meet Mog.

The DCC was curious about Mog and asked who was paying her. Tom explained that she was inexpensive and he was paying her cash out of his expenses but he did suggest that perhaps in view of the ever-increasing amount of internet crime, they form a more permanent arrangement with her. Tom was delighted when the DCC agreed and suggested a meeting with the three of them once the investigation was over.

Tom was now holding a delayed meeting of the team in the incident room.

'Morning all, I hope we all had a very productive day yesterday. I think it best if I give you my update first.'

'Newsum and I spent most of the day at the offices of Proteus which produced a great deal of information, most of which Mel is now wading through. Particularly interesting is the fact that there seems to be nearly two billion pounds missing from the Proteus bank accounts.'

There was a sharp intake of breath all round, the second in two days. This was followed by total silence that Tom eventually broke.

'So we have to find Michael Defreitas and a lot of money. I would suspect that if we find the money it will lead us to Defreitas.'

'So how did we get on yesterday? Jez?'

'I concentrated on doing a complete background check on Proteus and the directors. The fund has outperformed every fund in its sector since it began. What is particularly unusual about the fund's performance is that it seems to be recession-proof, offering consistent returns even in difficult financial times. That has made the Proteus fund very popular.'

He paused and re-visited his notes before continuing.

'The co-founders and main drivers of the fund are Michael Defreitas and Stewart McMillan. Defreitas is the figurehead of the fund and gives it glamour. He is often seen at film premieres and celebrity bashes. He was even at the Beckham party.'

Another pause for effect.

'McMillan meanwhile is the investment genius who produces the amazing returns. The fund's investment is focused mainly on hedging.'

Jez could see the puzzlement on his colleagues' faces and that greater explanation was required.

'Hedging is basically gambling on the future performance of a share, commodity or currency. It is the area of investment where most funds have lost heavily over the past year. I am surprised that Proteus hasn't been hit by the same difficulties. Only last month Proteus announced record dividends to its investors which attracted massive additional investment.'

'Thank you Jez, most informative, continue the good work. I want you to continue to work with David Browne of the fraud squad. I want to know how much money is missing and where it is as soon as possible.'

'Yes sir, just one other curious thing I have discovered is that there are no records for either Defreitas or McMillan before they went to Oxford. It is almost as though they appeared from nowhere.'

'Interesting, I was aware that our records on these two were incomplete. Thanks Jez, keep digging.'

'Mel? How did you get on with the Rajpoot?'

'Well I met Jeeva Singh the owner of the restaurant and then went down to the path lab and had a long chat with Helen James. Mr Singh is distraught, he cannot understand how it could have happened. I must say it does seem that Mr Singh runs a very tight ship and a very clean one. He is very well organised and I sense foul play.'

'We particularly need to find and speak to the temporary kitchen hand who worked that night as a matter of urgency. The problem is that we have very little information about him. We don't even know his name.'

Tom interrupted:'Mmm, I think this man may be a professional assassin in which case I fear we will never find him or even know who he is. How did you get on at the path lab?'

'Helen was very helpful and confirmed that they all died of botulism. Our tests in the kitchen confirmed that the batter for the onion bhajis was absolutely loaded with 'type E botulinum toxin.' It's fatal when consumed even in small quantities and was undistinguishable because it was masked by the strong flavour of the food.'

Tom took over again, 'So it looks like we have a hired killer who took advantage of the staff shortage to work just on the night that Travers was there and laced the batter with enough poison to kill half of GX. The question is, was Travers unlucky or was he the intended victim?'

Tom thought for a second and then continued.

'I think we have to work on the premise that Travers was the intended victim. It was very convenient that there was a staff shortage on that particular night. Too convenient. Mel can you find out more about the two kitchen helpers who went back to India?'

'I have already started preliminary enquiries based on the information Mr Singh had on their personnel files. I have spoken to their families in Mumbai who were surprised that they were on their way home. I intend to investigate this further today.'

'Well done Mel.' Mel beamed at Tom's compliment. *Another happy team member*, thought Tom.

Tom took a couple of seconds to think about this information. He suspected that they were going to end up adding another two victims to their total. Tom didn't like the thought of a hired killer loose in GX killing restaurant staff and poisoning people and he knew the Chief Constable and his wife certainly wouldn't.

'Okay Bill, your turn, how did you get on?'

'Well we all know about Peter the Plumber, small time burglar who tends to case his victims when he goes around doing his dodgy repairs to their central heating. He was definitely in the frame for the surgery burglaries, but his wife and kids had given him a concrete alibi we couldn't crack.'

'What happened in the Costa Del Sol?'

'Well I managed to talk to the surviving member of the family, Andrea, one of the daughters. She is obviously in a state of shock and struggling out there. She is only 19, in a strange country and can't speak the local lingo.'

Bill referred back to his notes and continued.

'Seems that they won a holiday for two weeks in a villa near Marbella. She said it was a bit odd because none of them could remember entering a competition. She survived because she had a late night at the local club and when she got back to the villa she couldn't wake anyone to let her in. I suspect they were already dead.'

'Has the cause of death been confirmed?'

'Yes, carbon monoxide poisoning from a faulty boiler.'

'Have you spoken to the police out there?'

'Yes I eventually managed to find a member of their force who spoke English. He confirmed the cause of death.'

'Any idea who owned the villa?'

'Yes the police confirmed that the villa was owned by a company based in the Cayman Islands.'

The Cayman Islands? Not another bloody coincidence. Tom thought before commenting.

'Interesting. Got your passport Bill?'

'Yes sir and I checked with easyJet, I can leave this afternoon and return tomorrow afternoon.'

'Excellent. I want chapter and verse on this. Oh and Bill, please don't stay in a five star hotel this time.'

'Err, no sir.'

'Okay so there seems to be the whiff of foul play everywhere at the moment.'

'Julia, what have you managed to find out about Adam Batstone?'

'Well he was a run of the mill accountant with the HSBC in Wolverhampton who had great hopes of living a more glamorous life in London. Proteus was very keen to take him on, in fact they were so keen that they invited him to take a medical before his interview. His family thought it was strange but in the end they all decided it was a sign of how keen Proteus was to give him the job.'

Tom interrupted. 'Yes apparently it was a new policy introduced by Stewart McMillan which was immediately dropped when Adam Batstone failed to show up for his interview.'

Yet another coincidence. Tom pondered on how many there had been in the case so far.

Julia continued. 'Adam Batstone left for London on the morning of the interview on the 8.25 train and hasn't been seen since. Adam was due to stay overnight in a hotel in London at Proteus's expense and then return to Wolverhampton the following day. Apparently they are a very close knit family and they were expecting Adam to call after the interview, so when he didn't they thought it strange but assumed he had got the job and was too busy celebrating with his new employers. When they hadn't heard from him the following day they called the police and reported him missing.'

'Okay I want you to check all the CCTV cameras at every station on the route the 8.25 train takes. I want to know where and when Adam got off that train and in fact whether he ever got on the train at all.'

'Yes sir.'

'Did you have a chance to check into the death of William Thornton?'

'Yes I spoke to the officer who attended the scene and he said it was a very straightforward scenario. Thornton died of asphyxiation as a result of the plastic bag that he had placed over his head to enhance his orgasm. Apparently it is a very dangerous, very pleasurable form of masturbation which does occasionally go wrong. You may recall a politician dying in similar circumstances some years ago.'

'Why the orange?'

'Oh apparently the orange was laced with amphetamines which again increases the pleasure.'

'Thanks Julia, very thorough as always.'

'One last thing sir. By all accounts William Thornton was a very private man who kept his personal life very much to himself. What I don't understand is why Thornton would do such a thing at his office. I have asked the mobile company for a record of all communications to and from his phone for the previous seven days just in case.'

'Good thinking Julia.'

Tom thought for a second and then gave out his instructions.

'Bill, off you go, have a good trip and see if you can track down the details of the competition and the company that owns the villa.'

'Julia, I want you to get a police artist to visit Mr Singh and get an impression of the temp worker. I also want photos of the missing staff and anything else you can find out about them. Please also continue checking out Adam Batstone and William Thornton. Leave no stone unturned.'

'Mel, you have a lot of paperwork to keep you going. May I suggest however that you start by looking at Adam Batstone's file?' He handed her the papers he had been given by John Davis the day before.

'Jez, When you have finished at Proteus, I want you to help Mel. Please pay particular attention to the bank account print-outs and statements. Try and see if there is a pattern of outgoing payments that might lead us to where the rest of the money has gone.'

'Right, see you all later, except you, of course, Bill.'

Geneva

Zolo was a happy man. The last two weeks had been very busy, very productive and, most importantly, very profitable. He had checked the internet continually over the past few days and had read with interest the results of his work. He was particularly intrigued by the Proteus revelations. He started wondering about his client and his identity.

It was one of his favourite pastimes. Some people did crosswords or Sudoku; Zolo liked to work out who his clients were.

It was obvious to Zolo, and anyone with half a brain, that the deaths of Travers and Thornton were linked and that the link was their employer, Proteus. He had read about the murder of Michael Defreitas and his initial reaction was to feel a little put out that he hadn't been hired to do the job. After a bit more thought, however, he realised why. Clearly his client had nothing to do with the murder of Defreitas or, bizarrely, Defreitas had faked his own death.

At the moment he was leaning towards Defreitas being alive and actually being his client. If he had faked his own death, Defreitas would need to cover his tracks. Zolo decided that this could only be good news for him as he might be called upon again in the near future.

He felt a tinge of sympathy that in killing Travers he had also killed fourteen other people, but it was only a twinge and a small one at that. Fate was fickle. The other victims had made the fatal mistake of being in the wrong place at the wrong time.

He knew his client was happy because he had received his monies on all the jobs. It was very unusual to get so many jobs, so quickly, off the same client. He wasn't complaining as he had received a total of four million so far but despite the huge money he had been paid, he was concerned.

His discreet enquiries had brought to light a connection between Proteus and organised crime. Zolo usually steered well clear of 'family business' and there he was bumping off their key employees! Something just wasn't sitting right.

He was also curious that the Costa del Sol job had been requested by the same client. He couldn't work out that connection at all. But he was a patient man and knew it would all become clear in time, as long as he wasn't caught in the crossfire.

Malaga

William Dean checked his face in the mirror every hour to see if he could spot any signs of recovery. He could see glimmers of improvement. He was also excited about his false leg. He had tried it on and whilst it was going to take some time he would eventually have virtually 100 per cent mobility. The next stage of treatment was the removal of all his body hair, of which he had in abundance. Electrolysis once was surely better than a lifetime of waxing.

Friday 29th October 2009

Having allocated his team members plenty of work the previous day, Tom cancelled the usual team meeting and he and Newsum set off for Mayfair first thing. He would catch up with his team later but knew he would soon hear of any important developments.

Tom was delighted to find Stewart McMillan in his office and immediately sat him down to ask him some questions.

'Thank you for seeing me Mr McMillan I am sure you are very busy in these traumatic times. I hope you don't mind me asking you a few questions?'

'Not at all, fire away.'

'I assume John Davis made you aware that Michael might not be dead?'

'Yes, what a bombshell that was.'

'How do you feel about that?'

'Well, Michael has been a close friend of mine since Oxford and I was devastated when I was told he had been murdered. The fact that it turns out that he is not dead and might actually be the murderer is obviously a shock but not a total surprise because Michael is totally ruthless and capable of anything.'

'Mr McMillan, you know Michael better than anyone, what do you think drove Michael to such drastic action?'

'I really don't know, although as in most things, time will reveal his reasons. Michael has always lived a very complicated life due to his propensity for married women.'

'Proteus seems to be a very dangerous place to work at the moment. The co-founder has disappeared in the most mysterious circumstances, two of members of staff have died in the past 14 days and a prospective member of staff left the Midlands for an interview here and hasn't been seen since.'

Tom let that sink in and then continued.

'Mr McMillan you are clearly a very intelligent man. Doesn't this make you wonder? Can this really all be just one unhappy coincidence?'

Stewart McMillan shrugged his shoulders.

'Of course I am shocked at what has happened in the past few days but the deaths of William and Julian can hardly be considered suspicious. Michael has always been an accident waiting to happen. It is all just fate I suppose. What's that phrase? Shit happens! John Davis told me you were enquiring about the Adam Batstone disappearance and I can assure you it has nothing to do with us.'

Tom noticed McMillan pause briefly as if searching for the right words before finally continuing.

'Adam Batstone's failure to arrive for his interview was a major disappointment to me.'

'Especially after you paid out all that money for his medical?'

'Yes he was a bit of a guinea pig for a new scheme I was trying out. Still you can't win them all. Is there anything else I can help you with Chief Inspector?'

'There certainly is Mr McMillan. I must advise you that, unlike you, I find the deaths of Mr Travers and Mr Thornton very suspicious indeed.'

Tom opened his notebook apparently to check his notes although in fact he was stalling the interview whilst he decided which direction to take next.

'Now tell me Mr McMillan, in your investment prospectus you make certain promises to your investors concerning your investment strategy. Can you please confirm how much of the fund is invested in cash at any given time?'

'We promise to keep a minimum of 25 per cent of our client's monies in cash at any given time.'

Tom looked at McMillan for a few seconds. Surely John Davis would have told him about the shortfall they had discovered yesterday. Perhaps John Davis had reasons not to tell but that was extremely unlikely. McMillan was clearly a very cool cookie.

'Would I be right in saying that at the moment you have around £8 billion invested on behalf of your clients?'

'I don't have the latest fund figures in front of me but that would sound about right.'

'I am not a mathematician Mr McMillan but I estimate that, in order to comply with your investment promise to your investors, you are currently holding around £2 billion in cash?'

'Yes Chief Inspector, that is correct, the cash is held in a number of banks and client accounts around the globe to achieve the best possible returns for our clients.'

'Yes, so I understand from Mr Davis. Mr McMillan, would it surprise you to learn that following an investigation of your computer records we discovered that as of yesterday Proteus was holding a total of just over £25 million in cash?'

Stewart McMillan looked shocked. He was either genuinely surprised or a superb actor.

'*How* much?'

'You heard me, £25 million.'

'But that is impossible. You must have missed a whole load of our accounts. I only checked the balances last week. I will have to check this out straight away.'

'Please do. I have some colleagues of mine who are happy to help you check the figures if you would like to come with me.'

They escorted Stewart McMillan from his office and introduced him to Jez, David Browne and Mog.

'Right, well I will leave you to it. May I suggest we meet back here at say 4pm? We can continue our discussions then.'

As he said it he realised he was committing himself to yet more rush hour misery and another evening of car-lag. A wave of tiredness swept over him. He would certainly be glad when this case was over.

'Oh, one last thing Mr McMillan, where did you go to school?'

'Oh London.'

'Precisely where in London?'

'Look Chief Inspector I have just had a terrible shock and really do fail to see how my schooling is a matter of great importance at this time. Can we discuss this later?'

'Yes, I can wait until 4pm.'

Tom turned and walked out of the building leaving Stewart McMillan standing there in stunned silence.

Tom and Newsum returned to Gerrards Cross, to Camp Road. He wanted to see Mrs Defreitas again to find out whether she could shed any light on her husband's whereabouts.

Mrs Defreitas was looking even better than when he and Newsum had visited her previously. She was clearly thriving on being a widow. Dressed in a bright multi-coloured top and tight white jeans, she showed them into the conservatory and offered them drinks which were politely declined by them both. Tom gazed at this beautiful and clearly very intelligent woman and then her tight jeans and sighed inwardly. Where had he gone wrong?

'I am so sorry to bother you once again Mrs Defreitas but there have been some important developments which I have to make you aware of.'

'I see.'

Her cheerful and almost flirty behaviour was far more subdued as she waited for Tom to continue.

'Mrs Defreitas, this is going to come as a shock to you but I have to advise you that we have reason to believe that the body found on West Common was not in fact your husband.'

'What!'

She put her hands to her face for a brief moment before looking steely-eyed at Tom.

'But I don't understand, how could you have made such a basic and appalling error?'

'It was an easy mistake to make in circumstances such as these.'

'Circumstances such as what?'

'Well we have reasons to believe that we were misled deliberately.'

'What reasons?'

'Well I cannot go into the full details at this time Mrs Defreitas, but there seems to be little doubt that the body found on West Common was dressed up to be your husband. Someone went to a great deal of trouble to make us think that your husband had been murdered.'

Tom finished talking and sat staring at Mrs Defreitas waiting for a response. She just sat staring at him seemingly grasping for the right words.

'Are you saying that my husband faked his own death?'

Tom was impressed by the lady's intelligence.

'Yes, I am afraid so. It appears that Michael had changed all his medical and possibly even his dental records to those of another man who he had kidnapped and then subsequently murdered.'

'Good grief I knew Michael would resort to virtually anything, but murder – surely you are mistaken Chief Inspector?'

'I am sorry I realise this is a huge shock but I can assure you that there is every reason to assume that Michael murdered another man in order to fake his own death. We also want to interview him about the murder of the dead man's girlfriend.'

'This is extraordinary. Why would he do that?'

'Well, we don't know for sure but there seems to be a considerable amount of money missing from the Proteus investment fund.'

'How much is considerable?'

'Just under two billion pounds sterling.'

Mrs Defreitas laughed loudly and continued for some time much to Tom and Newsum's discomfort. Finally pulling herself together Mrs Defreitas spoke.

'So let me get this straight, the cream of the great British Police force think that Michael murdered someone, made it look like it was him and then stole a huge amount of money off his clients. It isn't April the first is it Chief Inspector?'

She roared with laughter again. This really wasn't going as well as Tom had hoped his tolerance level had been reached. He paused and counted to ten whilst he fought to control himself. When he had reached nine and was feeling calm again Tom replied.

'I admit that it all sounds a bit far-fetched but this is deadly serious Mrs Defreitas and I am afraid it is definitely not a laughing matter. The evidence is becoming irrefutable. We believe your husband is a thief and a murderer.'

'I am sorry Chief Inspector for my reaction but these are extraordinary revelations.'

'We desperately need to find your husband before anyone else at Proteus dies.'

'Anyone else at Proteus?'

'Well yes, we are currently investigating the deaths of William Thornton and Julian Travers which we believe may be suspicious.'

'Yes I read about Julian in the local paper. Surely he died from food poisoning? Wait a minute, are you trying to tell me that he and the other fourteen who ate in the Rajpoot that night were murdered? Your accusations are getting more and more bizarre Chief Inspector, I am not sure what you are on but I could certainly do with some!'

'Do you have any idea where your husband may be? Has he been in contact with you?'

'No he hasn't been in touch since the day he disappeared which isn't that surprising if you are right and he wants everyone to think he is dead. He could be anywhere, especially if he has that kind of money.'

'Yes that is the problem we are facing. How many properties does Mr Defreitas own?'

'To my knowledge just this one and the penthouse. I think there is a company property somewhere abroad but I am not sure.'

'Not the Costa Del Sol by any chance?'

'Yes I think so. I am sure Stewart would be more helpful on that subject though.'

'Is there anywhere that Michael liked to go the most?'

'Well he liked Spain but whether he would go there when he has the money to go anywhere in the world, I don't know.'

'Is there anything else you can tell us that might help?'

'Nothing springs to mind but I will let you know if I think of anything.'

'Thank you Mrs Defreitas. I might need you to come and identify the body.'

'But if your theory is correct and it isn't Michael, what would be the point?'

'I am not sure yet. I will have to let you know. Goodbye for now Mrs Defreitas. I have a feeling we will be seeing one another again very soon.'

Tom turned and left the room with Newsum in tow and Patsy Defreitas sitting there open-mouthed.

————

Tom was slightly late returning to the Proteus offices and arrived to find Stewart McMillan in a state of high agitation.

'Ah Chief Inspector there you are, do you want to come into my office?'

'That would be a good idea. Sorry I am late but the traffic was murder.' Tom grimaced at the accidental pun that seemed to go right over Stewart McMillan's head.

'No problem Chief Inspector – at least it made sure that I could finish checking the company accounts and records.'

'How did you get on?'

'I regret to advise you that you are correct. Proteus is in breach of its investment prospectus and does not have sufficient funds to meet its commitments. I have notified the FSA and Proteus has ceased trading as of 3pm today. I am now waiting for the team of emergency receivers to come in and officially place us in administration.'

Tom was impressed. Stewart McMillan had acted quickly and decisively. Most importantly he was playing everything by the book. Maybe his initial opinion of McMillan had been wrong.

Tom then asked, 'The first and most obvious question is, of course, where has the money gone, Mr McMillan?'

'I honestly don't know Inspector. I have been busy meeting our legal requirements in such circumstances. Tracing the money is my next task. One thing I can assure you is that I will definitely find it.'

'There are two things that puzzle me Mr McMillan. You are co-founder, co- owner and the investment director of this fund and you can't tell me why or how there is nearly two billion pounds missing from your bank accounts nor do you know where that money has gone.'

'I know it may sound strange to you but, no I can't. I can only assume that Michael moved it before he disappeared.'

'My colleagues inform me that there are a myriad of different accounts. It would have taken ages to move that amount of money. I think the money has been missing for a considerable time.'

McMillan was staring at Tom with a look close to hatred and continued to do so before eventually responding.

'Chief Inspector, in the limited time since you dropped this bombshell, I have established that Michael, with the help of Julian Travers, had set up a dummy set of accounting information which misled everyone, including me, into believing that everything was normal and the funds were all where they should be. Julian had been working for us in some capacity of other for about year and a half, so yes you are right, Michael could have moved the money months ago.'

Tom inwardly raised his eyebrows at McMillan's impressive coolness.

'As you know, the fraud squad is already investigating Proteus and I am sure their investigation will go up a notch when they realise the extent of this massive fraud. I suspect they are going to require a considerable amount of your time Mr McMillan.

Tom paused for effect.

'In the meantime Mr McMillan perhaps you can tell me where you were last Wednesday between the hours of 5pm and 2am?'

'Am I a suspect Chief Inspector?'

'Everyone is a suspect Mr McMillan. Someone helped Defreitas commit the murders and whoever it was, is in grave danger. Now please answer the question.'

'Last Wednesday, now let me see, I think I was here until about 8pm and then went home and had some dinner and watched TV and went to bed at about 11pm.'

'Do you remember what you had to eat?'

'No I am afraid not, although it was almost certainly an M & S ready meal. I can never be bothered to cook during the week. Have you tried their Gastro Pub range? It is excellent.'

Tom shook his head but couldn't rid himself of the thought of how much he would like to eat an M & S ready meal instead of risking severe stomach problems from his mother's cooking. He waited for Stewart McMillan to continue.

'Chief Inspector, I lead a very mundane existence. My life is my work and my work is my life. Every day is similar to the next one and the one after that.'

'Do you have a girlfriend Mr McMillan?'

'A girlfriend? Good grief no. I don't have time for one and despite the trappings of my wealth my looks prevent me getting much interest from the opposite sex.'

'Are you gay?'

'I don't have time to be gay either Chief Inspector, nor for that matter do I have the inclination.'

'Thank you Mr McMillan, I am going to ask you not to leave the country and to surrender your passport to your local police station by 9am tomorrow morning. If you should decide to ignore this request we will immediately issue a warrant for your arrest.'

'This is excessive, Chief Inspector, I am not a murderer or a fraudster and I have no intention of leaving the country.' He sounded exasperated.

Tom left Stewart McMillan in a state of great agitation. He'd had enough, it had been a long week and he was feeling the effects. He wanted a beer with his mates.

He and Newsum headed for home doing battle with the rush hour traffic for the final time that week. Before leaving he got a quick update from David, Jez and Mog. Progress was apparently slow and would take a few more days.

David Browne confirmed that his boss Gillian Harris had been speaking to the FSA and was now in charge of the fraud side of the case. On the journey home he spoke to Gillian. They arranged to meet up at the Proteus offices at 11am on Monday.

Newsum dropped him off at the Apple Tree and he awarded himself a pint of Yorkshire bitter. It was only when he was halfway down his pint that he realised he had not asked Stewart McMillan about his pre-Oxford days. Tom was tired and was starting to feel old and vulnerable.

He had actually beaten the usual Friday crew to the pub for a change and it gave him time to reflect on the case. He really hadn't ever experienced a fortnight like it. A headless body, mass food poisonings, death by masturbation, stolen billions. And he used to think that life in GX was too dull.

It was finally the weekend and Tom resolved there and then to switch off for 48 hours and recharge his batteries.

Unfortunately things never quite go as planned.

Saturday 30th October/Sunday 31st October 2009

The relaxing Saturday morning Tom had planned was ruined at just after 7am by a frantic telephone call from Helen's sister, Phillipa.

Helen was missing and Phillipa was extremely worried and agitated. Tom tried to calm her down and agreed to meet her at Helen's flat in Old Amersham as soon as possible.

Phillipa was already there when he arrived and was in a hell of a state. Her usually immaculate appearance could be described as dishevelled at best. Tall, slim and blonde, a GX stereotype Phillipa was the spitting image of her sister but a lot more scatty but in a very attractive way, Tom had always fancied her but she had a string of admirers and treated them all badly.

'Hi Tom, sorry to call you like this but I am worried sick. I was going to call the police and then I thought of you. Oops! Of course you are the police too but well, you know what I mean.'

Phillipa wrung her hands together in a helpless way that just enhanced Tom's urge to put his arms around her shoulders. He managed to stop himself and let her continue.

'I know Helen was awful to you but I didn't know who else to turn to. I am so worried.'

'How long has she been missing?'

'Well we arranged for me to come round here at 7pm last night to have a girlie night in. I arrived at about 7.15 but there was no sign of Helen. Her cat Millie was in a right old state and had clearly not been fed. I don't understand it.'

'Have you spoken to your mother?'

'Yes of course, she hasn't heard from her either. What are we going to do?'

'Well as she is an adult Helen can't officially be reported missing for 48 hours unless there are signs that she has been abducted. But I will speak to DCC Jane Protheroe and see what we can do.'

Tom was hesitant as he dialled the DCC. She was not at her best at the weekends and would not be amused by the disturbance.

'Protheroe.'

'Ma'am I am so sorry to bother you.'

'This better be good Sparks,' was the frosty reply.

'Well we have a worrying situation here regarding Helen James the pathologist.' He said very formally.

'Worrying? In what way?'

'She seems to have disappeared ma'am.'

'What information do you have?'

'I am at her flat with her sister Phillipa. They were due to spend yesterday evening together and she never showed and never contacted her.'

'Mmm, this is not good, especially as she emailed me her resignation last night at about 6.30pm. Tom, I know it is against official protocol but Helen is one of us. Can you issue a missing persons report and do what you can to find her as quickly as possible please?'

'Yes ma'am, leave it with me.'

'Ring me later with an update please.'

'Will do.'

Tom immediately rang Newsum who said she would be there within five minutes. Apparently Jason was planning to take her to a football match and the diversion was just what she wanted.

Newsum arrived and was equally worried about Helen.

'Sir where do you think she might be? You know her well.'

Tom shrugged and replied, 'I haven't a clue. The worrying thing is that she is always very reliable and if she is running late for an appointment will always ring and let you know. This is most unlike her.'

'I can't believe she has resigned, she has never given any indication she was unhappy at work, in fact quite the opposite.'

'Lets start at her office.'

Tom told Phillipa that he was going to search Helen's office for any clue as to where she was but it might be necessary for him to return and search Helen's flat if she didn't turn up soon. Phillipa confirmed this was not a problem and took a spare key for the flat from the key rack on the kitchen wall. Tom stared at the key which was the very one that had been his proud possession until Helen walked out and left him decimated.

He turned and walked quickly away promising Phillipa he would call her with an update later.

Helen's office yielded little. Her assistant was there trying to catch up on paperwork. She was of little use as she revealed that she had left early on Friday afternoon, at which time Helen was still hard at work and behaving normally.

The strange thing was that Helen's car was still parked in her parking space. This worried Tom greatly. Had she been abducted? If not, then how did she leave work? By foot, or taxi or maybe she got a lift from a friend?

Surely if she had left work voluntarily she would have phoned Phillipa to say she was running late? She must have known she would be worried. Then there was the issue of her resignation. Why did she resign? Surely it wasn't over the Defreitas PM?

Tom didn't want to over-react but he was really worried and didn't know what to do.

He called Mog and asked her if she could pop over to Helen's office; she said she would be there within the hour. He might as well see whether Helen's work PC held any secrets.

Mog arrived looking dishevelled and tired, like she'd been clubbing til dawn; apparently she had – in Uxbridge until 5am. Tom asked Helen's assistant to provide Mog with a very strong, black coffee. Suitably revived, she quickly got to work and had soon accessed Helen's PC. She went through all her email accounts both business and personal. These didn't reveal much although they did reveal the resignation email she sent to DCC Protheroe.

'Well that was a waste of time and hangover. Seems Helen was careful what information she put on her work PC.' Said Mog to Tom as she closed down the PC.

Tom suggested they went to Helen's flat and checked her PC there.

'Are you asking me out, Tom?'

'Well I suppose I could buy you the hair of the dog afterwards.'

'And I *could* accept.'

Phillipa was still there and was happy to wait whilst they looked around. Helen's PC wasn't there. Tom had spent a great deal of time in Helen's flat over the previous months and knew where everything was kept. The PC had been removed. He asked Phillipa if she knew anything.

'I know she was talking about getting a new laptop but it was very much something she was saving up for and was hoping to get in time for Xmas. She wasn't a great gadget fan as you know, Tom, and it was not high on her list of priorities.'

Tom made their excuses and left again promising an update later. Phillipa thanked him and after a long lingering look at Mog turned and went back into the flat.

Tom was now very concerned. He had established a connection between Helen and Michael Defreitas and now she had disappeared too. He phoned Newsum from the car and updated her.

'Issue an immediate and urgent missing persons report. I want all airports, ports and railway stations alerted.'

Clerkenwell

Rocco was always happy to help someone as important as Tony Marciano but he was also aware of the dangers of failure. He had known Tony since he was five years old. Their parents had been friends and they were even distantly related as were most of his similarly employed colleagues.

Like Tony, Rocco was a trusted specialist for the families in the organisation. Whilst Tony dealt with finance and legitimising the illegal income, Rocco's speciality was more hands on and usually very illegal. He was basically a trained killer who had a flair for detection. He was also unquestionably loyal. This made him very popular and very busy.

Rocco sat himself down with a coffee and a cigarette and started to think about Michael Defreitas. Since his lunchtime meeting with Tony he had made some discrete enquiries about Defreitas and had built up a pretty good background on him.

Rocco assumed that money was no object for Defreitas and that he would have planned well in advance for his disappearance both logistically and financially.

What would he do in his shoes?

Rocco finished his coffee and stubbed out his cigarette and picked up the phone. He had dated a girl called Nicky who worked at the Civil Aviation Authority, better known by its acronym CAA. Nice girl. Pretty with a great body but a bit too clingy for a man in his profession.

'Nicky speaking,' said the familiar voice.

'Hi doll.'

'Who is speaking?'

'It's me Rocco.'

'I am sorry I don't know anyone called Rocco. I used to know a guy called Rocco but he turned out to be a complete bastard.'

'Oh babe don't be like that.'

'Be like what? You used me. You shagged me until you had had enough and then dumped me. Actually that isn't quite true – you never even had the courtesy to dump me, you just ignored me.'

'Something came up. I had to leave the country for a while.'

This was partly true. He had been sent to Sicily to find and kill someone who had ratted on the family, but that was another story.

'Well it was unkind and unfair and I don't want to talk to you.' It was essential that Rocco got Nicky back onside so he tried again.

'Oh doll, please can we try again? I know I should have contacted you and told you what was happening but there wasn't time and I was sworn to secrecy.'

'Anyone would think you were a secret agent or something instead of a wine shipper and by the way my name is Nicky not doll!'

Rocco now remembered the other lie he had told her.

'Sweetheart . . .err . . . Nicky, will you give me another chance? Dinner tonight at our special place?"

'Maybe but don't think that you are going to get your leg over.'

'Babe I know you ain't that easy. I will treat you with total respect I promise.'

'I was going to wash my hair and give myself a manicure but I could do with a decent meal. I can't believe I am doing this but do you want to pick me up, eight o'clock at my place?'

'Course, one other thing Nicky, I don't suppose you can help me with something?'

Gerrards Cross

The weekend was not proving restful for Tom at all, in fact quite the opposite. He was worried sick about Helen and had rung Phillipa and her mother regularly but there was still no word from her.

He went for a walk and tried to think about what could have happened to her. It was so strange, she was usually so sensible and reliable yet in the past few months she had turned her back on what he thought was a good, steady and loving relationship with him to go out with a man who was quite clearly a crook and a murderer; now she had uncharacteristically vanished without a word to her closest family.

As usual, he tried Kipling's six honest serving-men.

Why and who? He was certain that Helen's disappearance had to be connected to the Defreitas case but was her disappearance voluntary? His worry was that Helen was part of the Defreitas tidying-up exercise and she had been either kidnapped or worse. He had to find Defreitas. Where could he have gone?

When? Well that was easier. It was definitely after 6.30pm when she emailed the DCC and probably before 7.30pm when Phillipa was trying to get hold of her. That left a one hour window.

How? Her car was still parked at work so she had to have gone by some other means. He was already checking all the ports, rail stations and airports; he made a note to check all the local car-hire companies and taxi firms.

What? Wasn't really relevant and was covered by the others.

Where? That was the crucial question and hopefully would be solved by their enquiries into how?

Like Rocco earlier that day, he tried to think the way Michael Defreitas would think. Tom thought back to his conversation with Mrs Defreitas and whilst he had little knowledge of the Caribbean, he knew Spain well.

He decided to start his search with Spain before widening the net. If Defreitas had nearly £2 billion at his disposal then he would most likely have chosen the anonymity of traveling by private plane from a private airfield rather than risk the security of a major airport like Heathrow. Tom felt this mode of transport was more likely for a man with that kind of money than private boat.

He had an idea and started to think about the likely airstrips he might have used. He rang the CAA who was responsible for the nearest airstrip at Northolt. He spoke to a polite and perky young lady called Nicky who seemed eager to please and provide all the information she could. Tom was delighted by her enthusiasm. It was almost as though she had been expecting his call.

Tom was certain Defreitas would have flown out of Northolt on either the Thursday or the Friday. Nicky said that the only flight on those two days that matched his enquiry was a Lear Jet chartered by Mr William Dean at noon on the Thursday. The destination was a small private airfield just outside Malaga called Castiglio. He was the only passenger.

Gotcha! thought Tom.

On impulse, he rang and booked a flight to Malaga, Monday lunchtime by easyJet from Luton. He really wanted to fly from Heathrow with BA but felt that it wouldn't look good after making Bill travel cut-price.

Tom then started to worry that it might just be a wild goose chase. He was well aware that the police force's ultimate master, the bean counters scrutinised every penny spent but whilst they might query the cost of his traveling to Spain, he also knew he had to appear to be leaving no stone unturned. He could always use the excuse of following up on Bill's recent visit if push came to shove.

He started thinking about Stewart McMillan and wondering how all this could have been going on without him knowing. He had to concede that the way the bank accounts had been set up and the sheer volume of them would make even a casual inspection very time consuming and difficult. Even so, McMillan was the co-founder and co-owner and must have known something wasn't right.

Clearly McMillan knew more than he was telling. Tom decided that when he got back from Spain he was going to question him again but this time properly, at the station under caution. Maybe that would rattle him into an admission.

He then prepared a list of instructions of work to be conducted by his team whilst he was away.

The money had to be the key. Someone must have helped the cover-up of the shortfall at the fund. Travers was the obvious accomplice but how had Defreitas managed to fool the fund's auditors? He rang John, his banking buddy. John would give him chapter and verse on hedge funds and the like and would jump at the opportunity to get away from his wife and four kids to have a beer on such a lovely sunny Sunday afternoon. He would no doubt call it helping the police with their enquiries.

John was slightly red-faced and out of breath when he walked into the Apple Tree about 45 minutes later. If ever there was a man who was a prime candidate for a heart attack it was John. In his mid-forties, he drank too much, ate too much, smoked too much and did little exercise except the occasional running for a train.

The result was an extremely overweight, somewhat squat man who was never going to be a fashion icon. John's lack of style was however made up for by his wonderfully warm and generous personality. He and Tom had been at school together and had been friends ever since.

The Apple Tree was busy but they managed to find a quiet table in the garden away from the main body of drinkers.

'How have you been John?'

'Not bad Sparkie. Kids are revolting literally, bloody teenagers, wife has had enough of them and blames me. That is when she is not lecturing me about my drinking, smoking and of course eating habits.' He lit a Marlboro Light. Tom hadn't had a fag for over a year but at times likes this he always felt that familiar urge to light up. Once a smoker always a smoker.

'Things are pretty much as normal then. How is business?'

'Surprisingly good actually.'

Tom wasn't exactly sure what John's job entailed but he knew he was a director of a small but very respected merchant bank. He also knew that John detested the major banks and often vented his spleen about the way the government had bailed them out and still allowed them to continue trading as though nothing had happened despite nearly bankrupting the country. His favourite phrase that he used regularly, despite being one himself, was 'bankers are wankers!'

'How about the credit crunch?' Tom enquired.

'Unlike those idiots at the big banks, we had been nervous of the markets for a while and adopted a conservative view about five years ago. Whilst this affected our profits in the boom years, we held our nerve and have managed to survive the credit crunch quite nicely. But enough of that boring stuff. How are you keeping? Nice and busy?'

Tom was caught by surprise by the sudden change of subject and hesitated before replying.

'Yes I expect you have heard about all the shenanigans that have been going on in GX over the past two weeks.'

'Yes its all a bit worrying really, the wife thinks it has affected house prices and that the extra police work will drive up our council tax bills.'

'Well at least it gives you an excuse to be here.'

'Helping the police with their enquiries!' They both chortled together.

'And very pleasurable too!' John added, as he took another large slurp from his beer. 'So, how can I help?'

'I am keen to find out all I can about hedge funds and in particular Proteus International and I thought you might be the man in the know on these things.'

John looked pleased with the compliment.

'No problem, I am always pleased to help. Hedge funds have come to great prominence recently due to their lack of supervision which of course helped cause the credit crunch.

Hedge funds are basically funds that gamble on the future performance of stocks and shares and other investments. If successful, the profits can be spectacular but if the reverse then fortunes can be lost.'

He paused for another large intake of beer and a quick puff before continuing.

'Proteus is the top performing fund in the market and is very attractive to investors. To be honest we are all a bit jealous of them. They are glamorous and always beat the market, basically everything we aspire to but rarely achieve. Personally I can't see how they can perform so consistently at the levels that they do.'

Another pause for alcohol and nicotine.

'One thing about Proteus though is that they keep their operations very private and are ultra secretive about everything except how well they perform.'

This was all very well but Tom knew all this and needed more.

'Okay, so say I am an investor with £1 million and looking for the best place to invest my money. How would I know which fund to choose?'

'Well, all investment funds print lovely glossy brochures about their fund and how wonderful it is. These brochures detail fund performance and outline their investment strategies. You merely get the brochures for the funds you are interested in, compare them and then choose the fund you like best. It is all in their publicity documents.'

'Where do they get their figures from? Is there some kind of regulatory body that checks their performance and announces the results for each fund.'

'Hedge funds have not historically been policed particularly stringently although this has to change following the credit crunch and recent events such as the failure of Lehman Brothers. The problem the regulators face is that the very nature of these funds makes them very difficult to regulate.'

'Are you saying that they can do what they like and make whatever claims they like?'

'Well it isn't quite as simple as that. They do have to be audited. That would usually ferret out any false declarations.'

'Ah now that is interesting. So if a fund was making false declarations about their performance then the auditors would know?'

'Yes although most funds choose their auditors very carefully.'

'Do you mean the auditors are bent?'

'Not bent, let's just say they are interviewed stringently. I will give you an example. A CEO wanted to appoint a firm of auditors and interviewed three. The first one he asked him one question, what is two plus two, and when the auditor answered four he said he would let him know. He asked the second interviewee the same question and when he got the same answer he said he would let them know. The final interviewee arrived and was asked what was two plus two he answered: "What do you want it to be?" Guess who got the job?' John roared with laughter and Tom joined in before, turning serious, he said.

'I see. Now all I need to find out is who the auditors are for Proteus.'

'That will be easy enough. Tell you what, I will make a couple of calls when I get into the office tomorrow and let you know.'

'John thanks for that. Another pint of Summer Lightning?'

'Why not? You are only young once. What do you think the chances are of the Reds winning the title this year?' This was John's other great redeeming quality. He was a Liverpool supporter.

Monday 1st November 2009

Tom met Jane Protheroe at 8am on Monday morning and went through everything he knew. She was happy for him to go to Spain she said but trusted he would be back by Wednesday at the latest, and to keep in regular touch.

She did end the meeting by expressing the Chief Constable's dismay at the slow progress in solving the case and the ever rising total of dead and missing people. Tom felt the pressure crank up another notch.

Tom then held a brief team meeting dishing out his instructions before he left for Luton Airport.

Following his drink with John, he had phoned each of his team on Sunday afternoon and asked them to prepare written reports of their progress so far for him to read on the plane. This included Bill who was now back from his trip.

He was slightly mystified by the easyJet boarding procedures, or lack of them, but eventually he was on board albeit surrounded by excited holidaymakers and their screaming offspring. At least the plane left on time and he drowned out the neighbouring commotion by turning on his iPod and listening to some Pink Floyd whilst reading his team's reports.

The music was fitting; he felt comfortably numb. He started by reading Bill's report on his trip to the Costa Del Sol. As usual Bill had been very thorough.

He had met up with sole survivor Andrea at the villa and she had shown him round. She was clearly in a very poor state and suffering from shock but she had managed to answer his questions in a very helpful and comprehensive manner.

Apparently the family had won a competition where the first prize was a fortnight in a luxury villa near Marbella. They also had received a cheque for £1,000 for spending money. The cheque was written on a Cayman Island bank account. Whilst no one could remember entering the competition they were all so excited they did not worry about it. She hadn't actually seen the cheque close up so could not help with any account details.

Andrea did however know her father's bank details – he banked with the HSBC in Chalfont St Peter. Bill would be paying them a visit later in the hope of finding out more about the cheque.

It was on the third night of their stay that Andrea had gone clubbing and returned late to find herself locked out so had slept on one of the patio sun-loungers. It was early afternoon before she woke and made the shocking discovery.

She had little else to add except that she was surprised that the boiler had been faulty in view of the fact that the previous afternoon a man had turned up to service it. She gave a brief description of the man who she said was medium in height, tanned, wore a red baseball cap and drove a battered old white van. *Sounds familiar,* Tom thought.

Bill then enquired whether her dad had been responsible for the break-ins to the GX surgeries and she got very upset and almost abusive. Bill decided that he had as much as he was going to get and had ended his questions and gone to see the local police.

The local police showed little interest in him until he expressed his theory that it had been murder. They then took him to the senior officer who spoke very good English and agreed to help him with his enquiries.

The main lead and suspect was the man who had turned up to service the boiler but their enquiries had hit a dead end. They had found a battered old white van, which fitted Andrea's description, abandoned outside a local supermarket. They had quickly established that the van had been stolen but it had yielded no clues as it had been wiped clean.

Bill's final note was that the villa was owned by Mactas Ltd, a company registered in the Cayman Islands. He would be making further enquiries whilst Tom was away.

Apparently the Spanish police and Bill were now of the same opinion, that the boiler had been deliberately sabotaged and the family murdered. It was also Bill's opinion that the crime would have gone undetected if it had been left to the Spanish police.

Mel's report confirmed that they now had a police impression of the man who they suspected had poisoned the onion bhajis at the Rajpoot. Tom made a note to show the impression to Andrea as soon as she returned. He would also get a police artist to visit her and do an impression of the boiler-man in the Costa Del Sol.

Mel was also investigating what had happened to the missing Rajpoot staff and confirmed that she could find no record of them having flown home. They had simply disappeared.

Julia found it strange that Proteus wanted so much information from Adam Batstone before he had even been interviewed. It was in her view highly suspicious. She was still waiting for the CCTV footage from the stations en-route although she expected to have them by the time he got back.

Jez had been checking the Proteus bank accounts with Mel and they had made some progress. There appeared to be a regular withdrawal from each account at exactly midnight every night. The amounts taken were small, always under £50 and seemed to be done by some kind of computer program. The payments were then sent to an account in the Cayman Islands. They were checking more details on the Cayman Islands account but it appeared to be in the name of Deflan Ltd.

The withdrawals had been taking place at the same time each night for many days, weeks and possibly months or years. The number of accounts involved meant that even such a small amount added up over a long period of time. The size of each individual withdrawal however was small enough to slip under the radar.

So that was how he did it, Tom thought.

He smiled to himself. His team had done well and the net was tightening. He just hoped that his trip to Spain wouldn't be wasted.

Malaga

After a reasonable but noisy flight to Malaga, Tom took a taxi to Castiglio airfield. Tom felt quite shaken as he got out of the car; he had forgotten how badly the taxi-drivers drove in Spain and he vowed never to complain about the dreadful conditions of the roads back home.

Castiglio airfield was small, a collection of huts with a large conning tower that housed the radars, computers and other technical equipment. The good news was that there was a security office. The bad news was that it was shut. *Damn*, he thought, *bloody siestas!*

He waited and finally a fat bald man turned up in a beaten up pick-up with the word Seguridad on the side. He strolled across to Tom and spoke a lot of Spanish Tom didn't understand.

'Anglais?' Tom asked hopefully in his best French.

'A leetle my friend.'

Tom showed the man his badge and explained that he was a policeman from England and that he was trying to trace a man called William Dean who had arrived at the airfield ten days earlier.

'You are second man this day who ask for heem.'

'Second man?'

'Yah, a beeg Italian man in suit he try to find theees man too.'

'What did you tell him?'

'I tell you what I tell heem. He arrive by small plane get taxi to the clinic on the hill.'

'The clinic on the hill?'

'Yes, the clinic where people get changed.'

'Changed?'

'Yah they get changed.'

The fat man spread his hands over his face in a demonstrable manner. Tom was confused but could see little point in pursuing it as he would no doubt find out what he needed at the clinic. 'Would you be able to take me there?'

'Yah I go with you.'

The drive to the clinic on the hill took twenty minutes, twenty very unpleasant minutes in the very dirty, very smelly pick-up which had no air-conditioning.

Tom was delighted and relieved to reach the clinic unscathed. Getting quickly out of the pick-up he thanked and waved goodbye to his new friend, whose name he had discovered was Jose.

The clinic was austere and nondescript. It was very white. He found the front door and knocked loudly. Eventually someone came to the door and invited him in.

More indecipherable Spanish.

'Anglais?'

'No. We speak leetle.'

'Do you have an interpreter?'

'No.'

He soon realised that his security friend hadn't left and was sitting in his pick-up watching the conversation with great interest. He called him across.

'Jose, can you act as interpreter for us?'

'Certainly.' Tom had noticed a sudden dramatic improvement in Jose's English probably fuelled by sheer nosiness – or perhaps the possibility of a handy gratuity.

They entered the clinic and despite the communication problems caused mainly by the limitations of his interpreter, he finally managed to establish that William Dean had been treated but had left earlier that day. Apparently he'd had a great deal of plastic surgery, or plasteeek face as Jose called it, but the clinic refused to divulge exactly what. They did however confirm the visit of the Italian a couple of hours earlier.

They informed Tom that Dean had spoken a foreign language, which Tom assumed to mean English, and that he had left by taxi for Malaga Airport. *Oh brilliant*, Tom thought, *he could be anywhere by now.*

Finally he showed them a photo of Michael Defreitas and was dismayed to be told that whilst there were similarities, that it wasn't Mr Dean.

Not to be deterred, he rang Newsum and asked her to get Julia to trace all flights out of Malaga earlier that day and whether they had anyone called Dean on them.

It was a very long shot. Dean was now a new man, probably travelling with a new identity and a new passport

It looked as though the trail had run cold. The clinic had insisted that Dean was not Defreitas but his view of the Spanish was that they were unreliable and easily bribed. Tom decided that there was still every possibility that Dean was Defreitas.

———

Rocco, despite being one step and a couple of hours ahead of Tom, was also getting nowhere fast. A better knowledge of Spanish and a good old-fashioned cash payment had enabled him to establish that William Dean did not in fact speak English. This was strange and a real shock because Rocco had been convinced that Dean was his man.

Despite this he went to Malaga and tried to follow Dean's trail although he was assuming it would be pointless as the man would surely have changed his identity yet again as well as his looks. He was right. Dean had not caught a plane out of Malaga under his own name. It was like looking for a needle in a haystack.

———

Tom was at Malaga airport too but to get there he had endured another nightmare journey in Jose's truck. On arrival he managed to book on an easyJet flight leaving that evening. He could see no point in staying in Spain. He had too much to do at home. He had two hours to kill so he headed for the bar area and settled down to a large, very cold glass of San Miguel. Turning on his mobile for the first time since leaving the UK, he was delighted to find a text message from Helen. It read:

Hi all, sorry for the group message and not warning you but I had to get away. The strain of the last few weeks has been too much for me. Needed some sun. Will be home soon with lots to tell. Love you all Helen xxxx

He felt a strange mixture of relief and anger at the way she had treated everyone but then that was typical Helen. The more he knew her the more he realised how shallow, self-centred and money orientated she was. Then why did he still love her?

He then rang his team and gave them a quick update. Tom was aware that the call was expensive so kept the discussions short. After all he would be back first thing in the morning

He did however give specific instruction to Julia to check all flights out of any of the London airports since Friday to Spain, the Caribbean and more exotic locations such as The Maldives. Basically, anywhere sunny.

He asked Mel to run a search on the text Helen had sent, to try and find out where from.

He asked Bill to ring round all the local taxi and car-hire firms to find out if Helen had used them to disappear.

———————

Helen was lying on a sun lounger taking in the Caribbean heat. She had never been to the Cayman Islands before but had to say they were wonderful.

The hotel was just beautiful, the food excellent and the scenery amazing. She felt like she was in heaven and realised that the strain of the last few weeks had been worth it. Now all she had to do was wait for her lover to arrive.

She had woken that morning with a tremendous feeling of guilt and had gone online at the hotel and sent her loved ones texts from her mobile number. On a whim she had included Tom but had no idea why.

She had been given strict instructions not to use her mobile but she was sure that doing it online would be okay.

She closed her eyes and dozed off.

In flight from Malaga

Tom tried to sleep on the flight back but couldn't. He had never been a great flyer and sharing a small cabin with a load of Brummie holidaymakers was not helpful.

He kept running over the case in his mind. It really was turning into one of the most difficult cases he had ever had to investigate. Every time he felt he was getting somewhere he would come to a dead end.

He cast his mind over things and knew he was missing something important. What the hell was it?

As usual at times like these he started to scribble on his notepad. The notes he made were, as usual, more a series of questions.

⇒ Who is William Dean and why would he go to such lengths to disguise himself? If Defreitas isn't Dean, then who is Dean and where is he now?

⇒ Who is paying the assassin?

⇒ Where are the two missing Indians?

⇒ Where is the money?

⇒ Where has Helen gone and with whom?

He crossed out the final item; she was an adult, their relationship was over and she had moved on. He then changed his mind and reinstated the question. He still had this nagging doubt at the back of his mind that she hadn't told the whole truth and wondered whether her disappearance had been stage managed and planned in advance.

He decided finding the money was the key; the answer had to be with Proteus and he was going to concentrate all his resources on finding it. He looked at his watch and realised that he would not be home until 11.30pm so he started planning the following day.

———

Clerkenwell

Tony Marciano was getting unhappier by the second. Firstly, Rocco had phoned him and the news had been disappointing. Like Tom, he had been sure that Dean was Defreitas.

Then he had phoned Jeremy who updated him and the news sent a shiver down his spine. It seemed that not only had Michael Defreitas vanished into thin air but he had taken a lot of money with him, a great deal of which was likely to belong to the organisation.

Tony knew he was in big trouble and started thinking about his own exit strategy. He had always known that the organisation wouldn't just let him retire and had his departure plans in place.

He and Defreitas had been skimming off money from the organisation for years and he had managed to accumulate a very large stash offshore.

He had made sure the money would be impossible to trace and now he had more than enough to keep him in the style he had become accustomed to for the rest of his life. He just needed 48 hours and he would be gone.

He would be in Bogota by Wednesday at the latest.

———

Geneva

It was a wonderful Swiss morning. Zolo gazed out over the lake and mountains as he munched on his daily bowl of muesli. He would never tire of the magnificent view.

His phone buzzed signalling the arrival of a text. Excellent, he thought, more work and more money. He really didn't need the money any more; after all he'd had over 50 successful hits behind him and he charged 1,000,000 euros a hit. Not bad for someone who flunked his exams at school.

It had now become a game for Zolo. He loved the danger and got a huge buzz when he pulled off another successful operation. He had especially enjoyed the recent hits in England. Most of all he had enjoyed the killing of William Thornton and congratulated himself on his inventiveness in that instance.

He cycled down to the Post Office to collect his latest mission and returned up the hill and opened the file with great expectancy. The contents of the folder however were shocking and for the first time Zolo started to think about his future. He looked again at the photo of Tony Marciano and shuddered.

What was he going to do?

Tuesday 3rd November 2009

Tom started the day with a what was rapidly become the routine meeting with Jane Protheroe who was relieved to be told that Helen James was alive and well and enjoying the sun. Tom kept his reservations to himself.

He updated her on his progress in Spain.

'To some extent the trip was very informative. I managed to trace William Dean to a clinic just outside Malaga. Sadly I had missed him by a matter of a few hours. After some language difficulties, mainly caused by a hopeless interpreter, I did finally manage to find out that the clinic specialised in what they referred to as "personal alterations".' He paused for a second to refer to his notes.

'The clinic refused to give me any indication of the work they had performed on Dean. They did however inform me that his taxi had been bound for Malaga Airport. We ran a check of all flights from the airport but there were no records of a William Dean flying that day. I assume he has more than one passport.'

Tom paused and took a rather noisy slurp of coffee for which he apologised.

'The main problem is that the clinic said that William Dean is not Michael Defreitas. I showed his photo to all and sundry at the clinic and no one recognised him. It turns out that Dean arrived in great secrecy and the only person who actually saw him before the procedure was the owner of the clinic, who is also the surgeon, and his assistant. I am not convinced that they were telling the truth and that Dean is very likely to have been Defreitas. If so, I think we have to assume that he will be unrecognizable from the man he was. The further confusing thing is that the staff were adamant that he spoke a foreign language.'

'What? English?'

'I assume so yes.'

'Are you sure that's what they meant? In my experience most people in Spain have English as their second language.'

'Good point I will check up on that.'

As he said the word check, a light bulb went off in his head. *Surely it couldn't be? Nah.*

'Tom?' The DCC interrupted his thought process.

'Sorry ma'am. I just had an idea.'

More silence.

'Do you intend to share this idea with your boss?'

'Not at this stage, it's a bit off the wall, but if I am right I promise you will know soon enough. Oh by the way we aren't the only ones looking for Defreitas. An Italian had turned up at the clinic asking questions. Sadly I missed him too, but only by minutes.'

'Tony Marciano?'

'I didn't manage to find out the man's name but it certainly seems to fit with the business card we found on the body.'

'I have checked with the various authorities who are watching Tony Marciano. Defreitas is not currently on their list of known contacts but that means nothing. They were however most interested and asked to be kept informed as they know the families are legitimising their money somehow and a dodgy investment fund would be the perfect vehicle to use. Be discrete though Tom, these men are very dangerous.'

Tom nodded his head and made a note to delve a little deeper into Tony Marciano, but very quietly. He changed the subject quickly.

'Anyway on the flight back I had time to consider the case and the direction it needs to take, moving forward. The money, we need to concentrate on the money.'

'I think the direction the case needs to take is for you to solve it. The Chief Constable is on my case on this as he is getting a lot of pressure from his bosses, particularly his wife, and shit runs downhill.'

'Yes ma'am, leave it to me. Something is going to break this week, I can feel it.'

'I hope so for all our sakes,' she sighed. 'Well, keep me informed.'

Tom rushed out of the DCC's office and into the incident room. He found the contact details of the clinic in Castiglio and started dialling.

'Hello? Can I speak to someone who speaks English please?'

'Ya.'

Tom waited a few minutes and was starting to think that the line had gone dead when he heard.

'Ola? How I help you?'

'Oh hi, I was at the clinic yesterday asking about William Dean.'

'Ya, I remember.'

'I understand that Mr Dean spoke a foreign language. Can you tell me which one?'

'I afraid not.'

'Was it English?'

'No no, no English.'

'Czechoslovakian?'

'I no know. I sorry.'

'Listen what is your name?'

'My name is Juanita.'

'Listen Juanita I am going to fax a photo through to you and then I will ring you back in five minutes, okay?'

'Yes it okay.'

Tom shot over to the fax machine and faxed the grainy photo of Tomas to the fax number for the clinic.

He waited five minutes and then rang again.

'Allo?'

'Juanita?'

'Ya'

'Is the photo I faxed over William Dean?'

'The photo is very dark but my boss think so. You email me photo?'

She gave him her email address and he emailed the photo over. Five minutes later it was confirmed. Tomas was William Dean.

Tom was elated but mystified. How on earth and why?

Gerrards Cross

Tom needed some fresh air but it was hammering it down. He ran to his car and drove to Costa. Maybe some caffeine would get his brain moving.

If Tomas was Dean then Tomas was obviously still alive. But why would he have agreed to having such treatment and how could he afford it? They had already established that Tomas was a poor immigrant from The Czech Republic. He was in fact so poor that he would have agreed to anything for money, including drastic personal alterations.

So if Tomas was alive, who had been murdered and dumped on West Common? Was it Defreitas after all? Tom sighed; the investigation had taken yet another twist and he wasn't sure whether it was a helpful one or not. He felt a bit dizzy but put it down to drinking his coffee too quickly and the extraordinary case that got more extraordinary with every day, if not every hour.

Tom had already established that Defreitas had hired Shirley and must therefore be the one paying Tomas to not only have the operation but also all his expenses. But why? What was the point?

Defreitas had gone to great lengths to find a man with very similar looks and physical characteristics to himself? What was the point in then changing them? The more he thought about it the less he was convinced that Tomas could be William Dean or even for that matter still alive. Dean had to be Defreitas but that didn't explain the foreign language. He must somehow uncover more of Defreitas's pre-Oxford background. He would put his Rottweiler Julia on it as a priority.

He then turned his thoughts to the Italian. Just suppose the DCC was right and that Tony Marciano was laundering their ill-gotten gains through Proteus? They would be seriously pissed off if Defreitas had stolen their money! Pissed off enough to kill him and chop his head off? But why would they be looking for him in Spain if they knew he was dead?

He rang Stewart McMillan.

'Mr McMillan, DCI Sparks. Are you free this afternoon?'

'Yes, would you like to come and see me?'

There was something in McMillan voice that intrigued Tom. He knew he was hiding something and McMillan's voice gave away the fact that he knew that Tom knew he was hiding something. But did he know that Tom knew that he knew that Tom knew that he was hiding something? Tom got the giggles and paused whilst he recovered.

Tom thought about the rush hour traffic and said, 'No I will send a car for you.'

'But I can't leave the office.'

'I'm sorry sir but I must insist – a car will be with you in about 30 minutes.'

'Sounds like I don't really have a choice in this.'

'No sir, you don't. Oh and by the way do you know a man called Tony Marciano?'

'Not personally, no, although I think Michael had some dealings with him. I think he is one of our investors. Shall I check for you?'

Tom was taken aback by this offer and hoped that this new attitude of helpfulness would continue during the forthcoming interview.

'That would be great. Please bring details of his investments with you.'

Whilst waiting for Stewart McMillan to arrive, Tom called Jez and Julia into his office. He rang Gillian Harris of the fraud squad to find out how things were going.

'Good afternoon DCI Sparks, I am glad you called. Saved me ringing you.'

'How's it going?'

'Not bad at all thanks. We are making great progress and it's clear we have uncovered a classic Ponzi scheme here.'

'Ponzi scheme? You'll have to excuse me I am a bit of heathen when it comes to fraud.'

'Of course, sorry to use jargon. A Ponzi scheme is a scheme where people are invited to invest in a fund that is offering artificially high returns. The high returns aren't sustainable and as a result, the fund starts paying existing investors with funds received from new investors. Inevitably in the end the fund runs out of money but it can take many years in the case of a very successful fund such as this one.'

'I see.' Tom said uncertainly.

'Tell you what Tom, I'll send you over a book about it.'

'Thanks, that would be very helpful.'

'So who are the perpetrators of our Ponzi scheme and where has all the money gone?'

'I'm certain that Michael Defreitas knew all about it as did the IT manager Julian Travers, but whether Stewart McMillan is in on it too I'm not so sure about.'

'Stewart McMillan is on his way to see me. I was hoping to be able to go on the attack but maybe I won't be able to after all. Any sign of the missing money?'

'Well a large amount of it was used to keep the fund alive by paying out dividends to investors and returning monies to investors who wanted to leave the fund. The rest was siphoned off gradually over a number of months, if not years. Skimming we call it. Just taking a small amount every day, not enough to be noticed but enough to mount up to a substantial amount over a period of time.'

'Any idea who was taking the money?'

'Same answer as before I'm afraid. It could take months to sort this mess out and most of the people who would have been useful to us are dead.'

'Mmm, strange that. Oh, one last thing Gillian. Have you had anything to do with the Tony Marciano investigation?'

'I'm afraid not but Brian Small, one of my colleagues, has. He has some extremely thick files on Marciano but not enough to nail him. Well not yet anyway. Why do you ask?'

'Marciano was a Proteus investor and we're starting to wonder whether he and Defreitas were legitimising the families' illegal money through the fund.'

There was a momentary silence before Gillian replied.

'Interesting idea. Tell you what, I'll ask Brian to email us the list of known Marciano contacts and the companies he acts for. I'll then run the list through the Proteus records and see what I can find.'

'Great idea. If you can get the list to me before Stewart McMillan arrives it would help greatly.'

'I'll see what I can do. Speak to you later.'

Tom suddenly remembered John had left a message on his voicemail whilst he was in Spain. Apparently the auditors were a firm in Mayfair called Gerrard, Ashurst and Price.

'Before you ring off Gillian. Have you spoken to the auditors yet?'

'No but it is on my list of things to do. Do you know who they are?'

'Yes apparently they're called Gerrard, Ashurst and Price.'

'Are you sure?'

'Well a friend of mine found it out for me and I doubt he is wrong. Why?'

'Well they had a major fire about three weeks ago during which their senior partner Oliver Price died. Apparently he was working late and there was some kind of mechanical problem with a coffee machine.'

'Interesting. Any idea who the investigating officer was?'

'I am afraid not, there was no fraud involved.'

'No worries I have a contact with City CID I'll give him a call. Well thank you Gillian you have been most helpful.'

Tom turned to Julia and Jez and smiled.

'Well, we are getting there. Yes, Proteus was being run fraudulently, something called a Ponzi scheme, and yes someone was skimming money out of the accounts. We know who was doing the skimming all we need to do now is work out where the money has ended up and find out who stole it.'

'Oh and as you probably gathered we also have another connected death. I want chapter and verse on Gerrard, Ashurst and Price and especially the fire at their office three weeks ago. Phone Mick Brunton of City CID he should be able to point you in the right direction. That should keep you nice and busy.'

Tom sat back and prepared himself for the arrival of Stewart McMillan. He rang the desk sergeant and asked him to escort Mr McMillan to an interview room when he had arrived.

He made some notes and waited.

———

Gerrards Cross

Stewart McMillan was really quite indignant. Tom had deliberately kept him waiting for nearly an hour. Tom walked in and cheerily said.

'Hello Mr McMillan, nice to see you again. I trust they have made you comfortable and offered you tea, coffee and things?'

McMillan's face went purple as he shouted at Tom.

'What is the meaning of this Chief Inspector? How dare you treat me like a common criminal.'

'Oh I am sorry if you feel that way. I'm afraid I now have to read you your rights.'

Tom then turned on the tape machine. 'This is Detective Chief Inspector Thomas Sparks on Tuesday 3rd November 2010. We are in interview room 2 at Gerrards Cross station.'

Tom then read Stewart McMillan his rights. At which point McMillan completely lost it.

'This is absolutely outrageous. I want my solicitor here now!'

'Certainly sir. If you would like to give me his name and contact details I will make your solicitor aware of your request.' That seemed to calm McMillan down.

'Thank you.'

He wrote down his solicitor's details and passed them to Tom who in turn gave them to the police constable at the door.

'Please call Mr McMillan's solicitor and let him know Mr McMillan would like him to attend this interview.'

'I see it's a central London number so I assume your solicitor could be some time. Do you mind if I ask you a few background questions while we wait?'

'I think I should wait for my solicitor.'

'But your solicitor is going to be ages and surely you don't want to be here longer than absolutely necessary?'

Silence.

Stewart McMillian just sat there giving Tom his best stare. Tom continued, knowing that McMillan thought far too much of himself to ignore his questions, solicitor or no solicitor.

'Mr McMillan I was speaking to Gillian Harris of the fraud squad earlier today. As you know the FSA called them in late on Friday to investigate the finances of Proteus following the discovery that a lot of cash is missing. When did you first realise that there was a problem?'

'That is a strange question Chief Inspector, may I remind you that it was you who discovered that the cash was missing?'

'True but surely you do not expect me to believe that you weren't aware it was missing before then?'

'As I have told you before Inspector, I only concentrate on the investment side of the business and leave, sorry, left Michael to look after the finances.'

'For the benefit of the recording Mr McMillan can you please confirm that Michael is in fact Michael Defreitas.'

Again he raised his voice.

'Yes of course I am talking about Michael Defreitas. Look what is going on here? I don't know anything about what has been going on and yet you treat me like a common criminal.'

'Interesting your use of the word common when the body was found on West Common . . .'

Tom smiled at his wit but his smile quickly faded when he saw the furious expression on McMillan's face.

'Well from where I am sitting, we are investigating the multi-billion pound fraud of a fund of which you are one of the co-founders and the investment director. In my view it's very possible that you may be one of the perpetrators of what could be one of the biggest financial crimes in this country's history. For all I know you may be the brains behind it and responsible for the murder of many people. So that's why you may feel like you are being treated like a common criminal, because I think you may be a common criminal, Mr McMillan.'

'I think I'll wait for my solicitor.' McMillan repeated stonily,

'I am sure he is on his way. In the meantime, are you aware of exactly how much money is missing from the fund as of today?'

'No I don't, but I suspect you are about to tell me.'

'Early estimates from the fraud squad indicate a figure somewhere between £1.8 and £1.95 billion.'

'That's impossible, I would have known about it.'

'My point precisely.'

Tom decided a strategic pause was in order and counted to himself; when he had reached a very slow 30 he continued.

'So when did you and Michael decide to start fleecing your investors, Mr McMillan?'

'This is quite ridiculous, when are you going to get it into your thick head that I have had absolutely nothing to do with any of this. Michael was the one. He said the only way to break the mould was to offer people consistently high returns. At first we did it through pure skill and daring, but recently things have started to go against us. It was down to a few bad decisions and the credit crunch. I told Michael that the level of returns he was giving the investors was too high and was unsustainable.'

Tom waited to see if McMillan was going to dig this particular hole any deeper but he seemed to realise that he had said too much already.

'So you have lied to us already? You did know that Michael was acting fraudulently?'

'Well I suppose when you put it like that, but Michael was absolutely adamant he could guide us out of our difficulties provided we continued to attract new investors. The only way to attract new investors was to continue announcing superb performance figures month on month. Trouble was that despite the statistics we were releasing, people were becoming very nervous of the whole market and started to withdraw their money. It was only a trickle to start with but when that trickle became a flood and combined with a reduction in new funds being invested we were facing massive problems.'

'So finally the truth, you admit you knew what was going on?'

'I knew that Michael was declaring better performances than we were actually achieving and that he was using the new funds to repay people who were withdrawing.'

McMillan took a sip of water.

'Yes, I knew, and I was worried sick about it but Michael was such a strong character and so persuasive. He assured me that we were doing nothing wrong and that everything would be all right. My only crime is that I believed him.'

'Ignorance is not a defence in law Mr McMillan. You do realise that you are going to be charged with fraud and are likely to go to prison don't you?'

'I wouldn't know Inspector, I am not a great expert on the legal system in this country and my solicitor is still not here to advise me.'

As if on cue, there was a knock on the door and the desk sergeant walked in with Mr McMillan's solicitor. The man was a typical City lawyer of medium height, his black hair was Brylcreamed back and he was dressed in a pinstripe suit of which any Savile Row tailor would have been proud.

'Detective Chief Inspector Sparks I presume. I am Rupert Smithers of Smithers, Smithers and Smithers. I represent Stewart McMillan. Can you tell me whether you intend to charge my client and if so what the charge is?'

'Mr Smithers we have not arrested or charged your client yet but that doesn't mean we won't be doing so in the near future. At the moment your client is merely helping us with our enquiries and we have read Mr McMillan his rights and asked him a couple of background questions.'

Tom paused briefly to let that sink in and then continued.

'I know for a fact that the fraud squad are particularly keen to interview your client. I hope you are not too busy at the moment as Mr McMillan is going to keep you very occupied over the coming days.'

'I see.'

'May I continue?'

'Yes by all means.' Smithers said taking a seat next to his client and opposite Tom.

'Now where were we Mr McMillan? Oh yes I remember, we had just established that you were aware that Proteus was being run fraudulently and I was about to warn you that you are likely to be charged with at least aiding and abetting a major fraud depending on the evidence against you.'

'Enough!' Smithers interceded at once. 'You are clearly on a fishing exercise and have nothing incriminating against my client. I propose that we arrange a suitable day and time for you to conduct a proper interview with my client that I will attend from the outset. Now we are leaving.'

'That is of course your right Mr Smithers. I'll call you in the morning to arrange a suitable date and time for the interview which, I suggest, in view of the seriousness of this, should be as soon as possible tomorrow.'

'Agreed. I will be in my office from 7am tomorrow and will have my diary in front of me waiting for your call.'

'Thank you Mr Smithers. Oh, by the way, which Smithers are you? First, second or third?'

'Oh, I am actually the fourth the others are either dead or retired. I am waiting for my two sons to earn me promotion to number one!' he said laughing at his lawyerly sense of humour. Tom thought he was a pratt but had a feeling he was likely to be a very good solicitor who had been on retention for many months in preparation for this moment. He showed them out.

Stewart McMillan sneered at Tom as he left with a congratulatory arm around his solicitor's shoulders. Tom called out.

'Oh Mr McMillan, haven't you forgotten something?' McMillan turned and looked a bit taken aback.

'The details of Tony Marciano's investments?'

'Well,' McMillan said as he turned towards his solicitor. 'I am not sure.' His solicitor merely nodded and McMillan reluctantly walked over to Tom and handed him a rather thin beige folder with the name A Marciano on it.

'He is not much of an investor as you will see, about £15,000 in total.'

'Oh I have a feeling he is worth a lot more to Proteus than that, Mr McMillan. Tony Marciano is the main money man in London for the organised crime families. At this very moment the fraud squad are checking the Proteus records for any other investments in the names of known family members and their many companies. I have a feeling that the investments could be sizeable.'

McMillan had turned ashen. Tom realised he knew everything and was frustrated; if only Tom could have had another half an hour with McMillan before that bloody solicitor arrived.

Tom went back to his office and started working his way through his messages. Roger Townsend had called him five times over the past few days. Tom instantly felt guilty. He was aware of the pressure he had put on Townsend for a speedy PM and then had failed to contact him when he should have. Was he becoming forgetful or was he merely being distracted by the complexities of the case and the disappearance of Helen? Either way it just wasn't good enough. Tom felt distinctly uncomfortable as he rang Townsend.

'Dr Townsend? It's DCI Sparks. Apologies for the delay I have been abroad following up some leads on the case.'

Townsend answered in his usual unwelcoming manner.

'Oh it's you, finally. Did you know that mobiles do actually work abroad?' 'Yes true but there was no signal where I was.'

Tom could feel himself blushing at the lie and quickly changed the subject.

'Any news?'

'Well as usual Helen did a very thorough, very professional job. It is always difficult with a body that has been badly damaged. Who did you get to identify the body? There are no records on here.'

'Well we have been delaying the formal identification until the head turned up.'

'I see.'

Dr Townsend sounded totally unconvinced so Tom quickly continued.

'Besides all the medical details matched as did the personal effects found on the body.'

Tom had a eureka moment. He'd had the personal effects found on the body identified by Stewart McMillan – now his prime suspect. Tom didn't want to admit to Tooley's pathologist that he had been remiss so he changed the subject.

'Is there anything that strikes you as being unusual?'

'The only anomaly I have spotted is very minor indeed and would have been easy for Helen to miss especially if she was under pressure.'

'So Helen wasn't completely thorough and missed something? Mind telling me exactly what she missed?'

'The body has a couple of tiny moles on the left buttock very close together, very close to the anus. Helen should have noted these on the file as distinguishing marks.'

'Excellent, thank you Dr Townsend. What time will you be working until this evening.'

'Just had a teenage stabbing come in that Tooley wants done tonight so I will be here until at least 10pm if not later. Why?"

'I think it is time the body was formally identified, don't you?'

———

Gerrards Cross

Tom's next call was to Patricia Defreitas.

'Sorry to bother you like this Mrs Defreitas but did your husband have any identifying marks on his body?'

'Not really, except that is for two tiny moles on his bottom. Not very prominent, but he was very proud of them and liked to call them his beauty spots."

'This might sound rather bizarre but I was wondering if I could collect you as soon as possible to formally identify a body we believe may be your husband's?'

'Well yes I suppose so, but at our last meeting you said he was still alive. What is going on Chief Inspector?'

'I will explain everything when I see you Mrs Defreitas. I will be there in ten minutes.'

It was more like 15 minutes as Tom collected Mrs Defreitas and drove her to the Wembley morgue. She was pale and clearly apprehensive as Dr Townsend led them down a room lined with large steel drawers. This was a moment Tom never enjoyed and made him sometimes wish he was a traffic cop. Trouble was you had to be a sadistic bastard to be a traffic cop.

Dr Townsend found the drawer he was looking for and pulled the handle towards him. The drawer revealed a corpse covered with a grey sheet. When the drawer was fully extended he pulled back the covering sheet to reveal the headless body of the victim. Mrs Defreitas turned away.

'I can't identify him! It could be anyone! That is so horrible I think I am going to be sick.'

'Deep breaths Mrs Defreitas, you will be fine.' Townsend tried to reassure her in a very quiet and calm voice.

'Yes Dr Townsend.'

Tom interceded: this was why he had tried to avoid this.

'Can you turn the body over please Dr Townsend?'

'Yes of course, any reason why?'

'I would like to see the man's buttocks if you don't mind.'

Townsend gave him a strange look and a wink that made Tom blush. He duly turned the body over to reveal the man's buttocks that he then pulled apart to reveal two tiny moles close to the anus.

Tom turned.

'Mrs Defreitas, are these the moles you mentioned to me earlier?'

'Yes they are Inspector this is definitely my husband.'

'Can I just ask you to indulge me one final time?'

'Of course, anything to help.'

'Dr Townsend could you turn the body back over again please?' 'This is slight embarrassing but do you recognise the man's penis?'

Tom realised this was out of order but couldn't help himself. The strange look Townsend had given him earlier had nothing on the look he was getting now from the pathologist.

'Oh yes Michael had a tiny one. All the penises I have known have been different shapes and sizes and unless I am very much mistaken I can assure you that the penis I am looking at is my husband's'

Tom decided to change the subject.

'Thank you Mrs Defreitas, thank you Dr Townsend. I think we have our formal identification. As you are aware, Mrs Defreitas, I was hoping to spare you this experience but the circumstances of this case are such that I had no choice.'

Tom felt elated: he had finally solved the mystery of whose body it was. But he realised that he would have to answer some very difficult questions about why he didn't get the body formally identified by Mrs Defreitas earlier. He would need the DCC's advice on this one but he might have to do something he would hate doing. Blame Helen. He was jolted back to the present by Patricia Defreitas.

'Chief Inspector may I ask where my husband's body was found?'

'On West Common'

'But that was nearly two weeks ago! Why have you waited until now to have me identify him? Surely you could have saved yourself a lot of time?'

'Mrs Defreitas I can only apologise profusely for all the upset this has caused you and your family.'

'I think you have a lot of questions to answer on this. First you tell me it is my husband, then you tell me it isn't my husband and that my husband is a murderer and a fraudster. Now it turns out he was dead the whole time.'

'I know, but I can assure you that my force and I have acted responsibly and professionally at all times.'

'Well I find that very hard to believe. Were you aware that my parents live next door to the Chief Constable? In fact they are very friendly and will no doubt be seeking an enquiry into this shambles.'

Brilliant! That was all Tom needed. They travelled home in a stony silence and he was relieved when he finally dropped off Mrs Defreitas. He headed straight to the Apple Tree. On the way he radioed in that the body had been identified as Michael Defreitas by his wife, but this was not to be announced it to the media yet.

Tom sat at a quiet table in the corner of the bar and stared into his pint. He thought of Helen. He had always thought that money was the key to this investigation and it would probably turn out to be the case. He realised now, however, that Helen was also a key figure in his investigation.

It was Helen who had told Tom that the body was not Defreitas because she would have recognised him especially because he was so well hung – comments that had now proved to be totally false. Why would Helen do that? She had knowingly misled him and now she had disappeared. What did she stand to gain from all this? Surely she wasn't the murderer?

Tom had always realised that Helen would find out that the body had been moved and a second post mortem was being done. He had expected her to be indignant and throw a tantrum. But of course Helen knew Roger Townsend would spot the omission from her report.

At least he now knew why Helen had resigned and then disappeared.

Tom then did something that he had never done before and which was to be a talking point of the regulars at the bar for many months to come. He left, his pint untouched.

Wednesday 4th November 2009

Tom met DCC Jane Protheroe at her office at 7am. He had rung her briefly late the previous evening and had been deliberately vague as it was a conversation he wanted face-to-face rather than over the telephone.

'Morning Tom. You sounded most mysterious over the phone last night.'

'Yes, sorry about that but I felt this was a discussion that needed to take place face to face, ma'am. The time has come to have an official conversation about Helen James.'

'I see. I had a feeling it was only a matter of time. Would you care to explain?'

Tom opened his notebook and pretended to refer to it, his favourite stalling tactic. Now ready, he began.

'Ma'am, last evening I accompanied Mrs Defreitas to the Wembley morgue where I had asked for a second opinion on Helen's findings. Dr Townsend the resident pathologist there actually commended Helen James on her medical findings but was curious as to why she had not mentioned in her report one or two personal features that were unique to that person – Features which, as Defreitas's lover, would have been known to her. Well, one feature for certain.'

'I don't understand.'

'Ma'am the body found on West Common two weeks ago has been positively identified as Michael Defreitas by his wife.'

'But that means that Helen lied.'

'Precisely.'

'Why would she do that?'

'Well that is what I am trying to work out. It could only be for one of two reasons, money or love, or of course the fatal combination of the two.'

'But she was Defreitas's lover. Why say he was alive when he was in fact dead. It doesn't make sense.'

'She could of course be the murderer, but the very cause of death would seem to eliminate that unless she had an accomplice. This whole thing has got me wondering if she was even Defreitas's lover. We only have her word for that and a vague tip off from a neighbour.'

'This case is getting ever more bizarre Tom and things aren't looking too good from where I am sitting. The Chief Constable wants to see me at 10am and asked me to bring you with me.'

'Okay, see you at ten.'

'Oh and Tom, try and have some answers by then!'

Tom felt his stomach churn. The Chief Constable was a rail straight and proper man with ice running through his veins. The fact that Tom had been summoned to see him was not good.

Tom's brain felt like a bowl of disorganised spaghetti. He had all these threads and ideas but they were all tangled up. Nothing seemed to lead anywhere.

He knew that he had been cleverly manipulated and was desperate to work out who was behind it. Whoever it was had known that his relationship with Helen would cloud his judgement.

He rang Paul Smithers and arranged the interview with Stewart McMillan for 4pm at Gerrards Cross. He then called a team meeting.

'Right we have two hours to come up with a plausible reason why the Chief Constable shouldn't fire me for gross incompetence.'

There was a stunned silence.

'Last night Patricia Defreitas formally identified the body found on West Common as being that of her husband Michael Defreitas. We also know that two work colleagues of Defreitas, plus the Proteus auditor, are also dead, probably murdered. Julia, you were the one who interviewed Defreitas's neighbours weren't you?'

'Yes sir.'

'Which one was it who gave you the information about the silver Audi?'

'It was a lodger from one of the ground floor apartments. He was just leaving the building when I bumped into him. He apologised for being in a hurry and said that he didn't really know anyone in the block but he had seen the chap in the penthouse with a tall blonde woman who drove a silver Audi.'

'Did he say what the chap from the penthouse looked like?

'No sir, he was in a rush and we already knew what Defreitas looked like.'

'Okay, can you go back and see him please and get a description of the man from the penthouse.'

'Yes is there any reason why?'

'Well for a start there is more than one penthouse and we need to be sure it was Defreitas he was talking about.'

'I will get on to it now sir.'

'No, hang on a sec, let's finish the meeting first.'

'Jez have you made any progress finding out where all the money has disappeared to?'

'The trail is long and complicated but it looks like it ends up in the Cayman Islands and is then withdrawn in cash.'

'Cash? Two billion pounds?'

'Oh, it is nowhere near that amount sir.'

'It isn't?'

'Oh no, after propping up the Ponzi scheme I would say only £100 million is unaccounted for.'

'Oh well it is hardly worth looking for then is it?'

Jez blushed and Tom felt guilty he was allowing his growing apprehension to affect his normally polite approach to team meetings.

'Bill, is the plumber's daughter back from Spain yet?'

'Was due back yesterday.'

'Please take the artist round there this morning and also take with you a copy of the impression of the kitchen worker from the Rajpoot.'

'You don't think?'

'I don't know, I am just covering all the angles. You never know. See if she has seen the kitchen worker before. Also go and see Mr Singh and show him the artist's impression of the boiler-man from Spain.'

'Mel I have a task for you that is going to need some charm and persuasion. I want you to contact the surgeries that were broken into and I want you to find out which rooms were tampered with and get a list of the patients for both surgeries. Jez I want you to help her.'

'Right, well it has been great knowing you. I am off to be fired now!'

'Good luck!' They all shouted in unison.

Tom felt a tear forming in his right eye as he thought about his little team and how well they all worked together. Would he really be fired?

Geneva

Zolo was in a quandary. Not only did he know Tony Marciano, but more crucially Tony Marciano knew him. How on earth was he going to kill him without being recognised? Not that he was worried about Tony himself, rather the risk of the man's perpetual audience. This was the kind of danger he had always promised himself that he would avoid. But it was too late, he could not refuse the job without further risk.

He would have to be very clever and it would take some planning, but he comforted himself with the thought that he was, after all, the master assassin for whom no assignment was too difficult.

He started his preparations by shaving his head before taking a plane to London.

Gerrards Cross

Whilst Zolo was going through customs at Heathrow, Tom was entering the Chief Constable's office with DCC Protheroe.

The small, wiry, fastidiously tidy, uniformed man stood and welcomed Tom warmly.

'Ah Tom good to see you. Sorry it is in such circumstances. The Deputy Chief Constable has kept me up to speed with the latest developments. What a right balls-up if you don't mind me saying so. I had a phone call last night from Oliver Preston he says his daughter is distraught.'

'I am sorry sir but you have me at a disadvantage. Who is Oliver Preston?'

'Oh sorry, he is the father of Patricia Preston although she is of course better known to you as the widow of Michael Defreitas.'

'Oh,' said Tom wearily.

'Oh indeed.'

'Sir this has been a very difficult investigation with so many twists and turns but I have kept the DCC informed at all times. We are dealing with some very clever criminals who have implemented a well prepared plan to confuse us.'

'I know Tom and you are very well respected by all of us. The problem is Tom . . .'

He paused and Tom thought. *Here we go.*

'The problem is I think you may be too close to this. We all know about your relationship with Helen. The worry is that you are unable to be objective because of her obvious involvement.'

The Chief Constable looked at Tom and it was clear that Tom was not expected to defend himself and his position. Despite this Tom felt he must interject.

'Sir that really is not the case. I admit that I was taken in by her confession that she was Michael Defreitas's lover and that the body wasn't his but this was out of professional loyalty.'

'That's true sir.' DCC Protheroe interrupted. 'I interviewed Helen as well and I was completely taken in too. She had been a trusted colleague for many years who had always acted professionally.'

Tom was grateful for the support from the DCC and it seemed to calm the Chief Constable down and the worst seemed to be over when he asked.

'Do we know where she has run off to?'

'Not yet sir but I am checking all the airports for both scheduled and private flights. We have so far drawn a blank and we have to assume that she might have used a second passport and is traveling under a new identity and probably in disguise.'

'So where are we at the moment?'

'Originally my theory was that Michael Defreitas had staged his own murder in order to make a clean getaway. The subsequent deaths were, I assumed, him covering his tracks.'

'But that is not the case now is it?'

'No sir. Now we realise that someone else was behind the killings and we are trying to close the net on them.'

'Any suspects?'

'Defreitas has always been our main suspect and to be honest we have concentrated mainly on him. Obviously Mrs Defreitas's identification was a huge blow but we have a number of other directions our enquiries will now be taking.'

'Such as?' The Chief Constable asked doubtfully.

Tom paused, he could feel the pressure building again. He needed something good. He had a flash of inspiration.

'Well, I am very clear in my mind that Helen James and Stewart McMillan are now the key and may even be lovers. They have now become the main focus of the investigation.'

'Well I know all about Helen, what is Stewart McMillan like?'

'Well he seemed a bit of a nerd to start with but he is becoming increasingly aggressive and is proving difficult to crack. He is either a criminal mastermind or just the innocent nerd we always thought he was. I am interviewing him at his lawyer's office at 4pm.'

'What about the Italians?'

'Well they would be at the top of my list of suspects for obvious reasons except that they also seem to be desperately trying to find Defreitas.'

Tom paused to allow this all to sink in, but before he could continue the Chief Constable interrupted.

'What makes you think that Helen and McMillan are so key to this Tom?'

I don't really have a clue, Tom was thinking as he fiddled with his notebook to give himself time before responding.

'Well Helen deliberately misled us into believing that Defreitas was still alive. The only possible reason I can see for her to do this would be if she was involved in his murder. I have issued a warrant for her arrest on the suspicion of murder.'

'So you have a warrant out for the arrest of a Home Office pathologist on the most spurious of evidence and a suspect who is mainly under suspicion because he is becoming increasing aggressive during the many hours of questioning he is no doubt being subjected to. Is that it?'

'Oh not at all sir. I have managed to get a slot on *Crimewatch UK* tonight which I am hoping will bring in more information and maybe a sighting of Helen James. Her odd behaviour following the discovery of the body and her subsequent disappearance indicate to me someone with a big secret. I am absolutely positive we will solve this case when we find her.'

'Mmm you know I don't really approve of modern media publicity but sometimes I realise it can produce excellent results. I hope that this is one of those occasions. And McMillan?'

'Defreitas was clearly behind the fraud and his mismanagement and dishonesty have basically ruined Proteus, McMillan's baby. What better motive for murder is there than destroying a man's pride and joy and reputation? Stewart McMillan admitted to me yesterday that he knew what Michael was doing and that Proteus was about to go bust.'

'Of course it could be something even far more basic. They were in it together and McMillan killed him for his share. Let's see what the next few days bring. How did you get on in Spain?'

Tom relaxed slightly realising the worst was over.

'I thought that the man travelling under the name of William Dean was Defreitas and that I would find him there. Confusingly, the man I followed has been identified as our missing Czech, Tomas Kopecky.'

The Chief Constable scratched his head and frowned.

'I don't understand Tom.'

'Me neither, but if it was Tomas and that in my mind is still in question, it appears that someone has paid him a lot of money to be a red herring. What I can't work out is why? Unless the original plan was to sacrifice Tomas when the time came as being Michael Defreitas.'

'But wouldn't that have required Defreitas's involvement?'

'Yes. The only thing that makes sense to me right now is that the original exit plan was hatched by both McMillan and Defreitas and that McMillan and Helen James double-crossed Defreitas.'

'Sex and money, Tom, it is always one or the other. In this case it could even be both. Forget Tomas and concentrate on the sex and the money.'

The Chief Constable paused slightly before continuing.

'Well it is clear that you made a mistake trusting Helen James but you are in celebrated company there.' He glanced at his deputy before continuing. 'Tom, you are showing great flair in what is the most difficult case we have encountered in this constabulary.'

He stood up and shook Tom's hand.

'Keep up the good work Tom. I have every confidence in you. *Oh dear*, thought Tom, *the dreaded vote of confidence.*

Tom almost danced as he returned to the DCC's car for the return journey.

'Thanks ma'am.'

'Think nothing of it Tom, you are a good copper and I was telling the truth.'

Gerrards Cross

Tom's team, were relieved to discover he had returned unscathed from his meeting and clearly still had his job.

They had all returned from their assignments and reported to Tom one by one, Julia first.

'Sir, the man at the flats who identified the Audi is a Mr Ross who lives in the front ground floor flat, number one. His flat overlooks the car park and driveway. He reported that the man in the penthouse was shortish, balding and slightly overweight. I showed him a picture of Michael Defreitas who he confirmed he recognised but who he was certain was not the man he had seen with the blonde.'

'Mmm as I thought. Okay, do you have his mobile number?'

'Yes sir.'

'Okay well ring him now and ask him to pop in and see me immediately. If he refuses threaten to arrest him.'

'Bill, how did you get on with Andrea?'

'She was not 100 per cent certain but she seemed to think that the two men could be the same person.'

'Thanks Bill, not that it is going to help us too much as I am convinced this man is an international assassin who we have little, if any, chance of catching.'

'Can you please now try and trace these missing Indians. I suspect we are looking for two bodies.'

'Mel and Jez, how did you get on at the surgeries?'

'It was tough but we managed to get the information you wanted.'

'Excellent! Which rooms were broken into?'

'Well they are not 100 per cent sure but they know for a fact that Dr Drake's office was definitely broken into and his records tampered with and his computer was also hacked into. These doctors are all technophobes, they don't even have password protected PCs'

'Do you have a list of his patients?'

'Took some getting, but yes we did.'

'How did you get on at the dentist?'

'They reported that the main reception area was broken into but that Mr Worth, the dentist, keeps his patient records locked in a secure strongbox which had not been tampered with. His PC is password protected and there is no sign of the system being hacked into.'

'Now that is interesting and might explain the decapitation. Did you manage to get their list of patients too?'

'We did sir.'

'Okay I want you to compare the list and see if there are any patients on both lists.'

'We've already had a first look, sir.'

Tom smiled at them.

'Well done, did you find anything?'

'There were a number of people on both lists but three names jumped out in particular – Michael Defreitas, Helen James and Stewart McMillan.'

'Again exactly as I expected. This is all falling into place nicely.' Tom was about to wind up the meeting then remembered Helen's text.

'Just one last thing, have we managed to trace the text sent by Helen?'

'Waiting for Vodafone sir, they have promised a response today.'

'Okay, well done everyone keep at it. I think we are nearly there.'

Tom left them to get on with their other enquiries and went for a walk. He was trying to think about why the break-in would have taken place. Defreitas was dead so it couldn't have been to fake his death unless something had gone wrong. McMillan was still very much alive and so was Helen. An icy shiver ran down his spine. Or was she? Anyone could have sent the text – all they needed was her mobile phone.

He got back to his office and rang Gillian Harris.

'Hi Tom, how is it going? Did you get the email from my colleague yesterday?'

'Yes but sadly McMillan's lawyer had brought the interview to a halt before it arrived. Have you had a chance to work on it?'

'We have and whilst we haven't completed the final reconciliation, initial indications are that Tony Marciano, the organisation and their nominated companies have currently got over £2.5 billion invested in Proteus. I think we may have hit the jackpot. Thanks to your help, we are hoping we finally have sufficient evidence to bring Marciano to justice.'

'I am delighted to have helped. Well things are moving here too. We have made two big breakthroughs since we last spoke. Firstly, the wife of Michael Defreitas has now formally identified the body found on West Common as being that of her husband.

Secondly, in the brief time we had with McMillan before his solicitor arrived yesterday he did admit that he knew about the fraud but totally blamed Defreitas.'

Tom paused to let this sink in and then continued.

'So, Michael Defreitas has been murdered and we need to establish who would have a reason to want him dead. I'm hoping you might be able to give me some ideas Gillian.'

'Well it is still early days but it is clear that both Michael Defreitas and Stewart McMillan were party to this massive fraud.'

'Are you certain? McMillan admitted knowing what Defreitas was up to but totally denies having anything to do with it.'

'Well McMillan can protest as much as he likes but the fact remains that as co-owner and investment director he had to sign off all official paperwork which confirmed the results of Proteus and the fund's performance. He and Defreitas are therefore both equally culpable. We would like to talk to him as soon as possible.'

'Did he not come in to work today?'

'No, he left mid-afternoon yesterday and hasn't been seen since.'

'Well he left early yesterday to be interviewed by me.'

'The office manager John Davis has been trying all day to get hold of him but his mobile is switched off. Apparently he always keeps his mobile on. We are worried he may have done a runner.'

So am I, thought Tom and brought the call to a quick halt. 'Thanks Gillian. I am due to interview him at his solicitor's office at 4pm but I sense that maybe I should find him sooner if I can. I'll keep you updated.'

Tom called his team together again except for Newsum who was on a call.

'Okay guys, it looks like Stewart McMillan has gone missing. He did surrender his passport to us but I think he has a second one. I want you to put out a bulletin to all airports, including the private ones, ports and train stations. I want this man found as soon as possible. It is very likely that he could be travelling under a different name.'

Suddenly everything clicked into place: the burglaries, Helen, and the disappearance of Adam Batstone.

'Mel, get me a photo of Adam Batstone as quickly as possible and warn all points north, south, east and west that McMillan may be traveling under the name of Adam Batstone, and he may be travelling with a tall blonde.'

Tom was about to send his team on their way when Newsum burst in and shouted out excitedly and breathlessly.

'We found his car sir! McMillan's Porsche! It was abandoned in Burnham Beeches.'

'Lets go. Ring ahead tell them we are on our way and not to touch a thing.'

Burnham Beeches

Burnham Beeches is a naturally wooded area between Gerrards Cross and Slough. Its winding, narrow roads hampered Tom's speed despite his desperation to get there.

The Porsche had been abandoned in one of the many National Trust car parks in the wooded area. By the time Tom and Newsum pulled into the car park, there were nearly 20 officers gathered around awaiting his arrival, four dressed in the customary white outfits for forensics. The car was splattered with mud as though it had been driven at speed along the muddy roads. A car chase, maybe, Tom wondered?

The car park was an unmade level clearing in a lightly wooded area. The recent wet weather and the constant daily traffic of walkers and their dogs had created a muddy, slippery surface dotted with deep puddles.

Tom ordered the force of men to spread out and start searching the surrounding area. There was a clear set of footprints leading from the Porsche but these were quickly swallowed up when they reached an area of numerous other car tracks and footprints.

What was very clear was that whoever had been driving the car had left in a hurry. The engine was still running, the stereo was playing Magic FM and there were a number of personal effects abandoned in the car.

Two of the forensic team were working carefully and methodically through the car checking every millimetre and then bagging the contents. The other half of the team worked with just as much attention in the area around the car. They thanked Tom for making sure that the car and surrounding area had not been disturbed prior to their arrival.

Instructing the uniformed officers to widen their search to a five-mile radius, Tom decided little more could be achieved there and returned to his office to wait for news. He rang the DS in charge of forensics at Slough and was assured he would have a full list of the car contents and any other findings by midday the next day. This wasn't quick enough for Tom but he knew from experience that he had no choice but to be patient.

Newsum arrived back in his office, out of breath, and stammering.

'Th-they have found a body sir, it's about a mile from where the car was abandoned.'

Tom shot out of his chair.

'Okay, off we go again then, Newsum.'

This time Newsum insisted on driving. She was easily the best driver in the Uxbridge CID. Cool, calm and collected, she was always fastest on their track and training days.

She didn't hold the horses and they were soon back at Burnham Beeches. The lane and the car park were still a mass of police cars along with a newly arrived ambulance. There was a young Indian man in a green outfit waiting for them. It was Dr Sachin Shawazi, who Tom had met on a number of occasions both socially and professionally. He was, Tom knew, a first class pathologist.

'Ah there you are Tom, I have been waiting for you to show you the body. Please follow me.' He said as he bowed his head slightly.

'Have you had a chance to inspect it yet?'

'I had a quick look, bit of a bloody mess to be honest.'

'Is it intact?'

'No, why do you ask?'

'Head missing by any chance?'

'Yes it is as a matter of fact. It looks as though it was sawn off. How did you know?'

'Oh just put it down to intuition.'

Dr Shawazi looked confused as they trudged on through the wood and all thoughts of their previous conversation disappeared.

The body was draped front down over a tree branch. Shawazi was right, the head had clearly been sawn off. The body was dressed in a very boring pair of jeans and a check shirt. This man shopped at Asda or Marks & Spencer. The man's trainers were badly scuffed and the jeans torn in several places. The man's hands were covered in mud, all signs of a desperate attempt to escape from whoever was chasing him.

Back at the car park Tom strolled around for about 30 minutes letting Shawazi get on with his job. He rang the DCC to update her.

'Ma'am we have found Stewart McMillan's car abandoned in a car park in Burnham Beeches. There are signs that it was abandoned following a chase of some kind. Following an extensive search of the surrounding area, we found a body about a mile away.'

'Is it McMillan?'

'I would hate to commit myself after what happened with Defreitas but the MO is the same. Head has been sawn off although this time the head was sawn off at the murder scene. The size and general appearance of the body make me believe that it is very likely to be McMillan.'

'This really is getting out of hand Tom. I suppose we better have one of our dawn meetings on this. I will ring the Chief Constable and give him the news. I don't think he is going to be particularly pleased, do you Tom?'

'No ma'am.'

'To lose your main suspect once might be considered unfortunate but losing a second one is a disaster. Just do me a favour Tom, and get to the bottom of this fast!'

Phone calls made, Tom wandered over to where Sachin Shawazi was working.

'Initial opinion Sachin?'

'Cause of death was likely to be some kind of head injury possibly a gunshot before the head was sawn off. Caucasian about 5 foot 8 and 13 stone.'

'Time of death?'

'I will have to get back to you on that but maybe four hours ago?'

Tom thanked Sachin and confirmed that he would call in to his lab in the morning for an update.

He headed back with Newsum who declined his offer of a drink. Apparently Jason had made them spaghetti Bolognese. That was the trouble with working with women. They just weren't blokey enough.

Tom fancied a change and sat and drank in the cocktail bar of the Bull Hotel on his own whilst reflecting on another manic and horrific day.

They were running out of suspects and people to kill.

Thursday 5th November 2009

The morning dawned bright and crisp but winter was clearly just around the corner. Tom trudged to his car dreading another day trying to establish why Gerrards Cross had turned into Buckinghamshire's version of the killing fields. He was a bit jaded having enjoyed the change of scenery at The Bull the previous evening just a little too much.

The DCC, though, looked as fresh and as bright as usual.

'Morning Tom. You look a bit rough this morning.'

'I am ma'am, a bit too much research last night. It's the walking home afterwards that's the killer.'

'You bachelors amaze me. When are you going to meet your Miss Right and settle down?'

'You sound like my mother.'

'Oh dear, I think we should get back to business don't you? Right, so what do we know about our man?'

'I think it is either McMillan or it has been stage managed to look like it.'

'Interesting.'

'The car was parked with the door open and the engine still running. We were lucky the person who reported it was honest and didn't knick it.'

'There are still some honest people in this world Tom.'

'I am going to see Sachin Shawazi next and hope to have more to tell you after that. In the meantime, I am still continuing the search for McMillan and Helen until I am absolutely certain that McMillan is indeed dead.'

'Is it tonight you are on *Crimewatch*?'

'Yes ma'am.'

'Well good luck – or, should I say, break a leg?'

Tom went straight to the incident room and updated his team. They looked stunned. Like him they couldn't believe that the body count had reached 20 and was still climbing.

Tom asked for updates.

'Julia?'

'I have arranged for Mr Ross to come in at 8.30 to see you.'

'Excellent, please ensure that I have photos of Helen James, Defreitas and McMillan for the interview. I don't suppose we have a photo of her car do we?'

'No sir but I'm sure I can download a similar one from the internet.'

'Good thinking.'

'Bill?'

'I have been checking the airports, rail stations and ports and there have been no sightings of either of them yet.'

'Ring the CAA. There is a very helpful young lady called Nicky there. Ask her for details of any flights from Northolt containing either single people or couples in the past fortnight.'

Something occurred to Tom that in the chaos he hadn't considered.

'Bill can you also get a search warrant to search McMillan's flat and while you are at it let's get one to search Helen James's flat as well. I will come with you on both searches.

'Jez and Mel. I want to know everything about McMillan. I know he was bit of a workaholic but he must have had some other interests. Interview his neighbours, his family and his friends.'

Tom looked at his watch and realised it was already 8.30. On cue, Newsum announced that Derek Ross had arrived and was in the interview room.

Tom walked into interview room one and quickly sized up Derek Ross. He was suited and booted and looked like a salesman of some kind. It turned out he was a local estate agent who was a bit down on his luck, as were most of his profession at the moment.

Tom asked some routine questions whilst he waited for Julia.

'How long have you lived in your flat Mr Ross?'

'Only for the past five months. The flat actually belongs to my parents who are very kindly supporting me while I get back on my feet.'

'Tough times for us all sir.'

Just as Tom was wondering what to ask him next, Julia arrived breathlessly with a file that she handed to Tom.

'Thank you Julia, please stay. I am sure Mr Ross won't mind.'

'Not at all.' Judging by the smile on his face, Ross clearly liked the brassy looks of Julia.

'Right, well firstly thank you for coming in today Mr Ross. I am sure you are very busy and your co-operation is much appreciated. I will try to be as brief as possible.'

Tom opened the file and pulled out the photo of the Audi that Julia had hastily downloaded.

'Do you recognise what type of car this is sir?'

'Yes, it is an Audi TT convertible in silver. I had one in black before things went pear-shaped. Nice car.'

'Is this similar to the car you reported seeing regularly at the flats over the recent months?'

'Yes it is, it was driven by the blonde who was going out with the guy in the penthouse.'

Tom returned to the file and pulled out the photo of Helen with a heavy heart. Pushing the photo in front of Mr Ross he asked, 'Is this the blonde lady who drives the Audi?'

'Let me see. Yes I think it is.'

'Think? How certain can you be about this? It is very important.'

'Well it was usually at night or very early in the morning'

'Please look carefully and give it a great deal of thought Mr Ross. Take as much time as you like.'

Derek Ross took his time and then looked up. 'Yes it is definitely her. I recognise the cross she is wearing. I am sure it is her.'

Tom looked at the photo of Helen more carefully and could clearly see the necklace he had given her last Christmas. How ironic that his loving gift should be a key clue in his biggest ever murder case. Trying to sound as positive as possible, he turned to Derek Ross.

'Excellent.'

'Can I go now?'

'Not yet Mr Ross, I have a couple more photos for you to look at.'

Tom slid the photo of Michael Defreitas across the desk.

'Do you know this gentleman sir.'

'He is the guy who was murdered on West Common. I saw his picture in the local paper. He lived in one of the penthouses.'

'True. Is he the man you saw with the blonde lady?'

'Oh no, the man looked nothing like that. I could have understood it if he did but the guy she was with was a right nerd. I kept asking myself what she saw in him.'

Tom slid the photo of Stewart McMillan over to Derek Ross.

'That's him! You knew all along. The guy from the penthouse.'

'Are you 100 per cent sure of all the answers you have given me during this interview?'

'Yes I am.'

'Thank you Mr Ross, you have been most helpful. Now if you wouldn't mind going along with Julia here she will type up your statement and we can send you on your way. But we may need to speak to you again in the future.'

Derek Ross looked positively delighted to accompany Julia and give her his statement in full.

Tom left the interview room feeling exhilarated that his theory had been confirmed but also slightly deflated that Helen could have left him for a nerd, albeit a very rich nerd.

Newsum and Tom went straight to the path lab in Slough where Sachin Shawazi was hard at work on the murder victim.

'Morning Sachin.'

'Morning Tom.'

'How are you getting on? Got anything for me yet?'

'Well we need a bit of luck if we are going to get a quick result on this. The loss of the head is a big blow. We have cleaned up his fingers and taken prints. We also have made a note of all distinguishing marks. We will start trawling the national records later in the day.'

'I might be able to save you a great deal of time Sachin. May I suggest that before you start the national search you check out the records of Stewart McMillan, whose doctor is Richard Drake?'

'You have a hunch Tom?'

'You could say that, and besides, the Porsche is owned by Mr McMillan.'

'I will let you know later how we get on.'

'Time of death?'

'Well that is the strange thing, the time of death is much earlier than I originally thought. This man died at between midnight and 1am yesterday morning.'

'But how come? You seemed so certain.'

'I was basing my initial findings on the condition of the blood around the body. During the post mortem two things became clear. That the man had died much earlier than I thought and that he was killed elsewhere and moved.'

'But the blood around the body?'

'Planted there.'

'Planted there? How?'

'Easy really, just drain some of the blood from the body at the time of death. Store it in the right conditions and then spread around the area when disposing of the body.'

Tom was shocked. What kind of people were they dealing with?

Clerkenwell

Rocco was dreading his meeting with Tony Marciano. He had been summoned from Spain as a matter of urgency to report in person to Tony. This time he was going to the restaurant armed.

He had managed to find out little except that William Dean was not Michael Defreitas and was apparently a man from Prague called Tomas Kopecky. This information had been passed to him by a member of City CID, a friend of Tony's.

He had lost trace of him at Malaga Airport and the guy could be anywhere by now. He had decided to lie low in Spain for a few days in the hope that Tony would calm down and it would be safe to come back.

Little did he know.

Zolo meanwhile was taking a risk. He was sitting in Mario's watching Tony Marciano hold court and eat. He had seen farm animals with better manners.

Zolo was dressed as a cleric in a heavy robe that was very prickly and was making him sweat as it was covering his other outfit, a business suit with collar and tie. He was taking great care to ensure that the robe kept his real clothes well hidden.

He had specifically chosen the cloak for its hood. It was large and he had pulled it forward to cover as much of his face as possible. He was confident that Tony would not recognise him.

God he is a heathen, Zolo thought as he watched Tony eat his lunch. Tony had never really fully mastered the use of knives and forks and was frequently resorting to the additional help of his fingers as he ploughed through his spaghetti and side-salad.

Zolo did have one scary moment when Tony had looked across at him and shouted out.

'My friend how lovely to see you. I hope your wife and family are well and your daughters are fertile.'

He roared with laughter at his own joke. *Always a bad sign in any human.* Zolo merely bowed his head and moved his hands in a cross-like movement as if he was absolving him. He went back to studying the menu.

Whilst he had no specific plan, Zolo prided himself on his initiative and knew that an opportunity would arise which would be taken without hesitation.

He just had to relax, be patient and most of all stay positive. At that moment a very large man in a suit came in and Zolo knew this was his chance. He reached under the cloak for the gun and silencer in his jacket pocket.

Rocco and Tony greeted each other as Zolo slid silently out of his seat and approached them. Rocco never knew what hit him. Three bullets ripped into his back and neck. He was dead before he hit the ground.

Tony Marciano watched the bullets as they ripped into Rocco and stared at the man with the gun. It was then that he knew. Zolo! That was his last thought as two bullets hit him between the eyes. He was dead instantly.

Zolo looked at Tony and in particular at his mucky hands. He hoped the coroner liked garlic.

Then he was gone, leaving the remaining diners in a state of total shock. He could hear sirens in the distance as he ran down the road from the restaurant. He would be long gone before they arrived. He ducked into an alleyway he had checked out earlier and ripped off the cloak and gloves he had been wearing and dumped the gun and silencer in a bin then continued along the road as if he was just a normal business man strolling to lunch in Clerkenwell.

He walked for about half a mile before hailing a taxi to the airport.

Zolo was relaxed and happy. He had no doubt that his clients were 'connected' and they would use their contacts in the police force to cover it all up or use it in some way to their advantage.

Gerrards Cross

On the way back to the station, Newsum confirmed to Tom that the search warrants had been signed by the judge. They went straight to Stewart McMillan's flat where Bill was waiting, as arranged.

The flat was in chaos: it looked like four teenagers had spent the night there. Someone had been in the flat looking for something. The whole place had been turned upside down. All the mattresses, sofas, cushions and pillows in the place had been ripped open. Basically no stone had been left unturned. It made a quick search impossible and meant that the chances of finding anything vital had gone.

Tom cursed. He assumed that the killers had taken McMillan's flat key when they killed him.

He called Jez and Mel and asked them to come over. When they arrived he told them to help Bill go through the flat millimetre by millimetre. If there was anything still there of any relevance then he wanted to know. He also told them to speak to the caretaker and get access into Defreitas's flat next door to see whether the same thing had happened there.

He had previously rung Helen's sister and she was waiting when they arrived at Helen's flat. He explained that they had to conduct an extensive search which alarmed her greatly. Tom tried to put her mind at rest but it really wasn't that easy to do.

But the search revealed nothing at all.

'Did you find out what happened to her PC?'

'No, I asked Mum and she didn't know what I was talking about.'

'Maybe it is being repaired. Newsum, did you find any kind of receipt or ticket for such a repair?'

'No sir, the whole place is immaculate almost as though it has been stripped clean.'

'Helen always lived like this.'

Tom thanked the sister and left. *What now?* he thought.

He gave Tooley a quick ring.

'Hi Tooley, it's Tom. How is it going?'

'Fine, busy trying to crack a teenage shoplifting gang at the moment. See you have been busy.'

'Yes, waiting for official confirmation but I think Stewart McMillan was murdered yesterday. Doesn't really leave anyone at Proteus worth pursuing. The link has to be Proteus but I can't understand how or why if they are all dead.'

'Follow the money Tom, you know that. Unless it is sex or drugs, which it doesn't appear to be in this case, the only other motive is always money.'

Tom recalled the words of his esteemed leader. Sex and money.

'Thanks for the advice. Must get together for a beer when this is over.'

'Sure, give me a call.'

Tom stared out the office window. He had an idea. He rang Gillian Harris.

'Afternoon Gillian, Tom here, how is it going?'

'Hi Tom. It is going much the same as yesterday, plodding along checking the books, accounts and the like.'

'I don't know whether you are aware but we think Stewart McMillan was murdered last night. We're waiting for the official ID to be confirmed this morning.'

'Strewth, that doesn't leave us with anyone to prosecute. Looks like we could be doing all this work for nothing.'

'Gillian, you will recall we had a chat the other day about the auditor for Proteus who died in a fire last month? Did you manage to find out any more about him? I have been up to my neck in dead bodies and haven't had a chance to phone City CID.'

'Yes. I have spoken to Gerrard, Ashurst and Price and they have advised that the late Mr Price did all the work for Proteus, in fact he guarded it very jealously. They have yet to appoint someone to take over the file and at this rate will probably wash their hands of the whole thing.'

'Can you run a check on Mr Price's bank accounts for me?'

'Good idea. I will get onto it straight away.'

'One other thing, can you send me through a list of the investors in the fund, especially the main ones.'

'I have the list in front of me. I will fax it through straight away.'

'Thanks Gillian.'

Tom gave her the fax number and rang off.

Within minutes the fax machine was spewing out pages of print-outs that Tom passed to Julia to analyse.

Sachin phoned late in the day and confirmed that they couldn't find a match for the fingerprints. However, they had more luck with the medical records for Stewart McMillan which matched the body exactly, even down to the small identification marks on the body which were a small scar on the left kneecap and a deformed toe from where it had been broken and not set properly.

Tom was not surprised. It had looked authentic. In fact it was only the shenanigans with Michael Defreitas's identification which had even given him pause for thought. Tom decided it was time to prepare for *Crimewatch* and the inevitable press conference that the DCC would wish to call.

He had a headache.

BBC Studios, Cardiff

Tom had finally got home at 1.30 in the morning, completely exhausted. It had been nearly ten years since he was last on *Crimewatch*. That had been to help the search for the Chesham Building Society robbers. He had forgotten how long it took.

There was the rehearsal, then make-up and then the programme itself. He thought he had done rather well but knew he would be ribbed rotten by the boys at the station in the morning. At least he had a chance to have a chat with Kirsty Young and get her autograph for his mother who loved *Desert Island Discs*.

After the show it was a case of waiting around to see what information came in from the phones and to be there for the update that was broadcast just before midnight. It was the equivalent of *Match of the Day*, showing the highlights of the earlier show, briefly describing the crimes and announcing any progress made.

As usual, they had received a lot of calls, mainly from cranks, but there were a number of calls that seemed genuine.

His case had been given a 20 minute slot in the main show during which he had to describe the crimes and seek any witnesses. He briefly described the murder of Shirley Swift, the search for the black Hummer, the discovery of Defreitas's body, the chase and murder of Stewart McMillan and a photo of Helen. He was succinct and precise and even had time at the end to show the photo of the missing Indian kitchen workers.

It was only afterwards that he realised that the case was so complex that he really could have done with the whole of the one hour show to himself, or maybe make it a series.

The main subject of the calls received were sightings of Helen and the Hummer.

Apparently Helen had been seen in places as diverse as Margate and the Caribbean. The Hummer was parked in 23 different places across England and Wales.

The problem was that Tom's team would have to follow up every single call as from his experience at least one of them was likely to be genuine.

Friday 6th November 2009

'Morning Rossie.'

The desk sergeant chirped as Tom entered the station the following morning. He was of course referring to the ex-presenter of *Crimewatch*, Nick Ross.

'Very good Norm, been up all night practising that one?'

Tom got to the incident room having run the gauntlet of facetious remarks and enjoyed the brief limelight. Might as well make the most of his fifteen minutes of fame – well, twenty, in his case.

He called the team together.

'Morning sir, loved the make-up. Can you tell me where you got it from, I have been looking for eye shadow exactly that colour for ages,' Newsum chortled.

'Very funny, now let's settle down and go through what has come in from the show. Newsum can you update us?'

'Certainly sir, we have a number of people who have identified Helen James.'

'Yes, so I understand. I think we should eliminate Margate for the time being and concentrate on the more exotic locations – after all her text to me said she was getting some sun. Could be a bluff but I doubt it. Too much heat of the other kind in the UK, she is bound to be abroad somewhere.

'Actually, on second thoughts, Bill, take all the UK locations and check to see whether there are private airfields nearby and if so check what flights have left there over the past two weeks.'

'So what do we have otherwise?'

'Well we have the Cayman Islands. A lady on holiday saw Helen coming out of a bank there.'

Tom twitched.

'Which bank?'

'Not sure, we're checking as we speak. Lady was a bit vague to be honest but adamant it was Helen, apparently the lady bumped into her and she was very rude.'

Sounds like Helen, Tom thought to himself.

'Other sightings?'

'Switzerland skiing, scuba diving in the Maldives. Drinking in a café in Puerto Banus.'

Spain again – coincidence?

'Okay we need to follow up on all of these but for now prioritise Puerto Banus and the Cayman Islands. Anything else?'

'Yes sir, we have found the Hummer.'

'Where was it?'

'It had been abandoned on a housing estate near Millwall football ground. It is in a hell of a state as you can imagine but Hummers are made of stern stuff and it is intact internally. I have asked them to bring it to us by tow truck. I didn't think you would fancy a trip to Millwall.'

Bright lass, Tom thought.

'So my dalliance with TV celebrity fame has produced some information then, although time will tell whether it is useful or not.'

'Let's get Forensics on the Hummer the moment it arrives. Ask them to make sure they get samples from the floor matting, especially from the boot.'

'Julia how did you get on with the list of investors?'

'Well sir I would like to go and interview them all, especially George Michael, David Beckham and Justin Timberlake. It reads like a who's who of the world's famous people.'

'I am more interested in the less famous people at this stage. Who are the major investors?'

'Well Sir, I would say the biggest investor is Clerkenwell Investments and their associated companies. They have invested a total of £8.7 billion since 1984 and currently have in the region of £2.5 billion invested.'

'Can you repeat that?'

'Yes sir, Clerkenwell Investments has invested £8.7 billion over the past twenty-five years.'

Tom thought his conversation with Gillian Harris about Tony Marciano.

'I want chapter and verse on Clerkenwell Investments as soon as possible. I especially want to know who owns them as they have the biggest motive of all.'

'Mel and Jez, how did you get on?'

'We went through the flat with a fine toothcomb and found nothing. We also checked the Defreitas flat which didn't look as if anyone had been near the place for weeks.'

'Okay, thanks for that. I wonder what the intruders had been looking for? Okay, I want you to help Julia check out Clerkenwell Investments. But please be very careful; if these men are who I think they are, they are very dangerous.'

Thirty minutes later Tom was on his way to Clerkenwell with Newsum. Julia had found their office address via Companies House.

The listed headquarters for Clerkenwell Investments was a shabby building tucked down a neglected side street in Clerkenwell. It was boarded up and clearly hadn't been used for years. Despite this, Tom could feel the tingle of anticipation. Had they finally found the vital clue to the mystery of Proteus?

Tom and Newsum nosed around a bit and found a nearby corner shop where they asked about the boarded up building. Mr Patel the shop owner confirmed that he had owned his shop for over ten years and during the whole time the office building had been boarded up.

On his return to the station, he asked Newsum to dig up as much as possible on the office address, especially who owned the property. He also told Newsum to check with the Post Office to find out whether there were any arrangements to forward post.

Tom stayed late that night and reviewed the file. Clerkenwell Investments was a company registered in Gibraltar. There were ten equal shareholders all of which were companies that had also been registered in Gibraltar. These ten companies in turn were also owned equally by ten more Gibraltar companies. The list was endless. It would take ages to untangle the network of businesses.

Tom decided to concentrate on the office building. The Land Registry confirmed that it was owned by Clerkenwell Investments Limited of Gibraltar. *Bugger.*

Tom was driving home when he heard the news reader announce that police were concerned that the murder of Tony Marciano and an associate in Clerkenwell yesterday lunchtime was the beginning of a war between the mafia families that ran all the drugs and gambling in North London.

Marciano? Murdered? *Oh brilliant!* he thought, *not another death?* It seemed to Tom that every time he closed in on a suspect they ended up dead. The murderers were clearly one step ahead of him. Maybe this time there would be a clue and he would be able to finally solve this extraordinary case.

———

Wembley

Tom was sitting listening to Jeremy Ward who had been assigned to the Clerkenwell case.

'Tony Marciano was better known as Big Tony. He was the fixer for the families. His principal business was to launder the families' money,'

Jeremy Ward continued.

'From what you have told me I think it is highly likely that Marciano was taken out by the families because they thought he had stolen their money.'

'Do you think that they would have killed the others too?'

'Possible, very possible. Problem is we have no way of proving it and besides, those murders are more likely to be down to Marciano."

'So you think Tony killed them all trying to find the money and when he failed he in turn was killed.'

'Well it has a certain symmetry about it and it would definitely close the circle nicely for all of us.'

'But what about the Italian who went to the clinic in Spain? Why would he be looking for someone they had already murdered?'

'Maybe the solution to that is simple. He was actually looking for William Dean not Defreitas.'

'Well, it is all too neat and tidy and it leaves a nasty taste in the mouth.'

'I know, Tom, but life is too short. Police work today is all about results and statistics. You never know, you might get promoted on the back of this one. I have already been given the nod and the wink from my Chief Constable.'

Tom was aghast. Ward promoted to DCI? He knew he was bent as fuck but Ward was smart and very slippery and Tom knew he wouldn't be able to make it stick.

'Can you tell me who the main families are?'

'They are a matter of public record but my advice would be to leave well alone. These people kill for fun and they have half the police force on their pay roll. Take my advice Tom, move on.'

And you are probably one of the half, Tom thought as he looked Jeremy Ward in the eye. Mick Brunton had yesterday confirmed to Tom that Jeremy had been the officer in charge of the Oliver Price investigation and had clearly made little effort to ruffle any feathers in that instance.

Tom was frustrated, but he didn't want to move on. He had spent weeks following the trail of death around GX and London and knew there was more to this than met the eye. He went to see the DCC.

DCC Jane Protheroe was positively beaming.

'Well done Tom! What an excellent result!'

'I am glad you think so ma'am but I feel a bit cheated.'

'Cheated in what way?'

'Well we haven't actually caught the murderer have we?'

'Well I suppose not but let's face it, it is wonderful that it is finally over. The Chief Constable is delighted.'

'But there are things that don't fit and they need to.'

'Such as?'

'Helen, ma'am. Why did she do what she did?'

'Maybe she has a mafia boyfriend, she always was attracted to dangerous men.'

Realising what she had said, she quickly added.

'Or men in dangerous jobs.'

'So you think that Helen is a gangsters moll?'

'It's possible.'

'And very suitable.' Tom added.

Leaving the DCC to bask in the glory of their so called triumph. Tom decided to go round and see Mrs Defreitas but first asked whether Stewart McMillan's body had been formally identified. He discovered that they had yet to find a next of kin. He told them to dig deeper. He wanted to know his whole family background.

As they drove to Mrs Defreitas's house he asked Newsum, 'Have we got any further with the disappearance of Adam Batstone?'

'Funny you should ask that sir, I was just thinking about that myself. The last I heard we had established that he had left the train at Watford and had been met by a man in a hat. Apparently it was captured on the Watford station CCTV.'

'Any sightings since?'

'No sir, it seems as if he has vanished off the face of the earth.'

'A hat eh? Similar to the man at Marylebone. Let's get stills from both films and compare. You never know.'

They arrived at the Defreitas house to find the maid cleaning the windows.

'Good morning, we would like to see Mrs Defreitas please.'

'She no here. She go abroad.'

'Any idea where?'

'Sorry no, she leave yesterday afternoon.'

Tom couldn't blame Mrs Defreitas. After all she had been through, an extended holiday in the sun would be very attractive. They'd never had children so she had no real ties and of course she was now a very rich widow.

Back at the station he established that Stewart McMillan did not exist. They could find no records of him having been born, no birth certificate, nothing. He suddenly appeared from nowhere at Oxford. Further enquiries revealed that Michael Defreitas had never existed either. *Why hadn't they seen this earlier?* He thought. Maybe he was losing his touch.

Tom sat at his desk and felt the tiredness washing over him. His head was throbbing and he could feel yet another headache coming on.

He felt himself drifting off.

Wednesday 11th November 2010

Tom's first waking sense was that of a very bright light and the fact that he was lying down. He tried to move and couldn't. He tried again, same result. He started to panic. At that moment a head appeared in his view. It was DS Newsum.

He tried to speak to her and couldn't. His mouth wouldn't move. *Shit, shit, shit,* he thought. He began to panic. He tried to calm himself down but that didn't work.

'Sir, please don't try and move. I will get the doctor, please just stay calm.' She disappeared from view.

She was soon back with a man, youngish and in a white coat. He was Asian and in his thirties. Tom thought he had friendly eyes.

'Tom, I am Dr Patesh, you have been asleep for many days. I will be brief and then leave you to rest. Tom, I am sorry to say that you have suffered a cerebral haemorrhage, more commonly called a stroke. The stroke has left you completely paralysed and whilst this is likely to be temporary, we have no idea at present how long this will last nor the likely extent of your recovery. Sorry to be so vague but it is not an exact science.

'All I can recommend at this stage is for you to rest completely and let us do the best we can to get you better as soon as possible. In the meantime, you are getting all the nourishment you need from this bag here which we have connected to the vein in your neck. I am going to leave you now and hope you can get some sleep.'

Tom was terrified. He was a prisoner in his own body. He felt claustrophobic. He tried to calm down by counting to ten. That didn't work. So he started counting to 100 He had reached 43 when DS Newsum's face again appeared within his vision.

'Sir, don't worry sir, you will soon be back to normal. It is just the body's way of protecting you.'

Thursday 10th December 2009

It had taken over three weeks of rest and sleep but Tom was now finally starting to feel sharper and more relaxed. He felt incredibly frustrated but had no choice but to listen to the doctors and hope that the paralysis was indeed temporary.

Meanwhile, his brain had snapped back into real life and was he was starting to think things through. He was still tormented about the recent case and now had plenty of time to work out the truth. *Lets face it,* he thought, *I am not going anywhere for a while.* Besides it helped him take his mind off his situation.

He realised he had a number of questions that needed answering; the problem was he had no way of communicating them to anyone. He lay there and felt a tear leave his eye but where it went he had no idea as he had no feeling whatsoever in his face.

Newsum and Dr Patesh appeared in his vision and both smiled. Newsum had been fantastically supportive but little could cheer him. The case had beaten him, physically and mentally.

A third person, a lady, came into Tom's view. She was dressed starchily in a green and white uniform and Dr Patesh was gesturing to her. She looked familiar but Tom couldn't place her.

'Tom I would like to introduce you to your recovery therapist, Dr Victoria Steadman. She is going to supervise you from now on.'

A bell rang at the back of Tom's brain. The name sounded familiar, he thought of a woman on a horse. A bloody-minded woman on a horse to be precise! *Oh brilliant!*

The Epilogue

Tuesday 12th January 2010

Tom's spirits were lifted by waking up and sensing some feeling in his right toe and right fingertips. He would have shrieked with joy if he could.

It had been a month since that bloody woman had been re-introduced into his life although he had to admit that despite her starchiness she knew what she was doing. He also had to admit that she looked rather sexy behind her stiff façade. He was confused. One thing was certain, though: he kept thinking about those thighs.

Whilst he was plodding through his muddled thoughts Newsum turned up with some flowers, a humungous bunch in fact, a mixture of white lilies and blood red roses. Must have cost someone a fortune.

'Sir, these have arrived for you. Shall I sit you up so you can see them properly?'

Tom blinked once.

This was a signal system that Victoria Steadman had established so that he could at least communicate with his visitors. One blink for yes, two winks for no and three for I don't know.

Newsum called over a nurse and they sat him up. He was dazzled by the most extraordinary bunch of flowers he had ever seen. The nurse commented.

'Wow, what wonderful flowers, you must have an admirer.'

Tom thought about this and wondered who one earth held any admiration for him. He soon found out.

'Sir there's a card, shall I read it to you?' He blinked once.

Newsum read the card and stood there dumbfounded, before saying.

'Good grief, this is a surprise!'

Oh get on with it, Tom thought, now more than curious.

'Sir you are not going to believe it. The card says *Get well soon, with love from Helen, Michael, Patricia and Stewart.*'

Tom closed his eyes and would have roared with laughter if he could have. The clever bastards, they had outwitted everyone! The mafia, the financial authorities, Tom himself, EVERYONE! He really didn't know how he felt. Part of him was relieved Helen was still alive and had found happiness although this happiness was tinged with sadness that it wasn't with him nor on the right side of the law.

'Sir, they are all still alive, they conned all of us. You have to admire them don't you?'

Tom blinked once, then changed his mind and blinked again. He then thought that Newsum might think he was saying yes twice so blinked three more times and then thought, *oh sod it!*

'This pretty much goes along with the theory that has gradually been established at the station. The body that we found in Burnham Beeches matches the medical records of Stuart McMillan but it also matches exactly the medical records of Adam Batstone, the guy who disappeared on his way to an interview at Proteus. The theory now is that he was kept hostage somewhere all that time until he was needed. Poor devil.'

'We have spoken to Interpol and managed to establish that Tomas Kopecky had exactly the same medical records as those of the body assumed to be Michael Defreitas even down to the two moles on his buttocks. Tomas is still missing.'

Tom lay there feeling more frustrated than ever. The case had been broken whilst he was bedbound and useless. He felt vindicated in a way, but annoyed that the two masterminds had got away with it. They were now in the sun with the money and two lovely ladies to share it with.

The consolation that he felt was that in his experience, things would eventually go wrong for them. They would either all fall out, or the mafia would find them. He wondered where they were. As usual Newsum was ahead of him.

'We all reckon they are in either Spain or Cayman Islands or perhaps even somewhere like Brazil. The problem is they appear to have all left the country separately, using new identities. We are checking all the CCTV tapes at the airports and train stations but so far nothing at all.'

Tom thought about the assassin and the trail of murder and devastation he had caused. He wondered whether they would ever find him. Probably not.

'Well sir, I better be going. I wouldn't want to play gooseberry between you and Dr Steadman now would I? Have you asked her out yet?' She said with a wink.

'Oh one last thing, Mog sends her love and has promised to come in and give you a blanket bath soon.' This was followed by another even more outrageous wink.

Tom made a mental note to demote Newsum when he was fully recovered.

Newsum beat a hasty retreat winking a third time as at that moment Victoria Steadman swept into the ward and took over.

'Now Tom, how you are getting on today. My, what lovely flowers. An admirer? What mad woman could possibly have sent you those? She got out a needle and stuck it in the big toe of his right foot.

'Did you feel anything at all?' He blinked once.

She smiled, it was the first time she had smiled since he had met her. It was a lovely smile.

Geneva

Zolo had made up his mind, he would retire; that final hit on Tony Marciano was his last. He had hated killing a friend and he made it clear to his brother that he was retiring.

Nothing his brother said could change his mind.

His phone announced he had a text. Zolo heart raced as the adrenalin kicked in. Well it wouldn't hurt to look would it?

Somewhere very hot

Patsy Defreitas lay in the sun and gazed at the three people who were sharing the area by the pool.

The lovely Helen James who, to everyone's amazement, had somehow fallen in love with the man she was now holding hands with, Stefan. Stefan Bochinsky or Stewart McMillan as most people knew him. Stefan was Michael's brother, and the genius who had masterminded the whole thing. He had planned everything down the most minute detail and it had worked like clockwork. They had done it. £100 million!

She heard the front door bell ring. Stefan went.

Next, Patsy looked adoringly at her wonderful husband, Mihai Bochinsky, the Czechoslovakian refugee who had re-built his face and his life and made them both so rich. She didn't even mind the missing part of his leg. She had always thought it was overkill and told Mihai so on a number of occasions but he had insisted. He called it his insurance policy. Now she had to admit to herself that in fact she found it a bit of a turn-on, although she would never admit that to Mihai.

The whole thing had been tough and there had been times she had wanted to quit. She had missed Mihai so much and hated that everyone thought he was a womaniser. All the acting she had to do. Well, it was all worth it now.

Helen lay there in the sun feeling guilty about Tom. Poor Tom. He was such a nice solid man but she hated nice and solid. Stewart – she struggled to think of him as Stefan – was not everyone's idea of a hunk but he was smart and wicked.

Stefan returned.

Mihai lay and thought about the previous weeks of pain at the clinics. He had anticipated he might be followed so had switched clinics just in the nick of time.

The Malaga clinic had a sister clinic in nearby Ronda and he had been transferred there early one morning under a veil of secrecy. He had taken the precaution of leaving a considerable number of euros with the manager of the Malaga clinic with a promise of more to come the following month. In return, the manager was to create a false trail and give a positive identification of Tomas Kopecky's photo.

Mihai did not like to think of himself as a murderer it was more a case of self- defence. Kill or be killed. It had become clear five years earlier that Tony Marciano was a problem, a very dangerous problem. It had taken all this time to perfect their exit plan. He wished people hadn't had to die but there was no other way.

Stefan felt smug. He and Mihai had dragged themselves up from the gutter in Bratislava and having escaped the communists' regime had fought their way to the top via Oxford. One day he would write his memoirs and he would leave them to a newspaper on his deathbed. Stefan did not have a conscience.

He had not regretted killing Adam Batstone. It was Batstone's fault for bearing such an uncanny resemblance to him. Collateral damage.

Helen turned to him.

'Who was that at the door darling?'

'Oh it was only some guy who is here to service the boiler.'

THE END

Coming in 2015

Guts

Simon Hawkins

An introduction to *Guts* from the author

What can I say about *Guts*?

Well, it's a story that started formulating in my mind whilst I was recuperating from my operation. Inspired by my own experiences I started thinking about how the greed of the banks had destroyed many people's lives and how hard I had to fight to get the life-saving operation needed to save my life. I thought about the funding shortfalls in the NHS and of course how the banks had been bailed out by the Government and I thought. What if?

What if, a man suffering from cancer had a life-saving operation against the wishes of the NHS because of it's high cost. What if, the operation was so successful that it was a proto-type for similar life-saving operations all over the country. Operations that would save many many lives but prove to be a huge drain on the NHS.

What if, the man was also at the forefront of mis-selling claims that threatened the solvency of all the major banks yet again and possibly even threatened to bankrupt the country? Just what lengths would an unscrupulous Government department go to in their efforts to stop him?

Beginning in 2008, the year of the credit crunch, *Guts* covers events over the following seven years and wends its way through bank boardrooms, the corridors of political power, top secret and hitherto unknown Government security operational units that specialise in 'black ops', the NHS policies and hospital operating theatres with doses of humour, romance, sadness, conflict and above all intrigue, deception, danger and death.

The title is my inside somewhat childish joke . . . they're my favourite kind! My wonderful wife and I spend endless hours throwing words around when trying to name a book. Then one day we were travelling to my latest scan and my beloved just turned to me and said *Guts*. It was our eureka moment! You'll get it.

Writing this book has been a real journey for me as I've re-lived the past seven years, often savouring the little moments and re-living the life-changing. I hope I've managed to bring my struggles to life and equally that other cancer sufferers will gain courage and hope from my story.

Guts is a fictionalised version of my own making, and artistic licence has been used to entertain both me, the author, and you the reader. The skeleton of the story is true: I really did own all those cars. I was forced into bankruptcy as a result of the insatiable greed of the people that run our banks who drove the inappropriate sale of what have now been declared illegal financial products purely for personal gain. It's a scandal that has so far been suppressed, to a great extent, due to the Government's ownership of two of the main protagonists. The future will make interesting history.

Life is hugely precious and I continue to savour every day as if it is my last. I have fought for everything I now have and it's been tough, but those wonderful words from the immortal Norman Stanley Fletcher kept me going when the going got tough and the way forward seemed impossible.

Don't let the bastards grind you down!

I have suffered from cancer since 2008 and was very near death on a number of occasions. There is so much more I could write here but I don't want to give too much away but I can assure you that readers of *Proteus* will recognise a few of the characters. Everyone in the book is fictional and any similarities with those living is purely accidental.

I have included some of the early pages as a taster of the book that should be finished and published by this time next year. It is by no means the finished article, so please ignore any errors. I can assure you the end result will be properly polished, by John Makin of course!

The Prologue

'All those in favour of the proposal please raise your hands.' A quick glance around the room told the bank's chairman Sir William Dalrymple-Stewart all he needed to know. The 11 board members before him all had their hands in the air.

Some of the greatest men he had ever known, many of them friends, had all, unanimously, voted to accept the proposal. Fear had driven them to this place and decision. He cleared his throat.

'This is a very sad day. It was on the 12th July 1787 when the first of my ancestors opened the doors of his new savings bank to the Edinburgh public and in the 220 years since that fateful day Dalrymples Bank has grown and risen to become the largest Bank in Scotland, a bastion of trust, loyalty and honesty. I am proud to have served as chairman of this wonderful institution, carrying on the tradition of my ancestors, but I am not proud today.'

He paused and took a sip of water as much for effect as anything.

'The decision you've made is disastrous. Disastrous for the bank. Disastrous for Scotland. Disastrous for those who trust us and disastrous for us all personally. I've made you all fully aware of my feelings on this proposal and beseeched you to reject it as an act of treachery but you have decided to ignore my warnings and my advice. I refuse to be associated with this decision and tender my resignation with immediate effect. Goodbye gentlemen and good luck, you are going to bloody well need it, as is this country.'

Sir William stood up and left a room that had suddenly been sucked dry of life.

———

Sir James Spence read and re-read the letter in disbelief. Not again! *Fucking accountants* he muttered under his breath.

He picked up his mobile, opened his 'favourites file' and tapped on a well-used name. The call went to voicemail. 'Philip, it's Jim. You're not going to believe it. The fucking PCT turned us down again. They have just signed another death warrant, poor bastard. How can we save these people's lives if they don't even give us a chance to try! They're undermining everything we do. Anyway rant over. Catch you later.'

Sir James Spence was an eminent surgeon who specialised in the colon and surrounding organs and with other like-minded surgeons had put together a team that matched those of any hospital in the world. Patients travelled from all over the world to be operated on by Sir James and his colleagues bringing both acclaim and serious funding to the hospital.

Life was good in so many ways; they were improving their techniques and achieving better and better results all the time, but there was one cloud on the horizon and it was a very big dark cloud. This particular cloud was better known as the West Hampshire Primary Care Trust. Sir James and his team were close to a big breakthrough in multi-organ surgery that promised to save countless lives of people battling cancer. His problem was getting the PCT to agree to fund the operations and subsequent recuperation. This was proving to be impossible and this was a death sentence for so many people he was certain he could save.

No matter how good a case they put up for these operations, the PCT would reject them as 'speculative' or 'unproven', both words that in the PCT dictionary meant expensive.

Alex Stanhope loved golf. He played whenever he could and was very good at it. An ex-pro, he could still manage to break par regularly and despite being the wrong side of 50 was holding down a more than impressive handicap of two.

Today he was playing with his bank manager, Rob. Rob admired Alex greatly and would regularly show him off at company golf days as an example of how his bank helped their clients and in his case, Alex, to become the self-made millionaire property developer he was today.

Worth a little over £10m at the last count, Alex was indeed a self-made man. He had worked hard and could finally start to sit back and enjoy the fruits of his labour. Less battling with sub-contractors and more relaxing at his villa in sunny Spain.

Today they were crossing swords at one of Alex's favourites, the West Course at Wentworth. Alex had made his usual fast start and had the game under control. Rob was a keen player with a lot of potential but he was hot-headed and frequently lost his temper when things weren't going his way. They had played the front nine and Alex had a comfortable lead. Walking to the tenth tee through the avenue of trees, Alex started to feel a bit strange: he had became light-headed and his eyesight was blurred. There was a pain in his left shoulder. He stopped to clear his head.

'Are you okay Alex?'

'Yeah fine. Last night's claret just caught up with me that's all.' A bit of a white lie, Alex had gone to bed early with nothing stronger than a hot chocolate.

'You do crack me up Alex. What a life you lead, Château Lafite I assume!'

Alex shrugged not wishing to shatter the rose-tinted illusion Rob had of him whilst thinking that he really must go and have a check-up. This was the third time in as many days he'd experienced a funny turn.

Chapter 1

Scottish National Bank Regional Office in High Wycombe

Rob Hastings was a regional relationship manager of the commercial lending arm of the Scottish National Bank and he was late. It was hardly his fault: the email had only hit his inbox at 11.57 the previous evening informing him that he was required at a management meeting at 7am sharp.

The problem was he'd had spent the previous day playing golf at Wentworth with his client, Alex Stanhope. He got home tired and late after the usual gargantuan post-golf drinks and dinner. He'd checked his Blackberry briefly at about 10.30pm and then gone to bed. He only discovered the email following a call from his boss at 6.57am asking where he was. He knew if he didn't get a move on where he'd be and he didn't own a paddle.

Rob lived twelve miles from his office. It took less than twenty minutes for him to reach it including time to dress. Good job the tieless, unshaven look was in vogue for bank execs. Anyway it was an internal meeting and he would have time to smarten up later. The meeting room was full of the aroma of coffee, croissants and chatter as Rob breathlessly announced his arrival.

'Morning, sorry!' He grabbed a coffee, croissant and chair then looked around. There were five others at the table, regional director Tim Matthews, his assistant Brian Davis and his fellow relationship managers, three of them, Jane Searle, Mark Bryant and Doug Freeman.

Tim cleared his throat noisily and called for quiet, 'Thanks for coming in so early and at such short notice. Sorry if some of you missed my email, it was sent rather late in the day. The reason you're here is for, well, is for a number of reasons. All of which are top priority. There was an emergency board meeting late last night in Edinburgh and I'm instructed to inform you that due to the on-going credit crunch and the lack of liquidity in the money markets, the bank is having to take certain measures immediately to prevent a potentially damaging situation.'

He took a sip of coffee and quickly nibbled the nib of his croissant.

'The measures to be taken are strictly confidential and not to be discussed with anyone outside this room. If you can't keep your mouth shut you won't keep your job. Understood? Good.'

'Unfortunately I haven't had time to do death by PowerPoint for you so let's be old fashioned – I speak and you remember. Let's deal with this as directly as possible. *Starting immediately, all* and I repeat *ALL* your commercial clients are to have their portfolios re-valued. It won't be a popular exercise, especially as we've just increased their valuation fees by 50 per cent. The new rates will be emailed through to you this morning. You will also receive the details of our new reduced panel of valuation companies who are to be used in every instance *without exception.*'

The room was completely silent except for the rustling of jackets and shuffling of shoes as the bankers stirred restlessly.

'The anticipated result of each valuation is that all properties will have retreated in value considerably and in most cases the borrowers are now in breach of their banking covenants. We intend to use this as an opportunity to re-negotiate terms with some customers and place in administration those customers who we believe are in jeopardy.

'The next new measure is that effective immediately, it is the bank's policy that all existing facilities and any new lending are to be protected against interest rate rises through the purchase of an interest rate swap, better known I expect, by some of you, as a hedge.'

Rob had heard enough, 'Sir, at the risk of appearing thick, are you basically saying that the bank intends to milk our clients in every way possible over the coming months?'

'Of course not Rob, our clients are our bedrock and we will continue to provide them with a first rate service however, SNB must come first and we have to ensure that the bank is protected at all times. All our loan and mortgage documentation refers to the importance of the security for the loan and gives us the right to re-value the security at any time during the period of the loan. We are merely being professional.'

Rob responded, 'I realise that the actions proposed aren't illegal but these are difficult times and some of my clients will struggle to pay the valuation fees at the moment, let alone be in a position to pay any penalties or the higher interest rates it sounds like they'll be hit with and what is this about purchasing interest rate swaps? We all know that interest rates are heading through the floor, and staying there. Why on earth do they need to protect themselves from that?'

Tim Matthews smiled grimly at Rob, who was his favourite. 'Rob we all know that this is going to be very unpopular and affect a lot of customers but that's business, it's not personal. They were the ones who got themselves mortgaged up to the eyeballs. Mate, it's them or us at the end of the day. Their money or our jobs and bonuses. Whose side are you on?' He asked rubbing his thumb and forefinger together in a pretty good impersonation of Harry Enfield.

'Well obviously, when you put it like that . . .' Rob stopped and sighed.

'It's just that I am pretty close to a lot of my clients, they trust me.'

'There's no room for sentiment in this crisis, Rob, and that goes for the rest of you. I want you on the phone all day today advising every one of your clients of the re-valuations and getting their card numbers for the fee payments. In the meantime I'll be getting on with the hedging quotes.'

Another pause.

'Oh and one last thing. Sir William resigned last night. About time if you ask me the old fossil was 77 and was holding the bank back. News will hit the wires today. No news yet on his replacement but it's expected that Mark with take over as acting Chairman.'

Mark Tomlinson was the vice-chairman and CEO.

He paused for effect before adding. 'New era and you all know what they say about a new broom! Now let's get cracking!'

Chapter 2

Chalfont St Peter

Gold Hill Rectory was possibly the finest house in Chalfont St Peter. It was nestled in the corner of Gold Hill Common, hidden from view behind its own private copse. Having started as a tiny house for the retired abbess of The Grange convent, it had passed into private hands at the beginning of the 1900s and changed hands three times since, each change of ownership resulting in considerable extensions.

The original two-up-two-down now occupied one and a half acres and boasted an orchard, swimming pool, grannie flat in the grounds, gym, five bedrooms and a lounge the size of a tennis court.

Alex Stanhope was the present owner and he loved every square inch of it. It represented perfection in his eyes, and so it should. He had so far sunk in excess of £2.5 million into buying and modernising the property and the result was spectacular. He hoped the previous holier occupants approved and were looking down on him favourably.

Alex's office overlooked the wonderful walled garden and pool. He spent many hours each day running his property development empire from there. It was armed with all the latest equipment, Wi-Fi, Apple Macs – PCs and laptops, wireless printers and a 50 inch flat screen TV. The furniture was all des res and included his two coveted leather chesterfields. The idea was to impress visitors and it worked. No one could leave Gold Hill Rectory without being thoroughly impressed.

The driveway outside had two entrances, both electronically controlled, one being grand and for the visitors, the other being lower profile for tradesmen. The house had security lights throughout the property and CCTV cameras covering the exterior and gardens. Alex had been burgled two years before when a 4x4 was stolen from his driveway. He was taking no chances.

A large garage to the side of the house housed Alex's stable of cars, his one real indulgence. A new Bentley Continental sat there in all its silver glory alongside a new black Range Rover and Alex's personal favourite, a Porsche 911 four wheel drive convertible, in black, of course.

Alex was a self-made man. Tallish, darkish and handsome-ish, he liked to think there was a bit of Clive Owen about him although no one else could really see it. One thing was certain, he had the gift of the gab and a high IQ thanks to being blessed with the genes of two very, very bright and talented parents.

The combination of these qualities had made him a winner in the boom days of Tony Blair when property prices spiralled. He'd worked his way up the hard way. His occupational journey had taken him from premature school leaver to successful property developer via such jobs as insurance clerk, Prudential agent (he still had the bicycle clips), mortgage broking, stacking shelves at Woolworths and a mature student's degree at Southampton University, during which time he had also managed to get married and divorced twice, each time losing his shirt as a result.

Yes, he had definitely done it the hard way, but he was proud of his achievements and the fact that he had no worries about his retirement. He was secure.

He did however currently have two concerns, the first being that he was suffering increasingly from shortness of breath and light-headedness – so much so that he had not touched a drop of alcohol in weeks. Not that he was particularly a hardened drinker, Alex wanted to ensure he took every precaution. He was now 52 and the recent death of his father from a stroke often reminded him of his own mortality.

His other big concern was the credit crunch that, whilst it offered him a golden opportunity to expand and make some serious money, threatened to deprive him of the money he needed to borrow to pursue his expansion plans.

He tackled his first problem. He rang a very good friend of his, Jacques Van der Merwe, a highly regarded cardiologist with whom he regularly shared a drink at his local, the Greyhound. He explained to Jacques about the difficulties he was experiencing and his concerns. Jacques urged an immediate appointment and told him to get his doctor to refer him. That way he could go through the NHS rather than privately. This would, Jacques explained, save Alex a fortune in the future if tests and treatment were required.

Alex thanked Jacques and rang his local surgery. The put - upon receptionist informed him he would have to wait twelve days for an appointment with Doctor Carter, his GP. She was a nice lady and a very good doctor and he was reluctant to see anyone else. But bearing in mind the warnings of Jacques he opted to see one Dr Khan, the duty doctor, at 3.15 that afternoon.

———

Alex's partner Vicki and her mother were, as usual, lounging in the garden over tea, indulging in their daily moan about him. The old gal was well into her 80s and loved finding fault with everything, especially Alex. And so, to annoy, he joined them. The sun was shining and he was pretty sure the scotch would be out soon. The pursed lips and squinted eyes removed any doubt that *the Trouts, elder and younger* had indeed been feasting on his endless deficiencies and ability to provide lavish comfort in equal measures. The *whinge du jour* was the usual, his love of nice cars and his infatuation with Liverpool Football Club.

'Hello Millie,' Alex said as he air kissed Trout the elder's corrugated cheeks. 'You look younger every day.'

'Ah there you are, I was just talking about you. That bath you fitted in my flat is hopeless, absolutely hopeless. You should see me trying to get out of it,' she belted in a distinct Lancastrian accent.

'Mrs Howard, really! Not in front of the children! Such invitations should be made in private.'

Trout the elder glared.

'Goodness knows what you see in him Victoria. He really hasn't a clue how to talk to ladies and I won't forgive him for the way he split up your family. He's a hound! What on earth were you thinking?'

'Another Eccles cake mama?'. Vicki scowled as she slipped a dash of whisky in her teacup. The service on the Bentley could wait another day. Alex wouldn't notice, or to be honest, she wouldn't care if he did.

Alex had met Vicki during one of her internet experiments some six years earlier. She was then married to Julian. Despite the two teenaged kids, she was miserable and lonely so she decided to reach out for the comfort and love she thought she couldn't get from her husband. Julian had turned out to be a throwback to the Victorian age when men were men and women were non-entities. Vicki fell into the arms of the first man she met who was nice to her and with Alex it stuck. She'd worked hard to convince herself and everyone else that his money had nothing to do with her insatiable attraction.

The romance had been blissful if short-lived. Vicki moved in, filed for divorce and the fur started to fly. The proceedings were far from easy or amicable. Alex understood. He'd been there twice before. The battle between Vicki and Julian was long, bitter and expensive. Julian, being a retired solicitor, thought he could control the settlement. Vicky's lawyer and the law said differently. The result was heavy fees to prop up the local legal profession, a lot of blood-letting and acrimony and Alex being branded a villain of the piece by all.

From there everything went downhill faster than Franz Klammer. The kids sided with the devious and manipulative Julian and ostracised Vicki. Vicki, naturally and with full support from her mother, took it out on Alex. The love and trust had gone and all that was left was a shell of a relationship sliding inexorably and in slow motion over a cliff.

Chapter 3

Scottish National Bank Head Office in Edinburgh

Mark Tomlinson wasted no time in moving into the Chairman's office and enjoying the *en-suite* facilities. After a wash and brush up he was ready to start running the bank the way he had always wanted to run it. He'd respected Sir William but his head was well and truly buried in the past and these trying times required a modern dynamic approach to banking and business.

The dust was finally starting to settle following a hectic morning.

His phone had rung at just after 5.30am. It was Robert Peston, the business editor for the BBC and one of the most prominent and able of all the business journalists.

'Yes?'

'Mark. Hi, how are you? I hope you don't mind me calling at this hour but I've heard a whisper that Sir William has resigned, would you care to comment?'

'I have nothing to say Robert. I don't comment on rumours.'

'So you are not acting chairman of SNB?'

'No comment; any announcements will be made in the normal way and not over a mobile phone at 5.30 in the morning.'

'So you admit that there is going to be an announcement.'

'Rob, I admire you but you're fishing. We make announcements regularly; perhaps we'll make one today but then again perhaps we won't. What I'll do, and this is a promise, if what you say is true, I will grant you an exclusive first interview when I become the acting chairman.'

'So you aren't denying it.'

'Goodbye Rob and thank-you for the alarm call. Speak to you later, maybe.'

Mark had kept his promise and immediately following the announcement to the Stock Exchange at 8am, he rang his old friend Peston and granted him that elusive first interview. After all, they had been at Balliol together and he was best man at his wedding, it was the least he could do.

Mark buzzed through to his secretary and asked her to summon Mike Reynolds. Mike was group sales director and would prove to be a key member of the implementation of his new regime.

Mike was younger than Mark but the two had worked together for many years and had an understanding. Mark had used Mike as his stooge on many occasions in the past as he sought to wrest control of the bank away from Sir William. Last night had been a joint effort, a two-pronged attack that even Monty would have been proud of.

M&M, to their friends, and *The Sweeties* to their jealous competitors, were well aware of the precarious position of the bank and the need to generate profit and cash flow if only to protect the share price, their jobs and, most importantly of all, their bonuses. They had spent the best part of a week closeted together working out a strategy that would not only meet these needs but equally push Sir William over the edge to resignation: double bubble or win-win depending on which side of the Thames you came from.

The idea was simple. M&M, had been the architects of the bank's push into Personal Protection Insurance (PPI) an initiative that had brought the bank millions of pounds in profit, and earned them huge bonuses, and now they were turning their attention to their commercial clients, in particular those with borrowing facilities. The plan had four main parts.

One.

To insist on the revaluation of all commercial properties against which they currently had loans or mortgages outstanding or were using as security. These valuations were to be conducted under new rules introduced by M&M, the basics of which were:

✓ In future only four large national valuation firms were to be used in all cases, no exceptions. SNB were the majority shareholders of these firms having recently increased their holdings

✓ The valuation fees were in future to paid by the customer directly to the bank who would then pay a substantially reduced fee to the valuer.

✓ The fees were to be increased by 50 per cent across the board.

✓ These new valuations were to be based on a forced sale price only; a forced sale being basically the likely sale price of the property assuming it had been repossessed, boarded up and stripped of its fixtures and fittings. Previously valuations had been based on open market value – the value of the property in its current condition assuming a reasonable period of time to find a buyer. Forced sale values could be as much as 40 per cent lower.

Two

Once the properties had been re-valued SNB would re-assess their risk and change the terms of the loan to reflect the lower valuations and the perceived higher risk to the bank. The changes in terms wouldn't necessarily be just a higher interest rate but could include an administration or penalty fee of some kind. The bank even had the right to call in loans especially in instances where SNB no longer wanted the business or crucially if they were particularly interested in retaining the properties long term for themselves (see part four).

Three

As part of the process of each re-valuation and re-assessment of risk, every commercial borrower would be required to purchase an interest rate swap, or hedge, as it was better known. The premise was simple. SNB would express their concern that interest rates were about to explode and go through the roof due to the current economic crisis and it was essential for borrowers to protect themselves. They would do this with the purchase of an interest rate swap which capped the interest rate at a pre-agreed rate that was affordable for the borrower.

SNB's relationship managers would introduce their clients to the Treasury section experts of the bank. The 'experts' were in fact disguised sales people who sold the swaps on commission, a sizeable commission but only a tiny percentage of the huge commission the bank received. They all had sales targets to meet and the more they sold the higher the commission they were paid.

Their job was to convince the clients that interest rates were about to spiral out of control and drive them towards the highest commission paying products. They would frequently do this by dangling a huge carrot in front of the clients, pointing out that when interest rates went through ceiling, the clients would make a fortune.

Interest rate swaps were a highly complex financial mechanism regularly used by large multinationals as part of their financial strategies. They would now be aimed at unsuspecting small and medium-sized enterprises, SME's, who in their naïvety and desperation to please the bank would agree to anything to keep their businesses afloat and continue to be able to borrow the money they needed.

There were many different types of swaps but the bulk of them were potential time bombs for the borrower. Yes, they protected them against rises in interest rates but they penalised them heavily if rates fell dramatically. It was the risks that M&M were determined to keep as quiet as possible and hidden from the customers. In theory the bank would have been at serious risk if interest rates rose, but Mark had already been given the nod and the wink by a close mate of his at the Treasury that the

Bank of England policy was for interest rates to drop to 0.5 per cent and stay there for at least five years, possibly even ten.

In reality, the bank couldn't lose and nor could *the sweeties!*

Four

There was a 'Four' but it was very deeply buried, and only known by the two of them. Mark intended to keep it buried because if it ever did see the light of day . . .

All in all it was a licence to steal.

Mark didn't care, he was going to make a lot of money very quickly and no one would be able to stop him. He was, after all, chairman and CEO of one of the most famous banks in the world.

At that moment the other sweetie walked in looking very smug.

Chapter 4

Chalfont St Peter

Since returning from the surgery Alex had managed to call Jacques and make an appointment for the following day, ripped the head off his project manager Carl and had a blazing row with Vicki. Perhaps in hindsight it hadn't been a good idea to have referred to her mother as *Trout the elder* in Vicki's presence especially after the scotch.

Now sitting in his office and trying to calm down, he scrolled the internet. Alex might have a passion for cars but his first love was golf and he collected rare putters. He would daily check eBay for any worthwhile items and was currently bidding on a very rare Gary Player Ping putter. They were like rocking horse droppings and although he already owned one he was keen to purchase a second. His theory was that the more he owned the rarer they became and the quicker their value would increase. It worked for De Beers so why not him?

The problem with the theory of course was that whilst the value of the putters was indeed rising he was himself helping to drive them up and the latest one had already reached £720 with two days still to go. Alex estimated that the price was likely to rise to £1,500 but was fully prepared to pay whatever it took to claim his prize. His mobile buzzed.

It was Rob.

'About time.'

'Sorry Alex I am having a bloody nightmare of a day. You won't believe what's going on here. The chairman has resigned and everyone is running round like headless chickens.'

'No problem, I have had a bit of a day myself not to mention a pair of scotch-driven trouts!

Rob sniggered, he always enjoyed the banter with Alex and in particular the way he spoke about his partner and her mother. 'Been round again has she?'

'Yeah, at least I get an early warning. When her car turns into the driveway all the mice start throwing themselves on the traps.'

Rob roared with laughter. A call to Alex always cheered him up and was just what he needed after the day he'd had. Hours on the phone to clients explaining about the need for re-valuations and rogering them royally for their cash for the highly inflated valuation fees. There had been tears and recriminations and more than once he almost walked in to his boss's office and quit on the spot.

'So do you have any news for me?'

Sitting in his office Rob held his breath and crossed his fingers tightly. 'Yes, I spoke to head office about your request to increase your facility by two million to ten million and they've agreed it in principle. Subject to a couple of things.'

'Excellent, nothing onerous I hope?'

'Well there'll be a slight increase in the interest rate, they want an extra one per cent'

'On the new facility only I trust?'

'Sadly no, they want the whole facility repackaged at the new rate.'

'Robbing bastards, that's an extra £100k a year! Not thrilling news Rob. What else?'

'Well they want a re-valuation of your whole portfolio.'

'But we only did one a couple of months ago.'

'I know, I've queried this with them and we might be okay especially as you used one of our panel valuers. I think they're going to accept a letter with updated figures.'

'Cool. Last thing I need is to pay out another £25k in valuation fees.'

'Actually, it is more like £38k. We've just put our prices up.'

'The rise in the interest rate is coming straight off my bottom line.'

There was another pause whilst Rob steeled himself for the *coup d'état* and the inevitable explosion. He took a deep breath and blurted it out.

'They also want you to hedge the loan.'

'THEY WANT ME TO DO WHAT?'

'They want you to hedge your loan. It is probably a good idea really – after all what would happen to your business if interest rates shot through the roof?' Rob countered, somewhat unconvincingly.

'Rob you and I both know that that ain't going to happen.' Alex's command of the English language did tend to slip when he was cross. 'Interest rates are going low and are going to stay there for years and years, it is the only way out of this fucking mess.'

'I know, I know but you have to remember that the loan underwriters are Scottish and they are different to us southerners.'

'Yeah, tight as fook!'

'Sorry Alex I knew you wouldn't be happy and I have dreaded making this call. I will do what I can but in my experience when head office grab hold of something they don't let go.'

'No, it's me mate, sorry I don't mean to shoot the messenger. I'm in a good place and despite the bank's rather onerous requirements I am more than capable of meeting them. Let's press the button, shall we, so I can get out there and pick up some bargains?'

'Thanks Alex for being so understanding. I'll send you an email confirming our conversation later.'

'No probs, catch you soon.'

The call ended and Alex sat back with loudly proclaiming to himself. *Thieving bastards!*

Chapter 5

NICE HQ Office in London

The National Institute for Health and Care Excellence has changed its name three times since it was formed in 1999. Originally set up as the National Institute of Clinical Excellence, it was renamed the National Institute for Health and Clinical Excellence following its merger with the Health Development Agency in 2005. It adopted its current name in 2012. Throughout, though it has been known by its original synonym, now notorious, NICE. It has two offices, one in Manchester, the other in London, but its influence spreads throughout the whole country. NICE decides which drugs and treatments are made available to people through the National Health Service.

Sir James Threlfall had been the CEO since the merger. He was basically an accountant, a health management specialist who ran NICE, a non-departmental public body, using his status and influence. The power he wields is scary. Such headlines as *NICE refuses to sanction life saving cancer drugs* are common in the media but Sir James ignores them all. He is dedicated and focused.

He ignores the frequent accusations that he plays God with people's lives. He ignores the pressure exerted on him by the big PR machines of the pharmaceutical companies. He ignores the sob stories from the terminally ill and their relatives. He has a job to do and does it in the only way he knows how. It is basically simple statistics. He weighs up life expectancy versus cost.

The fact was he did play God and he did decide and, in some cases, seal people's fates. It was impossible to make everyone happy. But he did the best he could and he knew he was the man for the job. Occasionally there would be a revolt against his power but he would always bounce back and never lost control. Yes, control. *He* controlled the National Health Service, not the government, not even the Prime Minister. Nope, it was Sir James who made the big decisions and he loved it. He woke at 5am every day excited about going to work and the challenges ahead.

As usual Sir James had arrived at his London office at 6am on that particular day, and now sat nursing his third mug of coffee, his big addiction, whilst he grappled with the latest funding problem. This one was especially taxing and concerned the latest cancer miracle drug. Bevacizumab, trade name Avastin, was going through the consultation process and the preliminary results were in. Avastin was particularly effective for people with advanced bowel cancer and the makers Roche claimed that it could add an average of five months to the life of a patient and even reduce tumours sufficiently for them to be removed by surgery. These claims had been widely broadcast in the media by Roche, but the truth appeared to be very different.

The NICE trials suggested the difference was in fact only six weeks, making a course of treatment at £23,000 unviable and impossible to fund. Five weeks against £23,000? No, it just didn't compute.

Sir James knew that a decision was going to have to be made soon and it was one that would upset numerous people and organisation from the makers Roche through to the charities such as Beating Bowel Cancer and, of course, most importantly the oncologists and their patients. He stared out of the window at the London scenery. His office was located between the Mall and Pall Mall. He knew this was a big one and couldn't be fudged. He had an idea.

He buzzed his secretary who, being a single spinster in her sixties with only a grumpy cat to care for in addition to the needs of her demanding boss, was also an early starter.

'Miss Jones.'

'Yes Sir James.'

'Can you get me 10 Downing Street please.'

'Yes sir.'

There was a pause and then the call was answered.

'Prime Minister's office'

'Good morning, may I speak to the Prime Minister please?'

'May I ask who is calling?'

'Sir James Threlfall, National Institute of Health and Care Excellence.'

'Thank you Sir Thomas, and how are you today?'

'Fine thank you Joan.'

Sir Thomas had an on-off thing with Joan, the Downing Street receptionist, mainly for professional reasons. He would dine her and bed her once a month purely for moments such as these. Joan would, whenever possible, get his call through to the PM which was invaluable and worth an evening of self and financial sacrifice with Joan who was a plain, overweight middle-aged woman with expensive tastes and kinky needs. A split second later and he was through.

'Sir James.'

'Good morning Prime Minister.' Sir James got right to the point. 'I have an idea for you that might interest you. It won't be expensive but it is a real vote winner.'

'Interesting, please tell me more.'

To be continued